Prai...
and His...

"Frank Leslie kicks his story into a gallop right out of the gate . . . raw and gritty as the West itself."
—Mark Henry, author of *The Hell Riders*

"Frank Leslie writes with leathery prose honed sharper than a buffalo skinner's knife, with characters as explosive as forty-rod whiskey, and a plot that slams readers with the impact of a Winchester slug. *The Lonely Breed* is edgy, raw, and irresistible."
—Johnny D. Boggs, Spur Award–winning author of *Northfield*

"Explodes off the page in an enormously entertaining burst of stay-up-late, read-into-the-night, fast-moving flurry of page-turning action. Leslie spins a yarn that rivals the very best on Western shelves today."
—J. Lee Butts, author of *Hell to Pay*

"Hooks you instantly with sympathetic characters and sin-soaked villains. Yakima has a heart of gold and an Arkansas toothpick. If you prefer Peckinpah to Ang Lee, this one's for you."
—Mike Baron, creator of *Nexus*, *The Badger*, and *Detonator* comic book series

"Big, burly, brawling, and action-packed, *The Lonely Breed* is a testosterone-laced winner from the word 'go,' and Frank Leslie is an author to watch!"
—Ellen Recknor, author of *Bad Company*

## Also by Frank Leslie

*The Savage Breed*
*The Killing Breed*
*The Wild Breed*
*The Lonely Breed*
*The Thunder Riders*

# THE GUNS OF SAPINERO

*Frank Leslie*

A SIGNET BOOK

SIGNET
Published by New American Library, a division of
Penguin Group (USA) Inc., 375 Hudson Street,
New York, New York 10014, USA
Penguin Group (Canada), 90 Eglinton Avenue East, Suite 700, Toronto,
Ontario M4P 2Y3, Canada (a division of Pearson Penguin Canada Inc.)
Penguin Books Ltd., 80 Strand, London WC2R 0RL, England
Penguin Ireland, 25 St. Stephen's Green, Dublin 2,
Ireland (a division of Penguin Books Ltd.)
Penguin Group (Australia), 250 Camberwell Road, Camberwell, Victoria 3124,
Australia (a division of Pearson Australia Group Pty. Ltd.)
Penguin Books India Pvt. Ltd., 11 Community Centre, Panchsheel Park,
New Delhi - 110 017, India
Penguin Group (NZ), 67 Apollo Drive, Rosedale, North Shore 0632,
New Zealand (a division of Pearson New Zealand Ltd.)
Penguin Books (South Africa) (Pty.) Ltd., 24 Sturdee Avenue,
Rosebank, Johannesburg 2196, South Africa

Penguin Books Ltd., Registered Offices:
80 Strand, London WC2R 0RL, England

First published by Signet, an imprint of New American Library,
a division of Penguin Group (USA) Inc.

First Printing, October 2009
10  9  8  7  6  5  4  3  2

 REGISTERED TRADEMARK—MARCA REGISTRADA

Printed in the United States of America

*For my cousin Coleen,*
*with love and fond memories*
*of the hills above Bottineau*

# Chapter 1

The raptor did not know whether the man was dead or alive, and the man wasn't sure himself.

The man knew only darkness and burning misery and tooth-splintering pain that worsened occasionally, like the sudden raucous upbeat of a drunken four-piece Mexican band on a Saturday night in some smoky border-country cantina.

The raptor, a turkey buzzard, hovered low over the wagon being drawn by two burly mules across the sun-hammered sage flats toward cool blue mountains rolling back against the northern horizon.

The man lay spread-eagle on his back in the wagon box.

He wore a beaded buckskin vest over a brown wool shirt, red-and-white-checked neckerchief, patched dungarees, and worn black boots without spurs. His wide, seamed face was drawn taut with torment. Thick auburn hair flopped across his forehead with the wagon's pitch and sway. His bushy soup-strainer mustache was the same color as his hair, and his eyelids were squeezed shut, carving deep lines up into his temples.

His cracked and swollen lips were stretched so that his large white teeth peeked out from beneath his mustache.

Blood leaked from low on his right side—a large, matted mess of it staining his shirt and vest. It was this that the raptor sensed, as well as the blood leaking out around the man's hands and ankles, which had been nailed into the wagon's scarred oak bed so that the man resembled nothing so much as a frontier Christ crucified not on a hilltop but on a wagon bed and sent, lurching and squawking and clattering, across southwestern Colorado.

The land around was pocked with sage and cedars and ringed with craggy mountain peaks, some still tipped with snow.

The hungry raptor decided to take its chances.

Lifting its dusty black wings, it dropped down over the bouncing wagon. It lowered its spidery legs and lighted atop the man's broad, sweat-soaked chest, keeping its wings half spread to balance itself as the mules continued doggedly pulling the wagon across the meandering desert trail.

It cocked its bald head and stared with pelletlike copper-colored eyes up into the man's face as though waiting to see if the man would react to its presence.

He did.

One eye opened, showing the frosty blue iris and red-veined white around it. Both eyes bunched. The man said through gritted teeth, just loud enough for the bird to hear above the wagon's din, "Get off me, you filthy bastard!"

The man winced at the pain in his nailed palms and ankles as he tried, with minimal success, to arch his back and shake the bird from his chest. The bird only spread its wings slightly farther apart and canted its head to one side as it continued staring into the man's eyes.

"I said," the man raked out, tears of misery rolling down his sun-blistered cheeks, "get the hell off me, *vermin!*"

As if in mocking defiance, the bird skittered down to the man's flat belly, dug its three-pronged feet into his shirt and vest, and lowered its long, hooked beak toward the half-jelled blood on the man's right side, just above his cartridge belt and empty holster.

The man dropped his chin to watch the bird, horror showing in his eyes and dimpling his cheeks. "Don't you—goddamn it! *Don't* you—"

As the bird ground its sharp beak into the jellied wound, the man's angry, desperate rasp broke off, and a shrill scream rose from the wagon to career across the sun-seared valley.

The echoing cry startled the mules into a lope.

Two line riders from the Blackbird Canyon Ranch spied the wagon an hour later as it wound into the rocky, piñon-studded foothills of the Lunatic Mountains. By this time the wagon was nearly filled with the flapping wings and bobbing bald heads of turkey buzzards. Their squawks and barks could be heard from a mile away. A half dozen of the raptors hovered over the wagon like a cloud of giant mosquitoes.

The line riders rode down a steep slope and onto the switchbacking wagon trail in the shade of a sprawling boulder, stopping the mules and driving the enraged raptors away. The birds lighted on the ground or a lightning-topped cottonwood nearby, squealing and moaning with proprietary anger.

As the mules snorted and stomped, twitching their ears suspiciously and occasionally lifting a shrill, anxious bray, the riders approached on either side of the wagon and stared down at its grisly contents.

"I'll be damned," said Billy Roach. "Ain't that . . . ?"

"Trace Cassidy," said the other rider, a potbellied, sombrero-hatted man named Ralph Appleyard. "It sure as hell is. The old gunslinger his ownself. What the buzzards left of him." The middle-aged drover grimaced as he regarded the bloody, pecked remains of Cassidy—from his nailed wrists to his nailed ankles. "Someone sure gave him his due."

"For what, you s'pose?" asked the younger Roach, whose black-and-white-checked neckerchief fluttered in the dry breeze lifting from Sapinero Valley.

"For whatever he did. Had to be a while ago. Trace hung up his guns when he moved out here to take up ranchin' with his woman—a childhood sweetheart from Tennessee, I heard tell, though I never met her." Appleyard nodded toward the higher, fir-covered slopes of the northern mountains. "Has him a ranch up high in the Lunatics, another two hours from here."

"Key-*riist*, Hooch—someone sure had it in for him

bad. I don't know I ever seen a man treated this ugly, and I punched cows two years in Apache country!"

Appleyard stared grimly toward the northern peaks, which were now obscured by late-afternoon clouds from which a couple of thin, gauzy rain curtains danced. "They sure as hell must have. And they must have some mighty big *cajones*, too—sendin' ol' Trace back into them mountains like that."

"How's that?"

"Mountain people," Appleyard said, his eyes grave as they roamed the distant slopes and fissured ridges. "They take care of their own. Not folks to mess with. When they see that someone sent one of their own back to 'em in that condition, hell's gonna pop. Mark my words. Them mountain folks stick together, yield trail to no one."

Billy Roach followed Appleyard's gaze deep into the Lunatics, and his young eyes grew pensive, wary. He fingered the sandy down above his chapped upper lip.

"Come on, Billy," the older drover said, turning his horse down trail. "We got a herd to tally. Best leave these mules to their work."

When Roach sat his claybank mare beside Appleyard's, several feet behind the wagon, Appleyard raised his .44 Colt Navy and winced as the revolver roared, blasting black smoke at the sky.

The echo rolled across the valley.

The mules brayed and bolted forward, leaning hard against their collars, the wagon once more jouncing and clattering behind them. Mules and wagon raced off up the slope.

Appleyard stared after them, seeing Trace Cassidy's head bouncing and wobbling on its shoulders, the man's auburn hair sliding in the breeze. Screaming like a pack of enraged witches fresh from the bowels of the devil's own hell, the buzzards flapped clumsily into the air and headed after the wagon. It didn't take them long to catch up to it.

The old cowboy was glad when the wagon and its grisly entourage disappeared down the other side of a rise, its clatter and the buzzards' barks dwindling behind it.

Then there were only the ratcheting of cicadas, the soft rustle of the dry breeze against the rocks and yucca plants, and the ominous rumble of thunder over the Lunatics.

# Chapter 2

Colter Farrow jerked his head up from his pillow and reached for the Remington .44 he'd hung from the horn of his saddle, which was lying beneath his cot. He thumbed back the hammer as he aimed the gun at the line shack's plank-board door, and shallowed his breath, listening. . . .

Only the raucous braying of the cattle that he and Chance Windley had brought up from Mourning Squaw Creek.

Some of the calves had been separated from their mothers during the drive, and they were calling to each other desperately, while the two big, burly bulls were snorting and bugling and jostling for position with the bellowing heifers. Colter could see through the cabin's single front window a couple of the yearling calves wrestling around and mounting each other like drunken cowboys in a cheap whorehouse, and a thin smile shaped itself on the young man's lips.

In his sleep, he'd thought he heard a horse whinny, and that could mean anything from something as benign as a rider from a neighboring ranch moseying up for a cup of belly wash and a game of cards, to Ute braves looking to steal some beef and skewer a white drover with arrows fletched in distinctive Ute fashion.

An Indian would take Colter Farrow's long shock of dark red hair and hang it from a war lance to show the pretty Indian princesses around the lodge fires tonight, maybe buy himself a frolic between cool, cherry-colored legs under an old buffalo robe.

Dropping his stocking feet to the floor, the skinny young cowboy remembered the run-in he'd had with one such Ute on the drive up here three days before. He'd caught a stocky, scar-faced brave in tattered deer-skins and an army blue bib-front cavalry blouse try-ing to haze off two heifers and a calf.

Galloping toward the brave on his brown and white pinto, Colter had fired a warning shot over the Ute's head.

The Ute, armed with only stone-tipped arrows and a war hatchet thonged at his waist, ducked with a start. Then, abandoning his mewling booty, he rode to the lip of a dry wash and waved his arms and shouted at Colter, insanely enraged.

What little of the Ute tongue that Colter had picked up in his years here in the Lunatics—fully half of his sixteen years—told him the brave had been threaten-ing that the next time they crossed paths, Colter's red hair would be hanging from the bow he was hold-ing high above his head.

Shouting hoarsely in his guttural tongue, the Ute had pointed at the bow, then at Colter, reined his pinto pony around sharply, and galloped up a pine-covered ridge toward a rocky rim.

Colter had had run-ins with Utes before. Few drovers hadn't in the Lunatics, the tribe's ancestral hunting ground. But he'd never encountered one with eyes quite as poison-mean as this one. Colter had a nettling suspicion that he would regret shooting over the loco warrior's head and not plunking one through his brisket, which was what his older partner, Chance Windley, had warned him he should have done.

"Shit, we coulda just buried the red bastard in a gully, caved the lip down on top of him, and no one would be the wiser. And you wouldn't have to worry about losin' that pretty mop of hair o' yourn!" Windley had given his companion's hair a tug at the back and taken a long sip of his rye-laced coffee. "And we'd have us a fine Injun pony to show the girls at the dance barn!"

Now it was the angry brave that Colter was watching and listening for as, dressed in only his threadbare longhandles and socks and holding his cocked .44, he stepped outside the line shack and into the dusty yard scored with his and Chance's horse tracks and liberally littered with fresh cow plop.

The smell of sunbaked shit and sage hung heavy in the hot midsummer air.

Chance couldn't be out here, as Colter had watched his partner ride off toward the higher Sanderson Meadow with a dozen cow-calf pairs around noon, just before Colter, who had nighthawked the herd, had lain down for a snooze. No one *should* be out here except for Colter's string of cow ponies and the cattle he was up here to tend.

The young puncher had just turned to his left to start circling the cabin when a wooden rasping sounded behind him. He wheeled, raising the cocked Remington toward the cabin's far corner.

Holding fire, he lowered the gun as a cinnamon heifer scratched her neck against the ends of the hand-adzed logs, rolling her big dung-colored eyes back in her head in bliss.

Colter released a held breath, his hammering heart slowing. "Good way to become beefsteak, Mama," he told the cow.

As if in response to the waddy's warning, the cinnamon heifer suddenly stopped scratching her neck. She stood with only her head and a few inches of her neck sticking out from the far side of the cabin. She turned her head slightly to one side, glancing behind her.

With a startled snort and a sudden thump of hooves, she bolted straight out from the cabin and went running into the front yard, mewling indignantly, tail curled and back legs scissoring stiffly. Beyond, her black calf turned toward her and mooed. The heifer replied as she slowed near her offspring and began to graze calmly, lowering her tail. The calf moved toward her and dropped its head to suckle.

Colter stood frowning at the cabin's far corner. He raised the Remy again, and once more his heart quickened.

What had frightened the heifer?

The enraged Ute?

Colter didn't doubt the brave had been piss-burned enough to have followed him to the line shack. Maybe he'd been lurking around out in the pines, waiting for his chance to strike and give the young waddy one of those Ute haircuts Colter had heard so much about in the bunkhouse back at the main ranch headquarters.

Slowly, wincing as his right stockinged foot came down on a thistle, Colter backed away from the cabin's open front door. When he made the corner opposite the one the cow had been scratching on, he leaned back slightly from the waist to glance down the cabin's east side.

Nothing but sage, the side window, and the old sled Norman Holliday had hauled up here last winter for skidding logs up to the cabin for sawing and splitting. The sled was grown up with needlegrass and fescue. A mouse or a chipmunk was scratching around beneath it.

Deciding to circle the cabin and come up behind whatever had spooked the heifer, Colter glanced once more across the front of the cabin, flies swirling around the open front door, then turned and started down the side. He passed the sled, stopped at the back wall, and edged a cautious glance around the corner.

Nothing behind the cabin, either, except for the one-hole privy and the overturned corrugated tin tub that the line-shack waddies used occasionally for washing their clothes and, less frequently, themselves.

He slipped around the corner and scurried on the balls of his feet toward the cabin's opposite side. Half-way there he stopped.

Someone had kicked the sled.

Colter's pulse quickened. His hand grew slick around the handle of his .44 as an image flickered behind his eyes of the tall, skinny Ute in cavalry blues creeping up on him with his war hatchet poised for a killing blow. Wheeling, Colter crept back to the cabin corner he'd just left. He drew a deep breath and, squeezing the Remy in his hand, edged a look around the corner.

He caught a brief, fleeting glimpse of long chestnut hair and a denim-clad backside slipping around the front corner of the cabin, heading toward the door. As Colter stared past the sled, his red brows beetled over his light blue eyes, and a pensive cast entered those eyes half a second before they brightened devilishly and the corners of his long, thin mouth rose.

He scurried back toward the other rear corner and pressed his back to the cabin's wall, cocking an ear to listen.

Boots crunched brittle grass and gravel on the cabin's west side. Denim cuffs scratched together as someone walked toward the back of the cabin—slowly, furtively.

Biting his lip, Colter reached down and picked up a stone. He listened, gauging the position of the person moving toward him along the cabin's west wall, then winged the rock up over the roof.

He heard the rock thump up near the front.

The footsteps stopped abruptly.

Colter gently set his .44 on the ground near the base of the cabin, then peeked around the corner. Quickly but quietly, moving on cat feet, he ran up behind the figure now moving away from him—a slender, chestnut-haired figure in a blue wool shirt, black denims, and a tan felt hat—and grabbed her around the waist and hoisted her off the ground.

The girl's scream turned to a groan as the young man's thin but long-muscled arms squeezed the air from her lungs. She raised her pointed-toe stockman's boots and curled her knees toward her chest as Colter said, "Tryin' to sneak up on me, eh, Miss Claymore?"

"Colter Farrow, put me down!" she cried, half laughing. "You scared the *hell* out of me!"

"Ain't nothin' you weren't *tryin'* to do to me"— Colter bounced her around in his arms, planting one arm under her back and the other under her knees, until he was carrying her down the hill west of the cabin— "till that heifer gave you away. Damn lucky you didn't get shot. I figured you was a Ute come for my scalp and whatever else he took a mind to hack off!"

Marianna Claymore grabbed him around the neck, squealing and laughing as he carried her toward a line of wolf willows and yellow-flowered potentillas twisting along the base of the hill. "Colter, what are you doing? You're gonna spring your back, you crazy coyote. I must weigh as much as you do!"

Colter Farrow liked the warm, supple feel of the girl in his arms. He huffed and puffed. She was right— she probably weighed close to his 135 pounds, though every pound was in exactly the right place. He hadn't seen her for a month, and the thought of her had been about the only thing he'd been able to hold in his head for more than a few minutes at a time. He'd begun to wonder if she'd been a dream—a beautiful, blissful dream he'd conjured only in his sleep, no more tangible than stardust or forest sprites.

Belying his joy at seeing her again despite how, thinking she might be a Ute, she'd made him fear for his topknot, he said, "I'm gonna show you what happens to purty girls who come stalkin' around a Circle C line shack—long-loopin', for all I know!"

"*Long*-loopin'?" the girl said with a snort. "I wasn't trying to rustle your precious stock. I just came to see how you cow nurses spend your days, and by the looks of it, you spend most of them sawing logs—and I don't mean firewood!"

"That does it," Colter said as he approached the willows. "I was going to spare you, but you've pushed this cow nurse too far."

He barreled through the willows and potentillas, or "po-titties," as the old salts called them, tramping around cow pies and mud churned up by cow and elk hooves.

"Oh, Colter, no!" the girl cried, tightening her grip around his neck and kicking her high-heeled boots. "Don't throw me in the creek. Oh, please don't!"

"Why shouldn't I?"

"I don't want to get my clothes wet! Please, no. I'm up here for Pa, looking for mustangs!"

"You'll have to do it wet."

"Colter!"

Just before he would have sent her flying into a wide, tea-colored pool in the willow-sheathed creek, he stopped and looked down at her. Her pretty tan face with its brown eyes, long nose, and dimpled chin expressed anxiety and desperation.

Deep lines stretched across her otherwise smooth forehead. It was a heartbreaking look. Marianna was his first girl. In his inexperience, he was being too rough, he realized. You couldn't roughhouse with a girl the way you could with a fellow waddy such as Chance.

Colter gripped her more tightly against him and turned away from the creek.

She stared back at him, and a sensuous light entered her gaze. She dropped her eyes to his throat and said with a sultry thickness in her voice, "Let me take them off first." She touched her index finger to the spot on his throat that she was staring at. "Then you can throw me in."

She lifted her smoky gaze again to his, and the corners of her wide, full mouth rose. "But you have to come in, too."

He grinned and shrugged. "If that's the price I gotta pay, so be it."

# Chapter 3

After their swim and slow coupling against a beaver dam, the creek cascading around them, Marianna's legs wrapped around Colter's waist and her arms thrown back, hands clutching branches protruding from the beaver dam as she groaned, the lovers dozed on the mossy bank.

Colter felt something tickle his chin. He opened his eyes.

Marianna lay beside him, head propped on the heel of her hand. She brushed his chin with a single stalk of needlegrass. The sun behind her made her chestnut hair shine as though bathed in honey. Her tender breasts pressed against his shoulder, the nipples like wild rosebuds.

"Thought I'd seen the last of you," she accused.

Colter frowned.

"My sister told me that some boys get their first poke and go. Never see 'em again. I figured . . . after the dance at Hagen's Barn . . . you were gone." Marianna's brown eyes softened. "I wouldn't have liked that, Colter. You were my first, and . . ."

Colter pushed up on his elbow and slid her hair back from her cheek with the back of his other hand. "I wouldn't do that to you."

"You never came by."

"Your ranch is half a day's ride from Trace's place, and it just so happens us cow nurses got work to do. We don't have all day to dawdle and ride around sneakin' up on folks like you mustangers do."

Marianna dropped her eyes and narrowed the right one skeptically as she caressed his chest with the needlegrass. "You were gonna come see me? I didn't make no fool out of myself, hunting you down?"

He smoothed her hair back from her face, then walked his fingers down her long, slender back. A sweet feeling filled him—a feeling so sweet that he felt as though his heart would crack open and send up dew-dappled flowers from his chest.

He'd loved Marianna Claymore since he'd first laid eyes on her during a fall roundup six years ago. He'd been too shy to speak to her until last summer at a barn dance. He didn't know where he'd found the gall to do such a thing. She was a beautiful, beguiling young woman, as saucy and wild as the mustangs she and her father tamed, and trailed by nearly every moon-calf-eyed lad in the Lunatics.

Colter was just a scrawny, freckle-faced young cowpuncher, five feet eight inches tall in his boots, weighing barely 135 pounds fresh out of the washtub, with red hair he wore long to cover a birthmark on the back of his neck.

Now, here he was, lying naked with the girl of his dreams. The only girl he'd ever loved and could ever imagine loving if he lived a thousand lifetimes.

"I reckon I'm the fool, Marianna," he said, blinking back tears of sheer joy. She must have felt mighty strongly about him to come hunting him like she had—she, as beautiful a creature as God had ever made. "I reckon I'm the fool, not hunting you up to ask what I been wantin' to ask. I reckon I was afraid of the answer I might get."

Her eyes rose to his, brightening. "And what question is that?"

Colter felt a warmth come to his face. His innate shyness seemed to suddenly rise up to grab words away from him—simple words he knew he should know but that now sank like stones in a deep well. He looked down, saw her round, pale breasts sloping out from her chest.

They confused him further, caused his ears to warm, and he looked at a freckle on her shoulder as he said, "Trace has another claim. It's on Porcupine Creek just over the ridge from the home place."

He stopped. He knew he was circling the main corral instead of just riding through the open gate. His heart thudded. He could feel her eyes on him, sensed her consternation.

"And?"

He thought he detected a note of mockery in her tone, and this made his heart beat faster. She was enjoying his discomfort.

Suddenly he heard the voice of the man who'd raised him after his own folks had died in an epidemic. It was as though Trace Cassidy had burst through the brush behind him to exclaim with Trace-like exasperation and good-humored mockery, "Christ almighty, kid, will you go ahead and ask her before you're hemmin' and hawin' up here in a snowstorm!"

"And . . . I was thinking that, after the fall gather and we make the drive to the railhead at Durango . . ."

This time it was not the words that betrayed him. He'd felt as though he'd been getting to where he wanted to go, though more slowly than how he'd rehearsed it in his head. It was a sound somewhere in the distance, amid the bawling and mewling of the cattle, that had tripped up his concentration and interrupted the flow of his words.

He lifted his head to peer through the willows behind Marianna, beyond the half dozen heifers and calves idly munching fescue and switching their tails at the afternoon bottle flies. It came again—a wagon's clatter and a mule's bray.

"Oh, hell," Colter said, gaining his knees as he stared in the direction of the unwelcome noises. "Someone's comin'."

He usually never saw anything around the line shack except for cows, elk, moose, and a beaver he'd named Fred during the whole six weeks he was up here every summer. Now, just when he had his girl out in the shrubs . . .

"A supply wagon?" Marianna flushed with embarrassment as she reached for her clothes, keeping her head down behind the willows but casting quick, nervous looks over the green branches.

Colter shook his head as he stepped into his underwear. "Me and Chance brought supplies up on packhorses. Trace went to Sapinero for supplies, but he woulda taken the lower trail. Besides, he'd be home by now."

Breathless, he glanced southward, spying the mules and the dark gray wagon moving toward him from the main trail that cut along the base of the far ridge. Wagon and mules were within a hundred yards and closing.

When he'd scrambled into his denims, boots, and shell belt, and had donned his wide-brimmed, brown felt hat, which wore the stains of many mountain monsoons, he glanced at Marianna. Still topless, her pale breasts jostling, she'd sat down to grunt and swear as she squirmed into her skintight denims.

"Stay here till I check it out."

Colter jogged back through the brush toward the cabin, the girl's curses dwindling behind him. He ran back behind the cabin to retrieve his pistol. He dropped the Remington into the soft brown holster flapping down his right thigh, then turned toward the wagon's growing clatter, hearing something else now as well.

A mewling, barking sound.

He'd thought he'd seen something hovering around the wagon before but hadn't been able to make it out because of the distance and the dark pines behind the old freighter. Now he saw the large, ragged black wings and the small bald heads clearly.

Buzzards.

Several were riding in the wagon's box, while half a dozen more bobbed and pitched from their uncertain perch along the sideboards or fluttered in the air over the bobbing, pitching contraption and the two mules making a beeline for the creek. Mules, wagon, and buzzards traced an angle fifty yards in front of the wagon, heading for the willows, then disappeared behind a low knoll.

But not before Colter had been able to see that no one was in the driver's box.

He grimaced, his eyes following the wagon's course by the hammering and squawking of the wheels over the bumpy, rocky turf and the thunderlike jostling of the box's timbered bed. It bounded out from behind the knoll, crashed into the shrubs, only the tops of the mules' heads and the empty driver's seat showing, and blew forty yards through the bushes before stopping suddenly at the water's edge.

The mules' ears disappeared as the animals lowered their heads to drink.

"What the hell?" Colter muttered, jogging out from the cabin.

His heart thudded. He'd recognized Trace's supply wagon and the two mules—the only two mules Trace owned, which were used only for supply runs to town and to pull the chuck wagon during spring and fall roundups with the South Lunatic Mountain Pool.

Trace must have been using the wagon to haul salt blocks, and the mules had gotten away from him. Maybe they'd been scared off by a mountain lion, gotten lost, and were now heading for the nearest water on this dry shoulder of the Loonies. Mules were more frightened of mountain lions than they were of grizzlies or thunderstorms or anything else.

Trace would probably be along soon after walking back to the Circle C headquarters for a saddle horse. He'd be steaming mad, too. . . .

Colter ran, convincing himself that the driverless wagon was nothing to worry about, while at the same time the back of his mind cinched up cold and tight at the buzzards. Buzzards never got that excited about anything unless it was dead.

Dread was a buzzard's black wing fluttering against his back as he approached the stopped wagon. The raptors' barking and quarreling were almost a physical vibration amid the sheathing willows.

Several perched on the sideboards, their long, hooked beaks bloody or crusted with dried viscera. Two more were on the seat, shrieking angrily at Colter, while the heads and wings of two others bobbed amid something lying inert in the wagon's box.

Colter stopped as the smell of blood and viscera as well as the deathlike stench of the birds themselves slammed against him, filling his nose and lungs.

Wincing at the stink, dread now turning his knees to water, he continued slowly toward the wagon box. Several of the birds lighted, screeching furiously, while a few more held their ground, barking and screeching, their savagely hooked beaks opening and closing as they regarded Colter with challenge sparking in their flat, menacing eyes.

The remaining birds perched atop the wagon's sideboards and seat even as Colter reached the right rear wheel. Lips parted, lower jaw slackened with the intuited horror of what he was about to see, the young drover slid his gaze over the sideboard and into the box.

An iron fist squeezed his heart mercilessly as his eyes ran up from the black boots and denim-clad legs to the familiar buckle of the cartridge belt wrapped around the tall man's waist.

Bells tolled in Colter's head. His thoughts were so fast and confused that he couldn't get ahold of them. In fact, he *felt* more than he thought—as though the images his eyes were taking in were assaulting different parts of his body instead of being processed by his brain. The iron fist squeezed his heart even more tightly, more painfully, as his gaze continued up past the blood-matted shirt to the head that was turned sideways atop the wagon bed, the knotted end of a bloody red-and-white-checked neckerchief drooping over the pale, blood-smeared shoulder exposed by an open seam.

A squawking buzzard, eyes ablaze, dug one taloned foot into the bloody mess of what had once been the man's ear while it ground its other foot into the dead man's bloody forehead.

Fury burned like a wildfire ignited by a sudden lightning strike, and Colter was only half aware of his right hand sliding his Remington .44 from its holster, of cocking the big hogleg's curved hammer as he raised the gun over the wagon's bed and squeezed the trigger.

The gun roared.

The slug plunked loudly into the front panel of the wagon box after it had torn through the buzzard's breast, blowing the big, ungainly bird back against the bullet hole in the wood.

The bird shrieked and tried to right itself, but its head seemed a leaden weight. The head wobbled drunkenly atop its shoulders, making hair-raising bleating sounds. As the bird's broad wings flapped maniacally, the head fell into the wagon's upper-left corner and lay there, inert, as the life in the wings and the spidery brown legs slowly dwindled.

Meanwhile, Colter, seething, snapped the Remington up toward the wagon's seat, but held his fire. The bird that had been sitting there had already flown, squawking off into the brush.

The other two vultures glared at Colter from atop the sideboards on the other side of the box, dumb challenge in their small, hard eyes. Colter swung the gun toward them, and the Remington roared again, blowing one of the birds off the sideboard as the other leaped awkwardly up into flight, screaming like a warlock.

Colter fired two quick, enraged shots at it, but only the second bullet came close, parting the bird's wing feathers before it angled out over the creek and away.

Lowering the Remington, Colter heard the wounded bird thrashing its life out in the brush on the other side of the wagon. Through the wafting powder smoke, the young drover stared into the wagon's box once more, and what was left of the color in his broad, freckled face leached away like bone bleached by a thousand Southwestern suns.

Thudding feet and rustling brush rose behind him. *"Colter!"*

He wheeled. Marianna ran toward him, bulling through the willows, her arms up to shield her face from the branches.

"Stay back!"

Colter sheathed his pistol and moved toward her as she crashed through the branches of the last shrub. He caught her arms and used his body to block her view of the wagon.

"Stay back, Marianna!" he warned again, hearing his voice break with emotion.

"What is it?" Marianna tried to free her arms from his firm grasp as she craned her neck to look around him at the wagon. "What were you shooting at? What's in the . . . ?"

Her eyes touched his and held, and the question died on her lips. Fear flashed in her gaze as she tried to look once more at the wagon. Colter pushed her away and turned her around, keeping himself between her and the carnage in the wagon box. He didn't want her to have to see it the way he would see it twenty, thirty years from now.

The way he would see it on his own deathbed.

Marianna walked toward the wagon stiffly, no longer needing to be pushed. Her voice was hard, brittle with dread. "That's Trace Cassidy's wagon, isn't it?"

"Yeah."

"What's it doing here, Colter?"

"I don't know." His own voice sounded to him like someone else's. "The mules must have been heading up the mountain toward home and smelled the water. They're parched, I reckon."

Marianna was angling around the knoll now, still

moving toward the wagon. She didn't turn her head but held it straight forward. "What's inside it, Colter?"

He didn't say anything until they'd both reached the cabin. Marianna walked up to the front door as if she were going to head on inside. She stopped at the hard-packed depression just in front of it and turned around.

Her brown eyes were hard with fear, her cheeks were ashen, and the skin above her nose was wrinkled.

Colter sucked in a breath as he stopped and turned around toward the wagon, which he could no longer see because of the knoll and the willows. "I'm not sure. I think it's Trace."

He was sure. He'd recognized the boots, those long legs and lean horseman's hips, and the shell belt. That thick brown hair just starting to gray at the temples was Trace's, all right.

Colter just didn't want to be sure. He couldn't accept the fact that he was sure.

His heart hammered painfully against his rib cage.

"What do you mean you're not sure?"

He licked his lips and stared off toward the forest from which the wagon had come. His mind was trying to crawl away from the remembered image of the wagon and the buzzards and from all the rest that he had seen in the past few minutes. He wanted time to retreat and for him and Marianna to still be lying in the shrubs by the creek and for the wagon to not appear.

"It's him," Colter said, hunkering down on his heels, entwining his fingers and pressing his palms together until they ached. He nodded as he ran his tongue across his lower lip. "I reckon it's Trace, sure enough."

Marianna knelt beside him, ran a hand through his hair, and placed her other hand on his forearm. "He's dead?"

Colter nodded.

"What were you shooting at?"

He turned to her. She became a vague, indistinct image behind the tears washing over his eyes and dribbling down his cheeks. "The vultures. They were eating Trace, and there wasn't nothing he could do about it." He sucked a breath, sobbing. "Because some sonofabitch of a no-good scoundrel nailed his hands and his feet to the wagon bed!"

# Chapter 4

Trace Cassidy had no few friends in the Lunatics. Nearly every family in the South Lunatic Mountain Pool, and several others, turned out for his funeral four days later, at the Circle C headquarters along Big Spring Creek.

Even a couple of Mexican sheepherders came down from their rocky plateau to hold their sombreros over their hearts near the grave that Colter had dug on a pine-studded bench overlooking the stream.

Colter had built the coffin in which, weeping, he'd laid the badly mutilated body of the man he considered more a respected older brother than a stepfather, while Trace's widow—Colter's adoptive mother—Ruth Cassidy, had grieved silently inside the two-story log house with her two young children, David and May.

One of the ranchers himself, Owen Fussel, a lay minister, gave a sermon at the gravesite and led the crowd in singing two of Ruth's favorite hymns.

Marianna stood beside Colter, and he was glad to have her there. The girl said little, somehow sensing, rightly, that Colter needed her silent, loving presence more than her words.

When the crowd dispersed, the men and women and their children drifted down to their buggies or spring wagons at the bottom of the bench, and Colter walked down the hill with Marianna by his side. He saw Ruth speaking with four area ranchers, the black-clad men holding their hats in their hands. Pete Teagarden's thin gray hair blew in the late-afternoon wind under a gray, stormy sky, as he did most of the talking.

The other men nodded in agreement with Teagarden as they regarded Ruth Cassidy gravely. After Teagarden was finished with whatever it was he'd been saying—Colter had a good idea, and it drew his gut tight and made his heart flutter—Ruth Cassidy placed a hand on the gray-headed rancher's forearm and shook her head. She spoke for a time, regarding the others as well as Teagarden.

And then the men nodded to her in acquiescence to her wishes, donned their hats, and walked soberly toward their families waiting in their buggies and wagons.

Marianna looked up at Colter, her brown hair blowing in her eyes, the hem of her black dress—the only dress he'd seen her wear—blowing around her long, slender legs. One brown eye shone brightly as she squeezed his hand once more, gave a wan, sympathetic smile, then turned and strode over to where her father, the bearded, taciturn mustanger Titus Claymore, sat in their spring-work wagon, waiting.

Claymore looked uncomfortable in his ill-fitting

brown suit and bowler hat as he tried to keep his eyes respectfully away from his daughter and her grieving beau. As Marianna climbed up into the wagon, Claymore turned to Colter and pinched his hat brim.

"You know where to find us, boy."

Then he released the brake and shook the reins over the back of the gray mare in the traces.

Marianna and her father soon disappeared with the others, leaving Colter and Ruth Cassidy and young David and little May to their quiet, lonely ranch along Big Spring Creek, with the fresh grave looking down from the northern bench, and to the bald, bitter specter of their inconceivable loss.

For the rest of the day and evening, Colter occupied himself with the horses in the wrangler pasture, doctoring the usual brush cuts and cleaning out hooves. He worked in the breaking corral for a while, teaching a couple of the younger colts to respond to the rein.

While he worked he noted the deathly silence—a silence so heavy it was almost palpable, making him feel sick to his stomach—that hovered like a black cloud over the ranch. Every whisper of wind, gate squawk, bluebird call, and building creak was like a Ute war lance piercing Colter's heart.

After dark, it stormed—one of those violent summer monsoons with thunder crashing, lightning blazing, and rain hammering straight down—and he went inside the cold, dark, silent house.

There wasn't even a fire in the kitchen range. Ruth and the children had apparently turned in early. Colter nibbled a hunk of venison and a cold potato that one of the mourners had brought, and then crept quietly up to his second-story bedroom.

He crawled into bed and, physically sore and fatigued by sorrow and fury, fell almost instantly asleep.

He woke to the click and quiet squeak of his door latch. Lifting his head from his pillow, he saw a glowing, wavering lamp move into his room and, behind it, the ghostly, white-clad figure of a woman.

The lamp flickered redly across the gaunt, hollow features of Ruth Cassidy as she moved to the bed in her long cotton nightgown, with her deerskin moccasins rasping across the floorboards. The light winked dully in the woman's long, silver-streaked hair that fell straight down across her shoulders, curling slightly at the ends.

Colter thought he was dreaming until Ruth spoke his name.

"Yeah." He grunted, blinking his eyes, which ached a little from the light. He could smell the musky, piney smell of the coal oil, see the black smoke issuing from the soot-clouded chimney. "Did I oversleep?"

But he couldn't have overslept. His room's two windows were dark as pitch.

"No, you didn't oversleep. I'm summoning you early this morning, Colt."

She had called him Colt nearly since the day, when he was six years old, that she and Trace had taken him as their own in the wake of his parents' deaths in a milk plague. But this morning there was a strange, ominous tone in her voice.

She set the lamp on his dresser, sat on the bed beside him, leaned toward him, and swept a lock of his red hair from his forehead. Shadows flickered across the hollows of her cheeks and eyes, and her blue irises fairly blazed from those murky hollows.

"Why?" he asked. "You want me to head back up to the line shack? I thought—"

"No," she interrupted him. "I don't want you to return to the line shack. Chance will have to handle the herd by himself up there. There's something else you must do, Colter."

The cold, toneless pitch of her voice took him aback, and for a moment he wondered if it was Ruth who was dreaming and walking in her sleep. She had a dark, specterlike air about her, and he found himself raked with apprehension.

"All right," he said, his voice sounding inordinately loud in the silent room, and in contrast to hers. "Sure, Ruth."

"You saw Mr. Teagarden and those other men talking to me yesterday?"

"Yes."

"Do you know what they were talking to me about, Colter?"

He felt his heart flutter again like it had yesterday after the funeral.

"No," he said, though he had a good idea.

"They offered to send some of their men out after those who killed Trace."

She waited, as though for some reaction from Colter.

He nodded. "Figured it might be something like that."

"They even offered to go themselves," Ruth said.

"But I told them no. I didn't want them risking their lives to settle up for Trace. Those men have families of their own. Besides, they're not capable of handling the kind of man who did that to Trace."

Ruth's eye flickered, and for a moment she seemed about to lose her firm hold on herself. Then she set her lips in a hard line, and her eyes turned to blazing stones once more.

"It's our business, Colter—yours and mine," she said, her voice even harder than before as her gaze bored with what seemed an almost sexual passion into the young drover's, setting Colter back soundly on his figurative heels. "We're Trace's people. Where Trace and me come from—the Tennessee mountains—there's only one sort of folks who can settle a score like this. That's Trace's own blood. And you're every bit as much his blood as David and May and I are."

She stopped but continued staring into Colter's eyes. Her mouth was a long, thin slash across her face. Her swollen breasts rose and fell behind her night-gown. Colter could hear her breathing.

He'd never been afraid of Ruth Cassidy before—even when she'd been mad at him—but he was afraid of her now. He'd never seen her like this, and he'd been here when both David and May had been born after many long, agonizing hours.

Vaguely, he wondered if Ruth's sorrow had driven her insane.

"You want me to go . . . ?"

Colter's voice trailed off. His mind was still fogged with sleep, and all of this still owned a dreamlike quality.

But Ruth's desire was becoming clear to him, and his heart was quickening with both fear and renewed fury for those who'd taken Trace from him, Ruth, David, and little May. He'd thought of going after the killer or killers himself, but only half seriously. He was only sixteen. He wasn't a gunslinger like Trace had been at Colter's age. He was a drover, far better with cattle and horses than with a shooting iron.

Colter had never fired a gun at anything except animals for food, and at occasional coyotes and wolves caught harassing their cattle. Trace himself had preached to Colter that guns and knives were never to be used against other human beings.

Besides, Colter had figured Ruth wouldn't want him to leave the ranch. He'd figured that with Chance up at the cabin and with no other men on the roll until the fall gather, he was needed here.

Ruth swallowed and ran her tongue across her lower lip. "Trace is gone and he isn't coming back. I'm a widow. David and Little May will grow up without their daddy."

A muscle or a nerve in her cheek twitched. She lowered her dark eyes and bit down on her lip so hard that it turned white, and Colter thought she would draw blood. The twitch went away, and she raised her eyes to Colter once more.

"I want you to set things right, Colter. I want you to see that the men who killed your pa and my husband get the reckoning they deserve."

Suddenly Colter felt determined, confident. He felt buoyed by Ruth's unexpected show of confidence in him.

She placed a hand on his forearm as if to hold him back.

"It will be no easy task, Colter. The men who did what they did to Trace are demons. I know Trace taught you how to shoot, though he never spoke a word of it to me. He knew how I felt about . . . about his past. But I heard the shots down by the gulch when you two were shooting targets. And if Trace taught you how to shoot, you know how to shoot right well."

She paused, staring at him as though to cement her words in his brain. The lamplight flickered across her hair, slid hard shadows across her face.

"Don't depend on that alone, Colter. The men who killed Trace likely know how to shoot, too. And they probably know how to fight with their fists and with knives. You'll have to find some other way to settle up with them. You'll have to use your wits. But first you have to track them. And I want you to leave now, this morning, before David and May wake up. I have your breakfast waiting downstairs, and I've packed food for the trail. I want you to start tracking while the sign's still fresh. Follow them back to where they started. That's where you'll start to settle up for us and for Trace."

Colter stared at his adoptive mother in shock and wonder. Eagerness and confidence swept through him. But he also felt the enormous weight of this un-expected responsibility. It was a two-ton yoke on his shoulders, pushing him back against his pillow.

Ruth turned her head away and down for a mo-ment, as though she were sensing his thoughts, maybe even sharing the same feelings. "I love you, Colter." She turned back to him. "I love you like you were my own child born of my own womb. I would expect nothing less from my own flesh and blood. Do you understand that?"

Colter nodded slowly. "I understand. I won't let you down."

"Do not," Ruth said with a single, resolute shake of her head. "Ride back here only when you can bring word to both me and to Trace up there on the bench that his murder has been avenged."

Ruth leaned toward him, wrapped her arms around his neck, and kissed his cheek tenderly. He felt the wetness of her tears. She sobbed deep in her throat.

"I miss him, Colter!" Her voice was small and racked with pain.

A hard knot swelled in his throat. Tears welled in his eyes and dribbled down his cheeks. "I miss him, too, Ruth."

They held each other for several minutes, sobbing. He could feel her heart pounding, the rage and grief rocking every bone in her slight, work-toughened body.

She pulled away from him and wiped tears from her own eyes before rubbing them with the heels of her hands from Colter's. She cleared her throat and shook her head as if to clear it.

"There," she said, her tone hardening once again—that toneless pitch that caused a shiver to ripple up his spine. "Those are the last tears we'll shed. Like Trace said, all you can do about death is ride away from it. Ride away from it fast. Now, we've business to tend. I'll tend mine here. You'll tend yours out there."

Ruth rose from the bed, picked up her lantern, and strode stiffly toward the door. "Pack your war bag," she said, and opened the door. Turning toward him and holding the lantern up above her head, peering at him from beneath it, she added, "Don't tarry. Breakfast is waiting."

# Chapter 5

Colter Farrow had roped his best cutting horse—a blaze-faced coyote dun he'd raised from a colt and named Northwest because it always seemed to graze facing that direction—in the wrangler pasture shrouded in foggy darkness, hearing the storm's distant thunder rumbling in the south.

He'd saddled the gelding by lamplight in the barn while the milk cow mooed and kicked its stall, irritated at being rousted so early from its late-summer sleep. Now, having led the horse across the muddy yard, the fresh tang of rain-washed mountain air in his lungs, the young drover toed a stirrup and swung up in the saddle.

The Remington in the cross-draw position on his right hip somehow seemed heavier now than it had before when he'd only worn it to shoot snakes that threatened his horse or coyotes that threatened the calves. He'd slid his old Tyler Henry rifle into the boot on the saddle's left side, as he was left-handed, and it, too, seemed a more significant presence, its scarred, brass-plated stock angled up over the left stirrup fender, within easy reach from the horn.

Dawn had just broken, a pearl gray wash in the east, and fog hung in slender, ragged strips over the creek, with here and there a small cloud like an isolated puff of smoke hunkering low over the sodden, dripping pines of the surrounding ridges.

Crows cawed distantly. Those and the occasional bellow of the cattle scattered across the home pasture were the only sounds.

Colter glanced toward Trace's grave. In the misty light he could just barely make out the mounded rocks and the cross he'd fashioned from pine branches and rawhide. It was a sad, forlorn presence there at the edge of the dark pine forest a hundred feet above the cabin.

Colter wondered if Trace could see him from there and, if he could, what the onetime pistoleer thought of Colter's intentions.

Could he sense the trepidation in the boy's heart?

Colter himself would want a far more formidable figure than his own riding out to avenge his murder, he thought absently, feeling much smaller and lighter than even his own spindly frame.

He felt like a leafless twig in a gathering windstorm.

His rage at the killers suddenly nowhere to be found, he wanted nothing more than to ride the fifteen hard miles to Marianna's horse ranch and be cradled in her arms, to be caressed by her warm breath, to feel her cool breasts against his side . . . feel the beating of her heart against his own.

"When she comes by, I'll tell her where you've gone."

Colter looked down to see Ruth, a shawl wrapped around her shoulders, looking up at him. She'd draped a food sack around his saddle horn. He'd been so preoccupied with thoughts of Marianna and his own misgivings about his mission that he hadn't heard her come out of the cabin.

He flushed now and tried a confident smile, but it felt wooden. He longed suddenly for his old life here, with Trace still alive and everyone working hard and relatively happily, and for his occasional secret trysts with his girl.

"Thanks." He pinched the brim of his broad-brimmed snuff brown hat. He pitched his voice with manufactured confidence, but it still sounded like a boy's unconfident voice to him. "Don't worry, Ruth. I'll do what needs doin'."

For a second, he thought she would reach for him to give him a hug. But she merely crossed her arms beneath the shawl, her face a gaunt oval framed by her long hair, and stepped back toward the cabin.

She smiled grimly and said just loudly enough for him to hear amid the ticks of water dribbling off the cabin's shake roof, "I know you will."

That was it. Her only good-bye.

Frowning uncertainly down at the woman who watched him stoically—a woman made strange to him by rage and despair—he reined the coyote dun away from the cabin. He turned its head forward and put the horse past the barn and springhouse and around the breaking corral. Feeling the big holstered Remington flapping on his denim-clad hip, he headed for the creek's southward sweep through low willows and chokecherries.

As he thumped across the wooden bridge over the creek—several boards of which he and Trace had replaced just last summer, after the work wagon's left rear wheel had broken through a rotten plank—he glanced back once more.

Ruth was a slender, blurred figure still standing in front of the cabin, motionless. He started to wave to her, but she seemed too solemn for a gesture as superfluous as waving. So he turned his head forward again and put the dun into a lope along the soggy two-track trail.

He tried to ignore the hollow pangs of grief and loneliness assaulting his belly, and the hard, persistent hammering of his heart.

Colter's first day on the trail that wound slowly down the southern slopes of the Lunatics, he saw no one except for a couple of distant line riders and a raggedly attired drifter hunkered down beside a coffee fire in a secluded hollow fifty yards from the trail.

If the drifter spied Colter, the man gave no indication but only crouched over his coffee cup like a man wanting no company but that of his horse grazing nearby, the little sorrel's belly straps hanging free, its bridle bit slipped from its mouth. Smoke from the small fire wafted whitely in the late-afternoon sunlight.

Colter camped that night in a dry wash near the base of the Lunatics. It was as long and lonely a night as he'd ever spent, even including those just after his parents had died and he'd been left alone on their little shotgun ranch between Pine Butte and the north fork of Porcupine Creek.

Coyotes howled him to sleep and he woke once to the eerie screams of a distant jaguar, likely hunting the higher slopes for calves and jackrabbits.

Unable to fall back asleep right away, he lay there and stared at the stars that filled the sky like a million tiny fires. He counted seven shooting stars, one sparkling brightly as it careened over the valley before him, before his eyelids grew heavy. He turned onto his side, fitting his hip into the hole he'd dug out for it, and let sleep and its merciful escape from his worries overtake him once more.

He was on the trail again at the first flush of false dawn.

Making the last long pull through a winding canyon along the Sapinero River, the broad Sapinero Valley showing beyond the canyon's mouth in the bright midmorning light, he spied a wagon moving toward him. He saw the contraption—just a small brown speck at first—a long time before he started hearing its hammering rattle, which was louder when the wheels bounced over a chuckhole.

The wagon grew before him until he could make out the heads of the two mules in the traces and the lumpy, sombrero-hatted figure of the dusky-skinned man in the driver's box. He paid little attention to the man—just a prospector or a freighter heading for a claim or a little mining camp in the mountains—until, when the wagon was only twenty yards away, the driver suddenly hauled back on the mule's reins and regarded Colter through mud-black eyes under the broad brim of his steeple-crowned sombrero.

"Colter Farrow! Madre Maria, boy, look at you— you're all grown up!"

Colter checked down the coyote dun and regarded the man skeptically—a squat, round-faced Mexican with a sweeping salt-and-pepper mustache. He wore deerskin *chivarras* and a brown charro jacket, the gold stitching faded and torn, and Colter could see a hide tobacco pouch and a corncob pipe poking up from a side pocket.

Beneath the jacket he wore a faded blue calico shirt and a soiled red neckerchief. From the soft black holster on his left hip, the black grips of an old Schofield revolver jutted, while a hide-handled bowie was sheathed just behind it.

Three or four crooked, tobacco-stained teeth shone through his broad smile, and his brown eyes sparked with delighted recognition as they ran up and down Colter's lanky, corded frame.

"You remember me, don't you, boy?" the man said in thickly accented English when his eyes had returned to Colter's face.

The name slipped up from the depths of the boy's memory. He frowned, leaning slightly forward in the saddle as he drew the dun's reins up taut against his chest. "Juventino?"

The Mexican laughed with unabashed delight. "You remember your old Juventino Escobar, eh? The one who sneaked you all those biscuits reserved for the nighthawk riders!"

Juventino Escobar threw back his head and showed even more tobacco-stained gum as he guffawed at the memory.

Colter chuckled then as well, remembering round-up two falls ago, when Trace and the rest of the South Lunatic Pool had hired Juventino to run the chuck wagon and to look after the junior-most drovers, including Colter. The Mexican and Colter had taken a special shine to each other. Colter still remembered some of the trail songs the Mexican had taught him in his native Spanish while Colter had hauled water for the man and helped him wash the pots and pans.

"Look at you," Juventino said, when his laughter had died. "You're a whole hand or more higher than you were two years ago. What have they been feeding you up there—grizzly guts and puma *rinones*?"

"Trace is dead, Juventino."

The Mexican's face slackened, and the dark, deeply cross-etched skin above his broad nose wrinkled. "Took sick . . . or rustlers?"

"Neither. At least, he didn't take sick. Don't know about rustlers. Don't know who killed him. Only that whoever done it sent him back to the ranch in the work wagon. He'd gone to Sapinero for supplies."

Juventino studied Colter's features skeptically, as if only half believing what he'd been told.

Colter winced against another onslaught of emotion. "They nailed his hands and feet to the wagon bed. He'd been beaten and shot. Ruth thought it looked like they'd taken a quirt to him after he was down." He cleared his throat. "I'm backtracking the wagon. Looks like it came from Sapinero, all right. There's only a couple more forks in the trail before it leads on into town."

Juventino loosed a slow sigh and looked down at the cracked floorboards of the driver's box. Mining supplies and dry goods—dynamite boxes, files, chisels, a new pick, and bundles of flour, coffee, and salted meat crowded the wagon box behind him. Along the outside of the box still shone the faded, green-painted letters of the snake-oil salesman from whom he'd bought the buckboard several years ago.

Juventino prospected the canyons of the Lunatics and the Sapinero Valley between ranching jobs or trips down to Arizona to visit his married daughters. Sometimes he had a woman with him—usually an Indian or a half-breed girl. Sometimes he was alone. He was a good-natured though brooding, solitary soul who couldn't seem to find one place to sink his taproot.

Now he whipped the end of the reins in his hands with frustration as he shook his head and pursed his lips. Glancing up at Colter darkly, he said, "Don't go there, Colter. You're all grown up, uh? But you're no match for the kind of trouble one finds in town."

Colter canted his head to one side. "What kind of trouble do you mean, Juventino? Trouble in any town, or trouble in Sapinero?"

The Mexican held Colter's stare. Then his gaze flickered, and he turned his head to peer over his mules' twitching ears. "The kind of trouble in any town, amigo. Any town out here on the flats. You know the way it is between the town folks and the mountain people. It has always been that way, since I first came up here from Arizona." He glanced at the boy, squinting one eye and wrinkling his nose. "That's why your folks never let you go to town alone, uh? I bet they still have not."

"They have now. Ruth sent me, though I would've come anyway, in my own good time. Whoever killed Trace has got a reckoning comin'. A debt due to Ruth and me and to David and little May, and to Trace lyin' cold in his grave." Colter bunched his lips. "And gettin' colder every second we're sittin' here, jawin'."

Juventino shook his head slowly. "That's not you talking, amigo. That's Ruth talking. She's from blood-for-blood country. Like Mejico. She's going to get you killed, sending one young man to do the work of a half dozen seasoned pistoleers." He jerked his head suddenly. "Go on back home. Wait a day or two. Tell Ruth the trail went cold. Hell, I'll back you up. I'll tell her, too. Soon she'll realize what she's done and she'll change her mind, anyways."

"She won't change her mind, and neither will I." Colter paused, scrutinizing his old friend. "What is it you're not sayin', amigo?"

*"Que usted significo?"*

"What's so dangerous about Sapinero?"

"Huh? Nada." The Mexican shrugged, flushing beneath his natural leather color. "It is a town like any out here—unfriendly to the mountain people. Hell, it is unfriendly to any stranger. I don't let the grass grow under my feet there, either, I tell you, brother! You want to go and check it out, go ahead. See what I care. I warned you, Colter Farrow."

"Thanks for the warning, Juventino."

The Mexican cursed in Spanish and straightened his back, preparing to head out. "Watch the trail carefully, my young friend. Two days ago the mercantile in Sapinero was robbed. Three crazy gringo bandits—I guess they didn't know who they were dealing with—Paul Spurlock!"

He laughed.

"But they got away with it. Even killed a store clerk and pinked a sheriff's deputy on the way out of town. The sheriff led a posse after them, but returned without success. It is my feeling, though, that the bandits swung around the town and headed this way, toward the mountains. Probably holing up and letting that old, mossy horn badge–toter Bill Rondo sniff out the country around them before they surface and continue their journey into the Lunatics. One of them is riding a most conspicuous horse—a cream stallion with a double chain-link brand on its wither."

Juventino chuckled again. "I have to admit, it tickles my funny bone to know that Paul Spurlock got robbed in the middle of the day—successfully, to boot!"

He nodded at Colter, wished the boy luck in a darker tone than before, and flicked the reins over the mules' backs. "Stay away from the old Sanderson place," he warned. "I have a feeling they're holed up there. Thought I spied tracks someone tried to cover . . . but not well enough for this old chili-chomper's *ojos*!"

When the wagon had passed, Colter curveted the

coyote dun to look after his old friend. Juventino was probably heading to one of his half dozen mine shacks scattered throughout the Lunatics.

Colter scowled into the sifting dust, puzzled by the Mexican's uncharacteristic coyness. Juventino had said plenty, but he'd ridden around something, too. Colter was certain of it. It underlaid his overall apprehension with another layer of nervousness.

Then again, maybe he was just a frightened boy who really did have no business doing what he'd set out to do. The misgiving riled him, and he spat to one side, bunching his lips as he jerked his head away from the sight of the dwindling wagon, and urged the dun up the trail toward Sapinero.

# Chapter 6

The sign along the trail's right side was old, brittle, and sun-bleached. It stood about four feet up from the ground and consisted of two planks nailed together on a skinned cottonwood post.

The left sides of the planks had been broken off, so that the faded, painted words, one atop the other, announced SANDE CAN. It leaned to the right and was shaded by a tall willow and a rocky escarpment that stood a hundred feet above the trail. One of the willow's lower branches had been recently hacked off, leaving a ragged, pulpy scar.

Grass grew in this tight little canyon, and Colter could hear water trickling from somewhere in the rocks. The coyote dun could hear it, too. The horse lifted its fine, long snout and snorted hungrily.

Holding the dun's reins taut in his gloved fists, Colter stared at the sign.

He lifted his gaze to the trail forking off the right side of the main trail a few yards beyond the willow. The forking trail disappeared between two granite walls leaning toward each other like the heads of two skirmishing giants. It formed a corridor so narrow that Colter doubted two riders could pass through it riding abreast.

Colter put the fiddlefooting dun forward, turned it a little ways onto the forking trail, and checked it down. Dismounting, he held the dun's reins in his hand as he scoured the rocky trail.

His gaze stopped on a sliver of a shod hoofprint between two large rocks. Around it the sand and gravel had been swept clean, likely by the branch cut from the willow.

Colter stared at the print. His blood warmed.

He lifted his gaze to the narrow corridor just ahead, saw daylight on the other side of it, where the old Sanderson place likely lay. Colter had ridden with Trace to Sapinero a few times, and one such time Trace had mentioned that a man named Sanderson had built up a ranch in Sanderson Canyon because he'd found a good spring-fed stream there and enough graze for a couple of hundred cows. But the spring and the stream dried up about three years later, so Sanderson had abandoned the place and moved on.

Now it appeared the spring was running again. The creek likely was, too. And the old Sanderson place, being secluded and with the trail leading to it easy to cover, would make a good outlaw hideout.

Colter looked at the main trail pushing through a similar but wider corridor as it continued southeast toward Sapinero. Then he looked at the narrower corridor leading toward the old Sanderson place.

His mouth dried, and his throat grew heavy. His

left hand tingled as he realized his gloved fingers were caressing the walnut grips of his Remy.

If he could take down the three men who'd robbed the general store, the folks in Sapinero would welcome him with open arms. Since he'd been to town only a couple of times, and he hadn't been there in over a year, he doubted anyone would recognize him as Trace Cassidy's adopted son. As Juventino Escobar had observed, he'd grown quite a bit over the last couple of years.

A young man who brought down the three thieving killers and returned the stolen loot to the mercantile would most likely be the one rare stranger welcomed by the good folks of Sapinero.

Of course, the odds of bringing down the killers alone, when he'd never even attempted such a thing before, were long indeed. But if he could do it, maybe he had a reasonable chance of bringing Trace's killers to deadly justice as well.

Couldn't hurt to try.

He might even be able to win some confidence in himself.

Quickly, before he lost heart, he mounted the dun and rode it up the trail about a quarter mile. He tied the horse in a thick stand of mixed cedars and cottonwoods along a muddy freshet. He loosened the dun's saddle cinches, slipped its bit, then, shucking his old Tyler Henry rifle, made his way cautiously back to the trail fork.

He hadn't detected anyone watching the entrance corridor to the Sanderson place before, and now, hunkered down behind the willow, he scouted the es-

carpments carefully, his eyes probing every nook and
cranny of their stony surfaces. It would take only one
lone picket hunkered amid the rocks and boulders
running down the granite ridges to get him shot and
dragged off to a remote gully somewhere, food for the
same buzzards that had desecrated Trace.

After a few minutes of careful scrutiny, Colter became satisfied that the killers weren't watching the
narrow corridor. Maybe they were confident enough
in their own track-covering abilities, and confident
enough that they'd lost the posse east of Sapinero,
that they didn't feel they needed to.

Or maybe they'd already abandoned the place and
headed on into the mountains.

Colter rose and hefted the Henry rifle in his hands,
which sweated inside his gloves. He jogged forward,
raking his eyes back and forth across the terrain ahead
and pressing his back against the granite wall on the
trail's left side. He waited a moment, catching his
breath and pricking his ears, listening.

Hearing only occasional birdcalls and the tinny
trickle of the unseen spring, he edged a glance into
the brown-shaded corridor. About a hundred feet over
the rocky trail, the two leaning escarpments formed a
nearly solid roof, with only a sliver of blue sky showing between them.

The corridor was empty, with no one hunkering in
the shadows at the base of either wall.

Holding his rifle up high across his chest, his left
thumb caressing the hammer, he started into the corridor, wincing at the echoes his boots lifted as he
clomped across the rocks, inadvertently kicking sev-

eral. He stayed close to the corridor's left side, spying the slender, spring-fed freshet moving through the rocks and grass as he hurried through.

If they caught him in here, he'd have no cover whatsoever.

Gaining the other side, he drew a long, deep sigh of relief and continued forward into the canyon, staying just off the trail and holding his rifle high and ready.

The trail was longer than he'd thought, twisting between high stone walls, ragged aspens, and cottonwoods, and it was nearly a half hour after he'd started that he found himself hunkered near the crest of a cedar-stippled knoll, staring into the hollow on the other side.

There, a cabin, a barn, and a couple of connected corrals nestled, smoke curling from the cabin's tin chimney pipe.

In the corral connected to the barn across the yard from the cabin, a cream stallion milled with three other horses—a steeldust, a claybank, and a little skewbald paint. The stallion was drinking from a long, hollowed-log watering trough while lifting its back leg to scratch its barrel and twitching its tail at flies.

The other three horses stood in a clump at the corral's back fence, watching the stallion dubiously, like three boys wary of the schoolyard bully.

From his distance of a hundred yards away, Colter heard little from the cabin. But occasional intermittent yowls and catcalls emanated from the windows of the shabby-looking hovel, around which sage and wheatgrass grew high.

The three killers were there, all right.

Colter heard his blood rushing in his ears. Misgivings raked him.

Three or four times while hunkered there on the knoll, squeezing his rifle in his hands, he nearly convinced himself to abandon this crazy escapade, to head back the way he'd come and continue on to Sapinero.

But what then?

What would he do when and if he ran into Trace's killers? Would he turn tail and run like a donkey with tin cans tied to its tail then, too?

Studying the cabin, his mind racing, he bit his gloves off his fingers and rubbed his sweaty hands on his jeans.

Howls and occasional bursts of drunken laughter continued to rise from the shake-roofed cabin. From this angle, Colter could see the entire western wall and the partly shaded back wall. Against the back wall, an old wheel-less wagon lay tipped over on its side, overgrown with wheatgrass.

There was a window in the western wall, and another in the rear wall. The shutters of both windows had been thrown back, and flour-sack curtains could be seen licking out from the windows on a vagrant breeze. Colter couldn't be sure, but the curtains appeared to be closed.

The young drover jerked with a start as someone in the cabin laughed wildly and pounded a table. Getting himself calmed down once again, Colter ran a hand across his hairless chin and continued to study the cabin.

By the sound, the killers were drunk as coots and likely playing poker with the loot they'd taken from the mercantile.

Colter glanced once more at the chimney pipe that had caught the brunt of his attention the past few minutes. Thick white smoke—aspen smoke—continued to gush from the pipe. The smoke curled lazily toward the cerulean sky overarching the canyon.

A plan in place, Colter bit his lip, doffed his hat, and ran a hand back through his long, sweaty red hair, throwing it back behind his shoulders. Then he picked up his rifle, stole back down the knoll, and jogged around its base, making for the cabin at a crouch, hoping like hell he wasn't seen from the windows.

As he approached the hovel, the voices inside grew louder, began to separate and become distinct. He pressed his back to the rear wall, between the window and the corner, beside the overturned wagon, and heard the snicks as cards were thrown down on a table.

There was the sizzle of frying meat and the chugging of a coffeepot.

Inside, someone farted and was berated by another while the others laughed. There was the squawk of heavy iron hinges as a stove door was opened and a log was chunked into the firebox.

Colter turned to the wagon beside him and inspected it carefully, looking for the most solid places to set his feet. Then, grabbing a flat-bottomed stone from the brush, he stepped up onto the wagon, quietly slid his rifle onto the roof above, grabbed the roof's overhanging edge and, pushing off the wagon, hoisted himself up and over the top.

He set his knees against the crumbling shakes and stretched his lips back from his teeth with a wince, praying that the men inside hadn't heard the creak as his weight settled on the rooftop.

He listened.

Someone yowled happily beneath him. There was the angry clatter of breaking glass, and the man who'd yowled said in a mock placating tone, "Ah, it's okay, Standish. I'll stake ya to your first whore once we hit San Francisco!"

The voices continued, and chairs raked across floorboards, and for a second Colter, feeling his pulse beating in his temple, thought the men would leave the cabin. But then everything settled down again. Likely a new game was starting up.

Clutching his rock in one hand, and leaving his rifle behind him near the roof edge, Colter made his way on one hand and his knees toward the chimney pipe. He took his time, his face a mask of anxiety, as the sun- and snow-weathered shakes and rafters creaked and groaned beneath him. Certainly the men in the cabin could hear, but Colter prayed they were either too drunk to care or would pass it off as mice, birds, or the cabin's own natural settlings.

Finally, he made the chimney pipe. He could smell the aspen in the white smoke issuing from the dented, rusty tube. It smelled like new aspen buds in the spring. Hefting the rock in his hand and still hearing the low rumble of conversation beneath him, he set the flat-bottomed rock atop the pipe.

He waited.

His heart hammered. His thighs stiffened and ached with a fear like none he'd ever felt before.

Beneath him, the voice fell silent.

Someone exclaimed loudly, and there was the loud wooden raking of a chair across beat-up floorboards. The stove door squawked as someone opened it.

"Jesus, close the door, Clifford!" one of the killers bellowed.

Someone coughed. Coughed again.

Boots thumped and spurs chinged.

Quickly, figuring they couldn't hear him now, Colter scuttled back across the roof, picked up his rifle, and scrambled up across the middle of the roof to the front. Stretching himself out prone, he levered a cartridge into the Henry's breech, rested his right elbow on the roof, six inches from the edge, and snugged the Henry's brass butt plate against his left shoulder.

The cursing, yelling, coughing, and boot stomping was growing louder. He could feel the vibration in the shakes under him.

He'd just snugged his cheek up to the rifle's stock, aiming into the yard, when the front door scraped open nearly directly below him. A figure bounded into the yard on a puff of heavy gray smoke.

It was a tall, dark-haired man in a white-and-gray-checked shirt and a red neckerchief. He shambled into the yard holding his crooked arm across his face, coughing and cursing at the top of his lungs.

Colter lined up the Henry's sights on the man, ignoring his hammering heart. He tightened his finger against the trigger but held fire.

Another figure bounded out the door, with a third close on his heels, shoving him forward and yelling, "Get the hell out of my way, Chulo, you fat bastard!"

He and the second man—a big, broad-shouldered, thick-necked man with long, dark brown hair— stumbled into the yard in front of the cabin and away from the smoke puffing from the open front door.

"Hold it right there, you sonsabitches!" Colter heard his voice quaver and screech. "I got you dead to rights, so throw down those shootin' irons!"

He'd learned from reading a few dime novels that the good guys always gave the bad guys a chance to disarm themselves before greasing them. But suddenly, as the first man out of the cabin swung toward him, clawing a revolver from the holster thonged low on his right thigh, he wished he'd gone ahead and backshot all three of these hombres.

He gave a surprised, horrified grunt as the tall man bunched his lips angrily and raised the Colt in his hand toward the cabin roof.

The gun looked huge, its round black maw even huger.

Reactively, Colter drew a hasty bead on the man's chest and pulled the Henry's trigger.

# Chapter 7

The Henry's roaring whip crack felt like a cupped hand slamming against Colter's left ear.

The man in the checked shirt jerked suddenly, as though someone had just told him something he couldn't possibly believe. His big Colt stopped its ascent toward the cabin roof and dropped back down against his thigh, but not before it roared, blowing up dust and gravel between the man and the cabin.

As he turned and staggered drunkenly away before falling to his knees, the third man out of the cabin—a scrawny gent in a bowler hat—screamed, "The roof!"

At the same time, he slid a Schofield .44 revolver from behind the waistband of his checked wool pants and, thumbing back the hammer, began raising it toward Colter.

Colter blinked against the smoke now licking up into his face from the open door beneath him, stinging his eyes, and aimed at the scrawny gent's chest. He blinked at the same time he pulled the trigger, and heard a yowl beneath the Henry's explosion. He opened his eyes to see the scrawny gent staggering to one side while cupping his right ear with both hands, including the one that held the Schofield.

He was mewling like an enraged sheep, and cursing as he glared up at Colter.

The young drover ejected the spent, smoking cartridge from the Henry's breech. He was seating a fresh one when a revolver popped in front of the cabin. The slug hammered into the stout log wall only a few inches below Colter's face.

He felt the jolt of the heavy slug slamming into the log, and winced as splinters sprayed up into his face, which was wet from tears caused by the eye-stinging smoke.

He jerked a look into the yard and saw the big man, Chulo, moving around in the wafting smoke, sidestepping and canting his head from side to side as he cocked the Dragoon Colt in his right hand, trying to draw accurate aim on Colter.

Waves of terror shot through the young drover's bloodstream. He slammed the Henry's lever home just as Chulo fired his Dragoon once again.

*Thwack!*

The .44 slug slammed into a log just below and to the left of Colter's left elbow.

Colter held his breath as he centered a bead on the big Mexican's broad chest. He squeezed the trigger, and the Henry roared just as Chulo jerked back and sideways.

At first Colter thought he'd missed the man. Smoke

wafted in front of his face. When it cleared, he saw Chulo half running and half tripping away from the cabin and into the clearing before crumpling to his knees.

Facing away from Colter, he dropped the big Dragoon and held both hands across his belly, lowering his head nearly all the way to the ground. Then he straightened up again, throwing his head back and loosing a stream of Spanish epithets skyward.

Another pistol barked from Colter's right.

Ejecting another smoking cartridge casing over his right shoulder, the young drover jerked a panicked look toward the scrawny, bowler-hatted gent, who pressed one hand to his bloody right ear as he held his Schofield straight out and slightly up from his shoulder, grinning evilly.

"Why, you little *peckerwood*!" he screamed.

At the same time, the Schofield belched smoke and flames. The bullet blew Colter's hat from his head. The boy gasped and rolled sideways, angling back away from the edge of the roof while ramming another cartridge into the Henry's chamber.

The Schofield barked two more times, the slugs whistling over the roof.

Colter rolled up to the cabin's west edge, about five feet back from the front, and snaked the Henry down over the side. The scrawny man was sidestepping around the cabin's corner, looking for him. Now he saw him but before he could swing the Schofield around, Colter triggered the Henry.

"*Ach!*" The scrawny gent clapped the hand he'd been holding over his ear to his upper-right thigh, from which blood dribbled from the hole Colter had drilled in his checked pants, six inches below the man's cartridge belt.

Screaming, the man lowered the Schofield quickly and inadvertently tripped the trigger. Dust puffed from the toe of his right boot. The man howled louder and leapt straight up in the air, landing on his butt in the dirt and holding his right foot two feet off the ground, staring at it with horror, eyes wide as cow plops.

He'd drilled a round through his own foot, which quivered like a leaf on a breeze-jostled branch. Blood trickled from the smoking hole in the worn leather and dribbled down toward the heel.

"You little redheaded twirp!" the scrawny gent cried over his boot, spittle flying from his lips. "Look what you did to me, you son of a syphilitic whore!"

The man cursed again and grabbed his Schofield from the ground beside him. As he raised it, Colter pressed his chin against the roof, heard the two loud pops and then a metallic click as the revolver's hammer snapped against the firing pin, empty.

Colter levered a fresh round and aimed the Henry over the edge of the cabin. The scrawny gent stared at him, wide-eyed, as Colter planted a bead on the man's grimy, cream-colored shirt, between the flaps of his paisley vest. He wore a rawhide thong around his neck, with a tobacco sack attached. Colter aimed at the sack, which rested just over the man's heart.

"No!" the man screamed, flopping back in the dirt and throwing his arms up over his head. "Don't kill me. *Please!*"

Colter held fire as the man cowered in the dirt. Lifting his head from the Henry's stock, Colter crawled up toward the front edge of the cabin. The smoke curling up from the door was thinning, and through the foglike wisps he could see the big Mexican still on his knees about fifty feet from the cabin, his back to it, crouched over his belly.

He hadn't moved since Colter had shot him. His long black hair blew out in a sudden wind gust.

Neither had the tall gent in the checked shirt moved since Colter had drilled him. He lay on his back to the Mexican's left but closer to the cabin, legs spread, both hands resting against his bloody gut as if to indicate the wound that had killed him.

The scrawny gent continued to moan and plead for his life as he pressed his head into the dust and covered it with his arms.

Slowly Colter stood. His feet and legs felt like mush, and his heart hammered against his ribs. Crouching and holding the Henry low, he made his way back to the rear of the cabin. His face was flushed and stony as he scrambled down off the roof to the wagon, then off the wagon to land on the ground flat-footed, knees bent, a puff of air issuing from his throat with a hollow grunt.

He made his way around the west side of the cabin uncertainly, staggering slightly as though he'd been on a boat and had lost his land legs. Ahead, a few yards out from the cabin's front corner, the scrawny gent was on his knees, muttering furiously to himself as he thumbed cartridges from his shell belt and slipped them through his Schofield's open loading gate.

Six spent shells lay in the sage and red gravel before him.

Colter stopped and raised the Henry to his shoulder. "Hold it, Mister."

The scrawny gent, who'd lost his bowler hat and whose thin, sandy hair slid around the nearly bald crown of his head, glanced at Colter, snarling, "You hold it, sonny. I ain't gonna get took down by no snot-nosed *kid*."

He thumbed the last shell into the cylinder. "I'm guessin' you can't shoot a man up close, when you can see the whites of his eyes." He flipped the loading gate closed with a click.

Colter's throat was so dry he managed only a croak. "Hold it!"

The scrawny gent spun the cylinder and, bunching his lips and grinning defiantly, cocked the Schofield and extended the gun out from his shoulder.

The Henry's whip crack echoed off the cabin and hammered out across the canyon.

The scrawny gent triggered his Schofield wild as his head snapped back on his shoulders. He spread his arms and dropped the Schofield, which hit the ground with a thump as he gazed at Colter, thunderstruck.

The quarter-sized hole in the middle of the man's forehead turned dark red. Blood dribbled out of it to run down toward his right eye. But before it got there the scrawny gent grunted and sagged straight back against the ground. Curled beneath his rump and his back, his legs jerked for a time, as did his arms, and his head wagged from side to side as though in utter shock and disbelief of his situation.

Slowly, as the life left him, the spasms died. Then he just lay there, still, like some oversized bird in gaudy checked drummer's pants dropped from the sky.

Colter kept the Henry pressed against his shoulder for a long time, until long after the acrid black powder smoke had wafted away on the breeze. Slowly he lowered the gun to his side and stepped woodenly forward.

His ears rang. His feet felt as though heavy rocks had been strapped to each. His chest was raw. His stomach was turning flip-flops, and he felt like he had the day after he and Chance had sampled too much of the chokecherry wine they'd brewed up at the line shack last fall—thin, oily witch's fingers clawing at the back of his throat.

"Jesus," he heard himself mutter as he stopped and stared down at the scrawny gent.

The man's eyes were closed, blood pooling over the lid of the right one. The little finger and ring finger of his right hand were still twitching. His sweat-damp hair slid around in the breeze. A single gold tooth gleamed between his slightly parted lips.

Colter turned and, feeling as though he was slogging through quicksand, moved over to the Mexican, who, still kneeling, had dropped forward onto his face. His arms were crossed over his belly, and the ground around him was thick with liver-colored blood and viscera. His shoulders were still, and he made no sound whatever.

Colter swallowed quickly to keep his breakfast down, wrinkling his nose at the heavy, coppery, ammoniac smell of the man's insides, and moved over to the tall gent in the checked shirt. He didn't know why he looked down at the man—he knew the man had been dead even before he'd hit the ground—but something inside him, though appalled and horrified, was also fascinated by the death around him.

And by the fact that he'd caused it.

The tall man's blue eyes were wide-open and the corners of his mouth were raised, as though he was smiling up at Colter.

Colter dropped the Henry in a sage shrub, slogged away, dragging his boot toes, then dropped to his knees and convulsed violently, retching.

When Colter had finished "airing his paunch," as Chance called it, he crawled back up onto the cabin roof and removed the rock from the chimney pipe. After climbing down, he took his time retrieving his horse. He needed to clear his head, and the smoke needed to clear from the cabin.

He would stay in the old ranch house tonight, as he didn't have the stomach for preparing the three dead men for hauling into Sapinero still today. He'd have to wrestle each bloody cadaver up over its saddled horse and lash it down.

The very thought of the grisly task—of feeling the rubbery, dead flesh against his own, not to mention the blood—sent another shudder through his loins and threatened another dry heave.

It wasn't until after he'd retrieved the coyote dun and turned it into the corral with the outlaws' four mounts, and dragged the bodies about fifty yards into the canyon, that the gravity of his accomplishment began to sink in.

It drove out the lingering nausea and made his hands tingle with satisfaction. A muffled, addled satisfaction, but satisfaction just the same.

He wished Juventino was here to see the results of his rifle work. And Ruth.

After he'd dragged the bodies off, he washed at the creek that trickled through the gully near the canyon, trying to rid himself of the cloying death stench, then headed back to the cabin. Some of the smoke lingered in thin webs, and it was still thick, but Colter walked in and found the loot from the Sapinero mercantile in one pouch of a pair of saddlebags on the floor, near the overturned chair it had probably been draped over.

He didn't bother counting the two wads of greenbacks and the gold and silver in a small burlap pouch. He had no interest in stolen money and couldn't understand anyone spending money they themselves hadn't earned. How could they possibly feel anything but wretched for doing it?

Wretched, useless, and just plain no good?

He swept the money off the table where the three outlaws had been playing cards, separating the certificates and the coins from the pasteboards and putting it all into the saddlebags. He buckled the strap over the bulging pouch and tossed the bags into a corner.

Then he picked up the overturned chair and sat down in it. He dropped his hat onto the table and swept his hand through his long red hair, which was still damp from the creek. He held the hand out in front of his face.

It shook like an aspen leaf in a chill autumn breeze. He turned it into a fist and steadied it, staring at it.

Colter Farrow chuckled sardonically to himself.

He'd killed three men, and he hadn't even found the men who'd killed Trace yet.

Tomorrow he'd head for Sapinero.

# Chapter 8

Colter slept fitfully on a cot in the small three-room cabin, awakened about midnight by coyotes yipping and snarling around the three dead men in the canyon. He stumbled to the door and fired three shots into the night.

The coyotes fell silent. A moment later he heard brush rustling and breath rasping as the scavengers lit out toward the opposite star-hooded slope.

He was up at dawn, frying the side pork Ruth had packed, eating the thick, greasy slabs between biscuit halves, and washing them down with bitter black coffee. Loading the three dead men onto their saddled mounts was every bit as unsavory as he'd figured it would be—even more so now that they'd been nibbled on by the coyotes and were stiffening up and especially hard to lash belly down to their saddles.

When he finally had all three tied down as well as possible, enshrouded by their own blanket rolls, he mounted the coyote dun and started back the way he'd come, heading for the main trail. The fourth

horse, which the men had used as a pack animal—
Colter had found a wooden pack saddle and canvas
panniers in the barn—trailed along behind, nickering
occasionally, as did the other horses, at the cloying
stench of death.

He was certain now that Trace's wagon had made a
beeline from Sapinero. There'd been a chance Trace
had been robbed along the trail somewhere, on his
way back from town, but Colter had seen no signs of
a skirmish along the main trail and no sign of a
wagon pulling off anywhere.

That meant that Trace had most likely left the town
dead.

For that reason, Colter regarded the town rising
from the scorched sage flat before him with a small,
sharp hammer of trepidation and anger pounding the
back of his head just up from his neck. He supposed
the fear was a good thing, not something to be ashamed
of. Without it, he might have galloped into town like
one of Quantrill's raiders, shooting at every window
and swing door and calling out a challenge to the killers who'd beefed his kin.

And gotten himself promptly turned toes down
and no good to Ruth—or Trace—at all.

No, he'd have to play this with the skill of a seasoned gambler, slowly gaining the trust of the other
players and finding who held what before showing
his own cards. Only when he found out who'd killed
Trace—and there was probably more than one man—
would he figure out how to collect on the debt.

Suddenly, as the little sunbaked town sprouted
around him among the sprawling green willows, syc-

amores, oaks, and cottonwoods of Sapinero Creek, he heard himself whistling softly.

He smiled at that.

That was good. He was just a whistling drifter with no purpose here aside from turning the dead men in to the sheriff and maybe collecting any reward they carried.

He edged the caravan toward the center of the little town, the adobe brick shanties of which—and the central courtyard ringed with trees and bordered by a stout brown Catholic church—bespoke its Spanish origins. A fountain whispered in the middle of the square, and a couple of black-haired Mexican children stood around it, poking with a stick at something in the large stone bowl.

Colter kept his head straight forward as he edged along the square's right side, but he saw in the periphery of his vision people stopping along the boardwalks to stare. Several muttered hushed exclamations, while one old woman in a purple gown and a feathered picture hat drew a sharp, audible breath and pointed toward Colter with her cane.

Youthful chatter and laughter sounded behind the caravan. Colter turned to see three boys, between ten and thirteen, running along behind the last horse, exclaiming to each other and pointing at the dead men.

". . . and that one there—that's Chulo Espinoza," announced a towheaded lad carrying a small rifle carved from cottonwood. "He's the one that killed Mr. Herman!"

"Uh-*uh*!" objected a younger boy—a Mexican with close-cropped hair and sandals that made slapping sounds in the dirt. "That ain't Chulo—no, sir! Chulo's *way* taller than that!"

As the procession collected one more curious boy from a trash-littered gap between a drugstore and a squalid-looking cantina, and a handful of dogs, Colter angled the coyote dun toward a low, narrow building sandwiched between a bank and a harness shop and fronted by an arbor of peeled cottonwood poles.

A short, stocky man in a broad-brimmed tan hat stood leaning against one of the arbor's support posts, regarding Colter skeptically. He wore a tin star on the pocket of his wash-worn red-brown shirt, which was unbuttoned halfway down his broad chest, the sleeves rolled up past his heavy biceps. A black ivory-gripped Colt hung low on his right thigh, in a silver-trimmed cutaway black holster.

As Colter put the dun up to the hitchrack fronting the sheriff's office, the star-toter on the gallery rolled a stove match across his lips and turned his head slightly toward the open door behind him.

"Bill," he said, "you best get out here, take a look at this."

A man's voice said something from inside the sheriff's office, but Colter couldn't make out the words.

"Just get out here," the stocky gent said.

Colter gave the man a cordial nod. "How-do," he said, playing his role as self-effacingly as possible. Just a simple, drifting kid whom hard run-of-the mill frontier luck sent to riding the grubline. "Ran these hardcases down a ways west of here. They got stolen money on 'em. Thought you might wanna have a look."

The stocky lawman, still leaning against the post,

his thumbs hooked behind his shell belt, scrutinized Colter carefully through narrowed eyes. Colter wondered for a moment if the man recognized him, but nixed the worry. He hadn't been to town for two years, and he'd changed a lot since then. Besides, he'd never been in Sapinero long enough for anyone to get much of a look at him.

Boots thudded and spurs rang behind the stocky man. A taller, more menacing-looking man appeared in the doorway.

He was a good six inches taller than the stocky gent. He had longish silver hair and a sweeping silver mustache, with cold blue eyes and skin like ancient saddle leather. Despite the color of his hair and the seasoning of his features, something in the man's clear eyes and square shoulders told Colter that he was probably only in his early thirties.

"What the hell is this?" he muttered, scowling at the horses strung out behind Colter. He held his hands together in front of his belly, absently turning the large gold ring set with a green stone on his right middle finger.

The stocky gent said nothing. He just kept leaning against his post, regarding Colter with a sort of sneering disregard.

"You the sheriff?" Colter asked the tall man, who wore a silver-chased, pearl-gripped Peacemaker .45 positioned for the cross draw on his left hip.

The tall man stepped out the door, letting his spurs ring with an absent flourish. He stopped at the edge of the gallery and ran his gaze along the horses behind Colter.

By now, the three boys were closely scrutinizing the dead men, stooping to peer at their heads beneath the blankets, while several older men, some in the garb of shopkeepers, had strolled out from their stores to inspect the grisly cargoes as well. They were muttering among themselves in surprised, disbelieving tones.

"Sure enough, it is," said one man in hushed awe, elbowing the gent beside him. He glanced toward the gallery. "Hey, Sheriff. Get a load of this. This here stiff is Ralph Hodges! The one up there is Chulo Espinoza!"

Wearing a brown wool vest and armbands, the man regarded the sheriff with eyes lit with shock and pleasant surprise, his lower jaw hanging.

The sheriff glanced at Colter, scowling. With a skeptical grunt, he stepped off the boardwalk and moved around the coyote dun and over toward where the men and boys were inspecting the heads of the bodies dangling over the horses' stirrup fenders. The sheriff kicked at a dog sniffing around the horses.

As the dog yipped and jerked away, the lawman stopped at the cream stallion, ran his left hand over the double chain-link brand on the horse's left wither. Colter saw the man's scowl grow on his leathery face as he jerked up the blanket from over the head of the tall man in the checked shirt, whom Colter had taken out with a heart shot. He lifted the man's head by his black hair, and Colter saw the sheriff's cheeks turn red as a desert sunset.

"It's Heck Standish!" exclaimed one of the men who'd recently poured out of the saloon on the other side of the square to gather in a semicircle around the pack string.

A hushed roar rose from the crowd of shocked onlookers. One of the boys said to another, "Holy-moly—I told ya it was them!"

A dog barked.

"Thank Christ," said a man in a business suit and a low-crowned, flat-brimmed beaver hat. Walking up with a fat stogie in his beringed right hand, he looked at Colter still sitting the coyote dun before the sheriff's office. "Young man—the money. Did you find the money these killers stole from the mercantile? I'm Mr. Spurlock's attorney, and—"

"That's enough, Mabry!" the sheriff barked. He threw an arm out in a broad, sweeping gesture. "All of you—get on outta here now. Go on—*git*! This is a job for law enforcement, and if you will all haul your useless asses back to your shops or saloons or wherever the hell you came from, me and my deputy will ask all the questions necessary and see that the Standish boys are dutifully planted on boot hill."

"Hey, kid!" a man yelled from the opposite side of the town square, where he stood before a little cantina with three others holding soapy beer mugs in their fists. "Standish lost Sheriff Rondo and Deputy Bannon way east of here! Where the hell did *you* run 'em down?"

The man appeared disfigured in a way Colter had never seen before. Slumped slightly forward and to one side, the man had an enormous hump rising from his back, over his right shoulder, as though he were packing something under his grimy rat-hair coat. As though to hide the hump's effect, he wore a billowing red bandanna around his neck.

He grinned devilishly. The men beside him laughed mockingly. The men and boys around the dead men smirked.

Sheriff Rondo scowled at the man with the humped back. Large, blue-black veins forked above his nose as he jerked his piqued gaze at the crowd lingering around the packhorses.

"I told all of you to vamoose, goddamn it! Don't make me tell ya again, or I'll arrest every last one of you, including those damn mangy mutts—for *vagrancy*!"

The crowd, including all the dogs but one, reluctantly dispersed, the boys running off down the street and pretend-shooting at each other. As the sheriff walked down to the second horse, inspecting the face of the scrawny sandy-haired man, the deputy slipped his ivory-handled Colt from its holster and fired a round into the street near the wolflike dog lingering around the dead Mexican's horse.

The dog jumped nearly a foot in the air, twisting around, then ran, squealing, into an alley beside the saloon. Holstering the smoking hogleg, the deputy gave Colter a meaningful glance and went over to stand beside the sheriff, who was looking with disbelief down at the exposed head of the belly-shot Mexican.

Colter felt a tightness in his chest. Damn, he had figured this whole thing wrong. Way wrong.

He'd expected the town to welcome him with open

arms, once it had seen who he'd hauled in belly down across their saddles. And maybe the town itself had, but the ones who really counted, the ones who would decide the flavor of his visit—the *lawmen*—were obviously more than a little piss-burned.

Hipped around in his saddle and watching the two local badge-toters, Colter kept his face expressionless, belying the turmoil behind his mask.

Sheriff Rondo opened his fist to release the Mexican's long hair, and Chulo's head hit the saddle fender with a leathery slap. Squinting one cold blue eye up at Colter, and absently polishing his gold ring on his vest, the sheriff said, "You gonna tell me you"—he ran his sneering gaze quickly up and down Colter's lean frame—"took all three of these men down your ownself?"

"Yessir," Colter said politely, sincerely. He'd started the race; now he had to finish it. "I sure did."

The deputy looked at him sharply. It was like a slap from his flat brown eyes.

"They tried to run me out of a cabin in Sanderson Canyon." Colter hurried to explain, curling his left leg up over his saddle bows while leaning back over the cantle with feigned ease. He chuckled dryly. "I don't reckon they were ready for a dustup when they tried to run me off, but they got one. My daddy told me to never truckle to no man. I didn't see the saddlebags till later. I take it that money's been stolen?"

Rondo followed Colter's gaze to the saddlebags draped over the coyote dun's hindquarters. He unbuckled the strap over the bulging left pouch and peered inside. Plucking the bags off the dun's back, he draped them over his shoulder and squinted up at Colter again.

"Is it all here?"

"As far as I know."

Rondo glanced at his deputy. Returning his disapproving gaze to the young drover, he said out of the side of his mouth, "Chico, take these men over to the undertaker's while me and the redheaded shaver here . . ." He stopped to bark, "What's your name, boy?"

"Colter Farrow, sir."

". . . While me and Colter Farrow go on inside and have us a little sit-down chat."

# Chapter 9

Colter hesitated at the sheriff's invitation.

He looked at the stocky deputy as the man, standing beside the coyote dun, held out his open hand. Colter tossed the packhorse's lead rope to the deputy and glanced at the sheriff.

Rondo stood at the entrance to the sheriff's office, regarding Colter grimly, thumbs once again hooked behind his wide leather shell belt, black boots planted shoulder-width apart.

"See ya later, boy," the deputy said, chuckling and chomping down on his stove match as he began leading the horses up the street and around the square.

Colter glanced at the sheriff again. Then, that knot in his chest growing tighter and harder, he swung down from the coyote dun's back and tied the reins at the hitchrack. The thirsty dun started drawing water from the stock tank that stood on the other side of the rack.

Mounting the gallery and beating dust from his

jeans with his hat, Colter stepped through the jail-house's open door. Rondo had stopped a ways inside the dirt-floored room, which was cool and dark, with spiderwebs hanging from the low rafters. The sheriff of Sapinero County stood a good four inches taller than Colter. He grinned down at the young drover—a phony welcoming smile, no welcome in it at all.

When Colter had stopped just over the threshold, the sheriff said, "Now, then . . ."

He moved as if to close the door. Stopping suddenly, he turned back to Colter and, with a savage grunt, buried his left fist in Colter's solar plexus. Colter had been between breaths, and the unexpected blow drove out what little air he had in his lungs with a *"gnahh!"*

Colter's knees hit the hard dirt floor.

Clutching his belly with both hands, pain and nausea storming through him, he dropped his head nearly all the way to the dirt, and his hat tumbled off his shoulder. Red and blue starbursts obscured his vision as he gulped air like a landed fish.

Behind him he heard the door close. He looked slightly up to see Bill Rondo's long legs saunter in front of him, the man's pin-striped whipcord trousers tucked into his high-topped, hand-tooled black boots, the heels of which he slammed down as he walked with mocking flare.

"Now, then," Rondo said, rubbing the front of his ring across his cheek. "Let's get one thing straight, you little pip-squeak. You didn't take down those three owlhoots out yonder, understand?"

The man moved behind a desk that sidled against

the left wall of the narrow room, flanked by a stout-timbered door with a small barred window in it. The door to the cellblock. He tossed his hat on his desk and palmed a lock of his thick silver hair back onto his temple.

Colter sucked a breath and looked up at the man, teeth gritted. He flexed his left hand and was a little startled in spite of the savageness of the sucker punch to find the hand beginning to move toward the Remington holstered butt forward on his right hip. He'd never killed until a few hours ago, and now he was suddenly ready to kill again.

He stayed the hand, but bile boiled through him as Rondo smiled down at him from behind his desk.

"I asked you if you understood."

Colter glared up at the man. He wouldn't get anywhere defying the sheriff. At least not yet. Steeling himself against his own rage, he nodded.

"I didn't take 'em down," he said in a pinched, pain-racked voice.

"Nope, you didn't."

Rondo plopped down in his swivel chair and leaned back, crossing his black boots, his large-roweled Chihuahua-style spurs grinding into the deep notches they'd obviously already carved in the oak.

"You took 'em by surprise. Like I just took you. They penned their horses and started to the cabin, not realizing you were there. You'd heard about the robbery of the mercantile here in town and decided there might be a reward if you returned the money. And, of course, you'd be a hero in the townfolks' eyes."

Rondo stopped and arched a brow. Colter was still

down on his knees, arms crossed against his belly. As he glowered up at the sheriff, the boy's freckled, angular face was bleached as white as a bone in the desert, and his jaws were clenched so tight the skin over their joints dimpled.

He'd been hit before but never that hard. And never by a lawman. He was as incredulous as he was enraged. He still wanted to kill the man, and the knowledge that he would do it—or try to do it—if he didn't consciously suppress the notion, was almost as startling as Rondo's fist in his solar plexus.

"Are you following all this, or do I need to slow down?" the red-faced sheriff asked.

Colter said nothing, just knelt there in anguish, raking air in and out of his lungs.

"Answer me, boy! I won't stand for the disrespect I see in your eyes!"

Colter climbed to his feet, straightening his back slowly and feeling as though a tight knot was coming painfully undone in his belly. "I understand," he grumbled. He filled his chest with air, noted an abatement in the pain. "You want me to tell folks I drygulched those killers."

He wanted to add a snide remark but stopped himself. It might make him feel better, but it wouldn't help him find the men responsible for Trace's murder.

"You're smarter than you look, boy." Rondo threw his head back and laughed. He clipped the laugh and pointed at the door. "Now, what I want you to do is get back on that dun of yours. . . ."

He let his voice trail off as thuds sounded outside the open door. He glanced at the opening, and his thin silver brows beetled as boots pounded the gallery's floorboards. In the corner of his right eye, Colter saw a figure enter, breathing hard as though he'd run a long way.

"Rondo, where's that kid that . . ."

The newcomer's voice trailed off as Colter turned toward the door. He found himself facing a big-bellied man with broad shoulders and a high-crowned gray Stetson. The gallery's floorboards continued to pound until another man followed the first one into the jailhouse. He in turn was followed by a pretty blond girl about Colter's age or maybe a little younger.

The second man was tall, rangy, and handsome, wearing a cinnamon bullhorn mustache and worn but stylish drover's garb, including a battered tan Stetson, a pinto vest, brown chaps, a Schofield .44 on his hip, and another wedged behind his belt buckle.

The girl had a heart-shaped face with frosty blue eyes, and she wore a blue muslin dress under a green apron. It was not a crisp dress, but a dress that had seen more than its share of hard washings—maybe a favorite dress the girl couldn't part with in spite of its wear. Its ragged white sleeves were rolled carelessly up on her lightly suntanned arms.

The girl's thick, curly blond hair was held back from her forehead with a red neckerchief, and her eyes bored into Colter's. They were cast with curiosity and cool female interest.

She stopped just inside the door, then stepped back and to one side, folding her arms across the apron that could not conceal the full swell of her breasts, and leaned against the doorjamb. Her critical gaze raked Colter's slender, boyish frame up and down, and then she canted her head slightly to one side, as though in continued deliberation with herself.

The first man in the room said, "This him?"

"Who?" Rondo said, unable to keep the displeasure from his voice.

"The one that took down them owlhoots that robbed my store!"

The big man—between fifty and sixty years old and wearing every year on his broad, clean-shaven face, his gray hair cropped close above his ears—kept his eyes on Colter. They were the same blue as the girl's. His and the girl's jaws were similar also, but the father-daughter resemblance stopped there.

"This ain't him, is it?" the older man said, indicating Colter with a big, pudgy hand and glancing at Rondo.

"I'm the one," Colter said before Rondo could speak. "I'm afraid the sheriff here got it out of me." He feigned a sheepish grin. "I reckon I sorta surprised them killers."

"Where were they?"

"The old Sanderson place," Rondo said, holding a hand up to inspect his fingernails. "They musta circled around, just like I suspicioned they'd do. I was gonna head out that way . . . but then Junior here rode in. He surprised 'em on their way to the cabin."

Rondo looked at Colter. "Heard about the holdup in Mr. Spurlock's mercantile—that it, boy?"

Colter nodded, his sheepish half grin in place. He glanced at the girl, who was still regarding him critically, skeptically from her place against the doorjamb.

"I thought maybe there was a reward on 'em. Maybe one for the money, too."

"And, then, of course the kid was looking for a little respect," Rondo added, jeering. His mocking gaze fell on the girl behind Colter as he added, "Lookin' to turn a purty face or two, I 'spect."

Colter glanced at the sheriff. The sheriff glanced at Colter, smiling smugly.

Colter turned to the big man before him, flanked by the darkly handsome, slightly taller man in the pinto vest who was regarding Colter with mute interest, lips pursed beneath his shaggy mustache. Colter was burning inside, and his ears were as hot as the bricks Ruth used to warm their beds of a winter's mountain morning.

But he only shrugged and gave an awe-shucks-I-reckon-ya-caught-me grin.

"Son, I'm Paul Spurlock," the older gent said. "This here's my *segundo*, Blaine Surtees." He placed a hand on Colter's shoulder, casting the sheriff a mildly jeering gaze of his own. "And I don't care if you walked up on those men on a dark night and shot them in their sleep. I'm just glad to have the money back."

He nodded at the saddlebags draped over the cold woodstove in the middle of the small, dark office. "Those them?"

Rondo nodded grimly.

"All the money there?"

"Haven't had time to count it," the sheriff said, lacing his fingers behind his head.

Spurlock grabbed the saddlebags from the woodstove, walked over and handed them to the girl. "Jenny, count it, will you?" To Colter, he said, "They must've figured out when I had the most cash on hand. I pay my town wages through the mercantile, so every third Friday I have more cash in the store than usual. No vault, just a cash drawer."

Spurlock cast his jeering, disapproving glance at the sheriff once again. "That used to be enough. That and my name."

Rondo lifted a shoulder. "Maybe your name don't pull as much weight as it used to."

"Or maybe you're letting a bad element seep into the town," the girl castigated.

The outburst, as she knelt to go through the money in the saddlebag pouch, surprised everyone, including Colter, who turned toward her. She didn't look up but only started counting a wad of greenbacks in her hand, silently moving her lips. Her lightly suntanned forehead was etched with anger.

Spurlock chuckled as Rondo's face turned a darker shade of red. Behind Spurlock, Surtees chuffed and, grinning with bemusement, scratched at a mud stain on his vest.

"Maybe I oughta make the boy my sheriff," Spurlock said, smiling approvingly at Colter.

"Ah, no, sir," the young drover said, trying to keep as low a profile as possible under the circumstances. "I reckon I just got lucky with the Standish bunch, is all. Lucky I ain't facedown in a gully somewheres around the Sanderson place."

He was fervently regretting having taken down the Standish men. That had been a bad decision. He should have just wandered into Sapinero like any young grubline-riding drifter and kept his head down until he'd gotten the physical as well as political layout of the town.

"I reckon," Spurlock said. "But if you hadn't gotten so lucky, I'd be out a good five thousand dollars, and that ain't peanuts even for me. Not with the dry summers we been having the past several years. I settled here first as a rancher, you see. Later I opened the mercantile and the hotel and saloon, and I run the hotel while my daughter—Jenny there—runs the mercantile. But the ranch is still the cornerstone of my holdings."

He turned to Rondo. "How in the hell did Standish ever get around you, Bill? I figured you for a better tracker than that."

Rondo let a stretched second pass. His chest rose and fell as he breathed and held Spurlock's disapproving glare. "We all have a bad day now and then. You got your money back." He dropped his feet to the floor, those big spurs' rowels rattling raucously. "I hate to be rude, Mr. Spurlock, but I got work to do."

"I reckon we better let you get to it, then." Spurlock glanced at Colter, then jerked his head toward the door, before which Jenny now stood with the saddlebags draped over her shoulder. "Step out with us, son."

Colter cast a quick glance at Rondo, who regarded him with menacing dullness, then followed Spurlock, his daughter, and the *segundo*, Surtees, outside. He closed the door behind him. The girl turned to put her back against the hitchrack, and Colter's coyote dun lowered its head to sniff her hair. The girl smiled. It was the first smile Colter had seen from her, and he liked how it softened her features.

She turned to the dun and ran a gentle hand along the horse's jaw, and the dun nickered contentedly.

"What's your name, son?" Spurlock asked, standing on the gallery as he lit a long black cheroot and blew smoke toward the street.

"Colter Farrow, sir."

"Farrow." Spurlock frowned. "Don't believe I know that name."

"I'm not from around here." Colter thought quickly. He hadn't figured out a fictional place of origin, so he grabbed at the first place he could think of that was far away from here. "I'm from Nevada. Winnemucca, Nevada."

A couple of years ago Trace had hired a rider from Winnemucca.

"Winnemucca. Hmmm."

Colter's gut tightened. He thought the rancher was going to mention someone he knew from Winnemucca. But Spurlock merely nodded and blew smoke through his nostrils as he glanced at Surtees.

"S'pose the lad is due a reward, don't you think, Blaine?"

Surtees was obviously the taciturn sort. Staring with his cobalt blue eyes at Colter, he merely grunted and jerked his shoulders.

Spurlock looked at the girl, who was still running a hand down the dun's fine snout. "All the money there, Jenny?"

The girl nodded. "It's all here, Pa." She glanced at Colter obliquely, fleetingly, then turned back to the horse.

Spurlock reached into his pants pocket, flipped a gold coin to Colter, who caught it against his chest. "There's ten dollars for your trouble, son. Sorry it ain't more. Didn't have time to post a reward for the money or the Standish bunch, and these are lean times. I hope that'll do."

"It'll do, Mr. Spurlock. It's much appreciated, in fact." Colter swallowed, thinking fast. "But I was wondering, sir, if you might have a job for me somewhere hereabouts. I'm purty down-at-heel after ridin' all over Nevada and Utah lookin' fer drover work. Seems it's too late in the summer. Outfits ain't hirin' till fall."

"Same with us," Surtees said. His voice was low and soft, almost feminine. He was leaning into an arm propped high on a porch post.

"I already hired a fella over to the mercantile, Pa," Jenny said, not looking at Colter even fleetingly now.

Colter's stomach sank. He'd hoped the girl might help somehow, as he'd felt a vague, inexplicable connection to her.

"Well, there's the livery barn," Spurlock said with a contemplative sigh. "It's down a side street beyond the church, just across from the schoolhouse. You're good with horses?"

"Yessir."

"Very well, then. Tell old Charley Manuel over to the livery barn he has a new man on his roll. He has one wrangler already, the hunchback Wayne Kilgore."

Spurlock gave Colter a meaningful look. "Stay away from him. Steer wide, hear? The man's a trouble-maker."

Colter smiled with genuine gratitude. "I appreciate it, sir."

"Don't appreciate it too much till you hear how much Manuel's willing to pay you. I only own a half interest in the barn and, per our agreement, Charley sets the wages."

Spurlock removed the cigar from his teeth and blew out a long smoke plume. He was a roughhewn man, but there was intelligence and sophistication as well as smug confidence in his gaze. Colter had known a few like him before. They'd fought hard and scrim-maged well for what they'd attained, and they were not men to be trifled with.

Colter hoped neither he nor his men had had any-thing to do with Trace's murder. He'd have no idea how to take down a man of Spurlock's caliber.

"In a month or two, ride on out to the ranch and talk to Blaine here about a roundup job." Spurlock pinched his hat brim at Colter. "Thanks again for re-trieving the money, Mr. Farrow. Maybe we'll talk again soon."

Colter fingered the ten-dollar gold piece in his pocket as the three walked away. The girl fell back. Casually, she strolled over to Colter.

His heart thudded, and he was about to remove his hat when she said in a hard, bitter voice, glancing at the coyote dun standing hang-headed at the hitchrack, "The dun's brand is plain as day, Red. Better head back to the mountains you came from, or you'll sorely regret it."

Jennifer Spurlock's eyes flicked to Colter's. They were dark with portent.

Then, adjusting the saddlebags on her shoulder, she walked away.

# Chapter 10

As the girl sauntered down the street behind her father and Blaine Surtees, a saddlebag pouch sliding along her slender back, Colter stepped off the jailhouse gallery and inspected the coyote dun's left forequarter.

He ran his hand across the brand.

One of the reasons he'd chosen the dun to carry him after Trace's killers was because its brand hadn't held up well. In fact, it barely showed on the dun's wither. The brand would be noticeable only by someone scrutinizing the mount carefully, or by someone actively watching for a horse marked by the Circle C blaze.

Anxiety quickened Colter's blood as he looked over the dun's neck at the girl angling across the main street toward the big mercantile building on the west side of the town square. She wove through the small crowds gathered here and there to continue discussing the strange redheaded boy's grisly pack train.

If she were going to mention the brand to her father, wouldn't she have done so by now? Anyway, Colter had no intention of leaving town until he discovered who'd killed Trace and why, and until the man or men had gotten their just deserts. The town's learning who Colter was would make his job more difficult—would probably even put him in peril—but he was bound and determined to see his quest through to its bloody conclusion.

He untied the dun from the hitchrack and walked it over to the livery barn—the Federated Feed and Livery Stables—on a nearly deserted side street behind the big church, on the northeast edge of town.

There he found the barn's half owner, Charley Manuel, a half-Mexican graybeard in manure-stained duck trousers and a shapeless canvas hat, resetting a dilapidated corral gate. Manuel was a boisterous, foul-mouthed old gent who only reluctantly gave Colter a job and a free place to corral the dun, as well as the duty of mucking out the stalls and slinging feed and water while he and his wrangler, Wayne Kilgore, who had that day off, handled the tending of the livestock and rental wagons.

"You can share the side shed sleepin' quarters with Wayne," Manuel said, chuckling caustically as he removed a penny nail from between his bearded lips and began hammering it through an iron hinge strap. "But you might wanna keep that old Remy close to hand and sleep with one eye skinned! Wayne gets in one o' his sour moods, he's liable to cut your throat just to watch ya bleed!"

He laughed uproariously, blowing breath that smelled like a whiskey vat, while Colter led the dun into the barn.

For the next week Colter earned his nickel a day forking hay to the livery stock, mucking out their shit, and hauling water from the well out back of the place in two buckets attached to the ends of a long hickory pole that he carried across his shoulders.

The hunchback, Kilgore, didn't say more than two words to Colter during that entire week. But he felt the man's close, peculiar scrutiny, which often pricked the hair on the back of his neck so that he found himself absently touching the worn grips of his old Remington.

Like the old man had suggested, he slept with the Remy under his pillow at night and kept his ears attuned to Kilgore's stirrings.

But he soon discovered that no conscious effort was needed to detect the hunchback's midnight cries. When the wretched hump pained him, he fairly yipped and howled like a trapped coyote, setting the entire barn and all three corrals alive with the nickers and whinnies of startled horses.

Rarely did the hunchback's own cries wake him, but when they did he grabbed his crock of corn squeezings and stomped around the main part of the barn or the corral, cursing and howling at the top of his lungs until the whiskey relieved the pain. Then he stomped back into the shed, raking air in and out of his lungs and loudly clearing his throat, and plopped back down onto his cot.

Soon his raucous snores rose and fell regularly once again. As loud as the snoring was, in contrast to the man's mad yells and curses it was a welcome relief to Colter, who could then fall back into a restive sleep himself.

During his first seven days in Sapinero, Colter kept his head low. Though he spent almost all his time working, when he wasn't working he strolled the streets, hoping to overhear something about Trace around one of the saloons. He asked no questions and did not even engage in conversation with others. He wanted to speak to the girl, Jennifer Spurlock, but he knew that by doing so he might risk alerting the entire town to his true identity and his purpose for being here.

"Hey, little green shaver boy!" a familiar voice called late on Colter's eighth night in Sapinero. "Oh, *weeee* little one!"

Colter lifted his head up from his musty pillow in his and Kilgore's lean-to sleeping quarters. Heart thudding, he reached under the pillow and grabbed the Remington. The room was dark as pitch, but amber light shone through the cracks in the plank door.

Beyond the door a girl laughed softly.

Colter steadied the pistol in his hand and blinked groggily. "Who's there?"

"Santy Clause." Colter recognized Kilgore's voice in spite of its uncharacteristically jubilant pitch. Obviously, the man had been turning his wolf loose, which, Manuel had informed Colter, he did from time to time. "If you've armed yourself with that old hogleg, put the damn thing back under your pillow before you shoot yourself!"

Something hit the door with a clanging thud, and the light flickered between the cranks.

"Or, worse yet," the hunchback added as another girl's laugh sounded, louder than before, "me or one of my darling concubines. One of which"—now the door raked open across the earthen floor, spilling more wan light into the lean-to—"I have brought you, *mi pelir-rojo amigo!*" My redheaded friend.

Colter held the Remington negligently in his left hand as he stared at the lamp borne aloft in the doorway. Three shadowy figures staggered into the room. It wasn't hard to tell that the middle figure was that of the hunchback. Kilgore held the lamp in one hand while he draped his other arm around the long-haired figure to his right. Another girl stood to his left, and she seemed to be holding back slightly, tentatively.

"Boy!" Kilgore called again. "You are awake, ain't ya?"

The hunchback held the lamp higher. Colter winced as the lamplight danced across his cot and speared his eyes.

"Yeah, yeah," he said, turning his head away. "I'm here. What the hell . . . ?"

"The kid curses," Kilgore drawled. "But don't let that frighten you off, my dear Angelique. I've pegged him for a good sort, though something tells me he's from the mountains." Louder, Kilgore said, "Boy, I've brought you a damsel in distress!"

Both girls snickered, the one on his left leaning drunkenly against Kilgore, who stood bent characteristically forward, head cocked at an odd angle, his stringy hair hanging down to frame his long, angular, broad-nosed face.

"Well . . . maybe not in *dire* distress . . . but she will be if she don't get your ashes hauled soon. Cause she's been bought and paid for, but the good Madame Blanche don't know I swiped her away from the whorehouse. So, with that—and with all proper introductions left to the two of you—I bid you adieu . . . and do have a good roll, kid. You worked hard around here, and it's one hell of a black, rainy night, and even the redheaded sprout from the mountains needs a bit of the sublime under his buffalo robe once in a blue moon!"

As the hunchback and the girl on the left swung around and headed out, the girl drawing the door closed behind them, he added, "Or even a red or green moon or, hell, even a *periwinkle* moon!"

Kilgore continued roaring and the girl continued laughing and cajoling him playfully. Meanwhile, Colter felt more than saw the presence of the other girl in the room with him. He heard her chuckling softly, and he could smell her rosy perfume, heard her swear softly as she kicked the room's lone chair.

Colter said nothing. This whole thing—the hunchback's tirade and the two girls' presence in the doorway and being awakened at God-knew-what-hour—had a dreamlike aspect. The young drover sat up in his cot, still holding the Remington in his gun hand, speechless, as he heard the rattle of a lantern mantle. Then there was the scratch of a match, and a flame flashed to guttering life.

Just as quickly the match went out.

"Damn!" the girl cried, sucking in a sharp breath. "Burned my finger!"

Colter flung the buffalo robe aside and bounded out of bed. He felt his way to the bench that flanked the small sheet-iron stove and set the gun on top of it.

"Here." He felt around until he'd taken the lamp from the girl's hand. He was afraid she'd break it, and it was the only lamp he and Kilgore had in the lean-to. If it got broken, likely the old skinflint Charley Manuel wouldn't replace it.

He felt around in the coffee tin for a stove match, and the lamp finally sprouted to hissing, flickering life. The light spilled over the girl who stood beside him, found her white teeth as they appeared between rich, spreading lips.

"Oh!" she said, her sparkling brown eyes finding Colter's. "*Oui*. Much better." Her voice was high and musical and strangely accented.

Colter found himself staring at her, thoroughly taken aback by her beauty.

He'd seen sporting girls before. Most had been too fat or too skinny or missing teeth, and they often looked ten years older than they were. But this girl, dressed all in red velvet and black lace, with a black Spanish mantilla draped over the thick, curly brown hair that fell to her shoulders, was like an angel hand-picked by God to bless the smelly lean-to room of the livery barn in which Colter Farrow stood on a lonely, rainy night, thunderstruck.

Her face was oval-shaped and perfect, the exotic darkness of her eyes accentuated by deft touches of what looked like charcoal. Large silver hoops dangled from her ears, winking in the light of the lantern, which Colter still held aloft in his right hand. The creamy slenderness of her neck was accentuated by a delicate black choker adorned with a tiny bejeweled clip.

"So you are Colter Farrow." Her hair hung in her eyes, and she shook it away. "I am Angelique. And for the next two hours, or until Madame Blanche discovers Carlie and I gone, I am all yours to do with as you will." She arched a mock-admonishing brow and wagged a finger. "As long as it's not too rough. Don't want to damage the goods, *oui*?"

Colter felt as bashful as he had his first time with Marianna. It was her image that kept coming up between his face and Angelique's, chastising him now for the desire that hammered through him like Ute war drums and blazed in his loins like a bonfire.

Outside, in the main part of the barn, he could hear the laughs and lusty snickers of Kilgore and Carlie likely going at it on the cot that Charley Manuel kept in his office.

Colter jerked a quivering thumb at the door. "He . . . uh . . . Wayne paid you . . . for me?"

*"Oui."* The girl nodded, plucking what looked like a cigarette from the cleavage shoving up from her red velvet, black-trimmed corset. She poked the hand-rolled cylinder between her red-painted lips and, placing her hand on Colter's wrist to slightly lower the lantern, leaned forward and lit the cigarette against the chimney.

She straightened, blowing strange-smelling smoke. It didn't smell like tobacco smoke at all. It smelled verdant and fresh, like fresh-cut timothy, only slightly more pungent. The girl drew deep on the cylinder, and an inner lid seemed to close down over her eyes. The pupils expanded, and her gaze acquired a deeply sensuous, dreamy cast.

"Have you ever done this before?" she said, rising up on her toes and planting a hand gently along Colter's cheek. "Made love to a woman?" Leaning forward, she nudged his hair away with the hand that held the strange-smelling quirley, and kissed his neck just below his ear.

"Yeah," he said, hating the uncertainty in his voice. "Sure I have. Several times."

"Ummm," Angelique said, nuzzling his neck and chuckling. "I should feel quite lucky to be spending the next two hours with one so experienced."

"Look." Colter hesitated, swallowed. "Look . . . I . . . got a girl. . . ."

"Yes," Angelique said, drawing away from him and staring up at him as she took another deep drag on the quirley, her eyes going even more dreamy than before. "You have a girl. Make no mistake, Colter Farrow—I am no girl. And what you are about to experience . . . for free . . . you will remember for a long time to come. Now, off with those longhandles and climb into bed, and I will show you how it feels to have the blocks thrown to you by an expert. *Oui*?"

Colter stared at the sensuous creature, incredulous. Her creamy cleavage rose and fell. His heart drummed in his ears.

Colter breathed a silent prayer for forgiveness to both God and Marianna as he wasted no time in stripping down to his birthday suit.

# Chapter 11

Colter tossed his longhandles into a corner and, embarrassed by his pale scrawniness, headed back to the rumpled cot.

"It is cold," the girl said as she, with almost religiouslike somberness, removed the mantilla from her head and draped it over the back of the chair.

Colter hesitated as he leaned over the cot. He looked down between his legs and flushed.

"Aren't you the shy one," Angelique observed. "I've seen them before. That's a nice long, hard one. And I'm glad I won't have to work to get you ready for me. Some of the old prospectors—*oh!*"

His ears ringing, Colter padded barefoot to the stove, keenly aware of his jutting, swinging member. He plucked a couple of split logs from the box beside the stove and opened the squeaky door, sort of squatting down to hide his crotch from the hot stare of the girl standing close beside him, undressing.

"Where are you from?" she asked.

He blew on the ashes in the grate until they glowed

and a small flame flickered. Then he crossed the logs on the flame and turned to the girl just as she peeled the red-and-black corset back from her shoulders, exposing her bosom.

He'd been about to speak, but as the full, deep breasts jostled free of their stays, the sides bathed in golden lantern light, the tips alluringly shaded, a giant frog leapt up into the back of his throat and croaked.

He nearly lost his balance, weight shifting between his bare feet and haunches, but managed to keep himself from tumbling straight forward into the stove.

Angelique laughed as she stooped to begin removing her garter belts and black net stockings. Her breasts swayed, pink nipples jutting slightly.

Colter's face was burning now. He quickly slammed the stove's door without making sure that the logs had caught and, turning away from the girl, hustled over to the bed.

"Here and there," he said, trying to put some nonchalance into his voice as he sat down on the cot and pulled a corner of the buffalo robe across his lap. He leaned his head against the wall on the other side of the cot and half propped himself on his outstretched arm. His toes brushed the floor.

"'Here and there,'" Angelique repeated, tossing her stockings onto the chair. "That is many places for a boy so young. How old are you, Colter Farrow?"

She moved toward him slowly, her hair slightly mussed about her head and her beguilingly beautiful face. Almost absently, she cupped her breasts in her

fine-boned hands and lifted them, rolling them together.

"I'm . . . uh . . . sixteen . . .," he heard himself say.

Her eyes were smoky. She stopped before him and
shook her hair from her forehead, slowly, gently
kneading her breasts. Colter watched her from his
limbo world of erotic ecstasy in which time stopped
and reality became a dream of unimaginable bliss.

"Sixteen," she said, just above a whisper, her voice
thin and dreamy. "That is only one year younger than
me."

After a time, she crouched over him and wrapped
her arms around his neck. She pressed her forehead to
his and stared into his eyes from an inch away, wrinkling the skin above her nose playfully.

Fine pits of copper in her irises sparkled brightly.

Then she kissed his forehead, then his nose, and
then she pressed her lips to his.

Each was a long, lingering, warm, wet kiss, the kiss
on his mouth most of all. As she kissed him, her tongue
making quick, probing dashes between his lips to ca-
ress his teeth or his own tongue or to lick his lips, he
lifted his hands to her sides.

He felt the ridges of her ribs beneath the marble-
smooth skin, and the curved sides of her breasts sloping down toward the cot. He rolled his thumbs across
the jutting nipples, then pulled his hands away quickly,
finding himself almost afraid or ashamed to touch
such an exquisite creature, as though he would soil
her, or she would break like a fragile, timeless figu-
rine.

She chuckled, stretching her lips back from her teeth and wrinkling the skin above her nose again. She reached down for his hands and placed the palms firmly against her breasts, and as he massaged her, she slowly leaned toward him, lifting one leg to straddle him.

Kissing him, cooing softly, she pressed him down flat against the cot. Then she was on top of him, with his hard, aching shaft thrust up inside the warm, wet depths of her, and she was leaning forward, brushing his hair back with her hands and closing her mouth over his once more, caressing his tongue with her own.

She began to rock slowly, purposefully, forward and back, forward and back . . .

Later, when Angelique had shuddered with spent passion, she lowered her head to Colter's chest.

When she raised it again, she sandwiched his flushed, sweat-damp face between her hands. "Now it is all over except for the guilt."

She smiled sadly, pressed her lips once more against his, kissing him tenderly. Keeping her smoky eyes on his, she swung a leg to the floor. He tried to hold her down against him, but she gave a little wiggle, grunting playfully, and pushed up from the cot.

Colter propped his head on his hand and stared up at her. "What do you mean?"

"All men who have other girls—other girls they are in love with or are married to—feel guilty as soon as it's done." Firelight flickering across her naked, voluptuous body, still wearing the slender black choker around her neck, she moved over to the shelf where a tin coffeepot sat in a rusted tin washbasin. She flipped the pot's squeaky lid, looked inside, and glanced at Colter. "To wash with?"

Colter nodded.

As Angelique poured water from the pot into the basin and began to wash herself with a ragged cloth, Colter said, "That was so good I don't reckon I got much room to feel any guilt."

Running the cloth down her neck and across her breasts, she chuckled without mirth. "You will." She said nothing more until she sat on the chair and started to pull her stockings on. "All men feel guilty. It is in their nature." She sighed and clipped a garter belt closed. "Then they hate me like their worst enemy— until the next time they come to me."

Colter frowned. A bleakness was suddenly crawling over him. "Why is that?"

Angelique lifted a shoulder. "Because they are men. You will see." She extended her leg to pull her second stocking on and glanced at him wistfully. "What is her name?"

Colter dropped his eyes. She was right, he thought, as guilt nipped at him in the form of Marianna's face flashing up before him in all its tender, loving sweetness. He'd asked her to marry him only a few days ago. Now he'd lain with a sporting girl, and during their passionate coupling, Marianna had been the farthest thought from his mind.

"Marianna," he muttered just above a whisper.

"Who?"

He cleared his throat and kept his eyes down, feeling the heat of shame on the back of his neck. "Marianna's her name."

"Where is she?"

"Up in the Lu—" He stopped abruptly, flushing slightly and lifting his gaze to Angelique's as she stood to snap her second garter. "Back home."

"When will you go back to her?"

"When I'm finished here, I reckon."

"Finished with what?"

Colter's heart thudded. A sense of danger churned with his guilt now. He had to be careful of everything he said and did in this town, or it could cost him his life. For all he knew, Angelique might be an informant for someone powerful.

Colter grasped at lies, glad a right-sounding one revealed itself so quickly. "Enough money to get back home on. I been out ridin' for ranchers, and now I'm makin' my way back to Winnemucca."

Angelique stood and turned to him as she shrugged into her corset. Brashly, she showed her breasts to him one more time, and even amid his guilt and trepidation, he felt a renewed warmth in his loins. Then she pulled the corset closed, making the tops of her breasts bulge up under her neck, and laced it.

She crossed to the cot and sat down on its edge.

Again she slid Colter's long hair back from his face and sandwiched his cheeks between her hands. "Colter Farrow," she whispered, wrinkling her brow with deep concern, "this is no place for you."

Colter just stared up at her, confusion and apprehension on his hooded brow.

She caressed his cheeks, then lowered her head

slowly to press her sweet, full lips against his once more. When she pulled away, she let a few seconds stretch, her face deeply troubled, before she whispered, jerking her head slightly, "Go home."

Two loud thumps on the door made her lurch with a start.

Kilgore's voice shouted, "If you two ain't had a mattress dance yet, I'm out two silver dollars fer nothin'!" The door scraped open, and the hunchback stumbled in, wearing only his longhandles and his mule-eared boots. His stringy blond hair hung in his eyes. "What're you doin' in here—playin' patty-cake?"

"No, we ain't playin' patty-cake," Colter retorted indignantly, rising up on his elbows. "We . . . why, we . . ."

"Had one hell of a romp," Angelique finished for him, smiling down at him. "It's not the amount of noise that counts—is it, *mon cherie*?"

*"Mon cherie?"* said the hunchback, leaning back against the open door—or as far back as the hump would let him. "I paid you for a poke, girl. Not to go tumblin' for the boy." Kilgore laughed his raking laugh, his eyelids hanging over his drink-bleary eyes. "Wouldn't wanna piss-burn all the menfolk in town!"

Colter chuckled but clipped it off when Angelique jerked her head toward Kilgore, her face blanching slightly in the lantern's soft glow. The hunchback stopped laughing, and his expression soured. He hung his head to stare at the floor with obvious chagrin.

"That's not funny, Wayne." Angelique rose from the cot. Giving Colter another, somber glance, she turned to the chair and donned her mantilla. She spoke softly to the hunchback standing like a chastised child against the door. "Where is Carlie?"

"Lit out," Kilgore muttered. "Saw nothin' to linger for, I reckon."

Angelique stepped toward the hangdog man and placed her hand on his arm. "Is it still raining?"

Kilgore shrugged.

Angelique leaned toward him, kissed him gently on the cheek. She said something too softly for Colter to hear clearly, but he thought it was simply, "I'm sorry." Then she turned, blew Colter a kiss, her expression brightening only slightly. Then she rustled on out the door and into the darkness of the barn.

Kilgore held his position against the door, his head canted low, his eyes still on the floor. From the barn came the scrape and thump of a door opening and closing. The sound seemed to jolt the hunchback out of a deep reverie. Lifting his head, he glanced at Colter.

"So, how was it?"

Colter felt his shoulders lighten with relief that the inexplicable tension had suddenly, at least partly, been sprung. "Not bad. Not bad at all."

"Oh?" Kilgore picked up the stub of the strange-smelling cigarette that Angelique had left hanging over the edge of the table, and poked it into his mouth. "You've had better, I suppose? Better than the best whore in southern Colorado?"

Colter sat up on the cot and leaned back against the wall. "What was that all about?"

Kilgore lit the cigarette stub on the glass chimney,

puffing the sweet-smelling smoke. "Bitch gets only the best," he chuckled. Then he glanced at Colter through a thick cloud of webbing smoke. In a pinched voice, coughing slightly, he said, "What was what about?"

Colter canted his head toward the door. "The look she gave you."

His voice still pinched and waving a hand at the smoke, Kilgore stooped to drag a fresh whiskey bottle out from beneath the table, then staggered over to his cot just beyond it, abutting the outside wall. Above the cot, coats, chaps, and a calendar hung from nails.

"It wasn't about nothin' that's any concern of yours."

Kilgore's voice sounded impatient now. Nettled. His heavy brow mantled his troubled eyes. He sagged onto the cot and leaned back against the wall, wincing at an obvious pain in his hump. The toes of his boots brushed the straw-littered earthen floor. "No, sir, ain't nothin' you'd wanna trouble yourself about, boy."

Colter hesitated, not sure the hunchback was in any mood to be pushed. But curiosity rippled through Colter like small earth tremors. "Why wouldn't I?"

"It's personal."

Colter nodded, not sure he was satisfied by the answer but resigned to it. "Then I apologize for pryin', Wayne." He slid lower on the cot, punched his pillow, and lay down, turning onto his side facing the wall. "Oh," he said, glancing over his shoulder. "I do appreciate the poke. You're right. It wasn't half bad."

Kilgore blew smoke out with a sigh. It was suddenly so silent that Colter could hear the soft ticking of the rain. He could smell the freshness of the sage through the cracks in the barn's outer walls. A burned log fell through the stove's grate with a thump.

"Hey, kid," the hunchback said at length, "why don't you go on back to the Loonies where you came from?"

Colter had closed his eyes. Now he opened them. His blood quickened.

He glanced over his shoulder at the hunchback still sitting across his cot in his longhandles and boots, head resting at an awkward angle against the wall. Kilgore took another deep puff from the quirley, the coal glowing brightly in the shadows above the cot.

Smoke puffed, filling the room with its cloying sweetness.

The hunchback kicked a boot out absently as he added, "Around here your only true friend is the undertaker."

Colter turned full around until he was resting belly down, propped on his forearms. His lips were parted as his breath came hard and a cold prickling broke out along his spine. He slitted an eye at the hunchback. He could tell from the man's wry, sneering expression that there was no point in playing cat and mouse.

"The brand?"

"Nah." Kilgore shook his head slowly. "I seen you and Trace up in the Loonies around a year ago. You were out hunting a mountain lion that had been feedin' on your calves. I was runnin' my wolf off its leash, packin' a couple bottles up to an old mine shack I knew about. Planned to get drunk there, blow my brains out. Turned out I didn't have the balls."

He chuckled dryly. "You two came by the spring I was sittin' at. You probably don't remember because you didn't see the hump. Everyone remembers the hump. I was leaning back, like I am now, against some jumbled rocks. Plum drunk off my ass. Trace, he give me a dollar for more hooch. Trace usually slipped me a dollar in town, because I always tended his mules when he stayed overnight and I helped him load his supply wagon."

Colter's heart thudded against the cot beneath him. It was like the blow of a blacksmith's hammer on an anvil. His temples throbbed. Here it is, he told himself. Am I ready to know the answer to my question? Am I ready to act on it?

"Who killed him, Wayne?"

"Tellin' you that would be as good as killin' ya."

"Who killed him? Tell me, goddamn it."

Kilgore rolled his head around on his shoulders, curling his upper lip. "Hell, boy, five minutes after I told ya, the undertaker up the hill on the other side of the creek'd be dancin' a jig while fittin' you for a wooden overcoat."

Colter swallowed. He felt his shoulders trembling, his thighs hardening. Slowly, as though his joints were chinked with wet limestone, he reached under his pillow for his Remington. He stood and, heedless of his nakedness, walked over to Kilgore's cot, and ratcheted back the Remy's heavy hammer.

Gritting his teeth, he raised the pistol to Kilgore's head.

The hunchback rolled his eyes up toward Colter's. He curled his lip even more, so that his large, tobacco-stained front teeth shone in the lantern light. "You be careful, young'un, or I will tell you."

Colter noted the strange hollowness in his own voice. "You've got three seconds."

He opened and closed his fingers around the handle.

Kilgore stared at the revolver's maw. Then he raised his eyes to Colter's. He grinned, his eyes flashing evilly. "You're threatening the wrong cripple, boy. You've mistaken me for someone who gives two dollops of fresh dog dip for another day on this miserable wart on the devil's ass."

Colter leaned forward and pressed the Remy against Kilgore's forehead, pushing his face to within inches of the hunchback's long, broad nose. Rage burned through him, and his gun hand trembled as though he'd dipped it in snowmelt.

He loosed a sob of rage and grief as he remembered the buzzards hovering over the bloody wagon. "Tell me who killed Trace Cassidy, you drunken hunchback freak, or I'll drop this goddamn hammer on your sneering face!"

Kilgore narrowed his eyes at the Remy's barrel. Then he looked up at Colter and pushed the revolver away from his face with the back of his hand.

"Just for that, kid," he snarled, "I'm gonna tell ya."

# Chapter 12

"Bill Rondo and his sawed-off sidekick killed Trace Cassidy. Who'd you think?" The hunchback took a long swig from his bottle.

"His deputy?"

"Chico Bannon—you got it," Kilgore said, pulling the bottle back down and loosing a long, liquid sigh. He stared up at Colter, a semi-sneer on his wide mouth, showing his front teeth bathed in whiskey.

"Why?"

"Who knows?"

"You know."

Kilgore chuckled. "How do you know I know—or think you know I know?"

"Cause I think you're all over town," Colter said. "I think you know a little bit about everything and everybody in Sapinero. A cripple has the advantage of bein' . . ." The young drover searched for the word. "Inconspicuous. Just like a boy does."

"Damn, you're a smart kid! Maybe too smart."

"You think so?" Colter heard his breath rasping

slowly, heavily in and out of his nose. He'd lowered the Remy to his side. Down at his other side, his right hand was a raw, red fist, the knuckles turning white. "Why?"

The hunchback blinked slowly. His head wobbled drunkenly. He took another pull from the bottle and set it down on the cot by his side. It turned over and spilled, but he didn't notice in spite of the soft, tinkling, chugging sound the whiskey made as it poured out over the edge of the cot and against the wall.

He stared up at Colter uncertainly, as though he was having trouble focusing.

"Rondo don't need no good reason once he gets it in for you," the hunchback drawled. "Maybe Trace beat him one too many times at poker over the years. Maybe . . ."

"Maybe what?"

"Maybe I just don't know, kid. All I know is, if you go after Rondo and Bannon, you better bushwack 'em like you done the Standish bunch." Kilgore wrinkled his brows and canted his head to one side, closing an eye. "Say, is that true how you took 'em down? Like Bannon told around town? Shot all three like ducks on a millpond?"

"It was almost that easy."

Colter's face was expressionless. Inside, rage burned, tying his gut in knots.

"I knew who they were, so I smoked 'em out of the cabin. Gave 'em a chance to give up, but they threw down. They were nearly as drunk as you are now, so it wasn't all that hard pinking each one as he drew.

Took a couple shots with the smallest one, because my hand was shaking and there was a lot of smoke. They were the first men I'd ever killed, you see. But I killed him deader'n hell eventually. Just like I'm going to do to the men who killed Trace."

He paused and dipped his chin, his lips pursed so that they formed a straight white line across his lower face. "As soon as I find out why they did it."

"Good luck." Kilgore began to sag sideways.

"Tell me, Wayne, or so help me . . ." Colter squeezed his Remy until he could hear the old walnut grips cracking.

"Good night, kid." Kilgore hit the cot on his shoulder and instantly began snoring.

Colter watched him for a time, debating whether it would be worth trying to roust him. Doubtful. Either the hunchback didn't know why Rondo and Bannon had killed Trace, or he didn't want Colter to know the reason. The former seemed most likely. Otherwise, why tell him anything at all?

He didn't doubt that the hunchback had told the truth about the Sapinero lawmen. Colter had suspected them the moment he'd laid eyes on them. Now he just needed to know the reason they'd killed Trace.

And the best source for that information was the two killers themselves.

Colter turned from the hunchback's sleeping form, Kilgore's snores resounding loudly around the small room. Suddenly he realized he was naked. Inexplicably self-conscious—the hunchback would be out cold till morning—he tossed his Remington on the bed and struggled into his longhandles. The room had cooled now that the fire had died, and the still-falling rain added a penetrating dampness.

When he'd buttoned his longhandle top up to his throat, he pulled on his socks and, because he was lost in thoughts of bloody revenge, automatically donned his broad-brimmed hat, the braided rawhide thong brushing his chest. He sat on the edge of the cot for a time, staring into space and trying to sort out what he had learned.

But instead of being able to think, he mostly only felt a burning need to kill.

He felt himself drawn out into the chill night, toward the sheriff's office. He wanted to get another good look at Rondo and Bannon. He wasn't sure why—he doubted that he'd kill them tonight. He needed time to find out their reasons for killing Trace, and to plan his attack. Going off half-cocked would only get him killed, leaving Trace and Ruth and David and little May unavenged.

Rising from his cot, he slipped into his brown wool trousers and boots and, lifting his suspenders up over his shoulders, wrapped his cartridge belt around his waist and filled the cross-draw holster with the Remy. He looked down at the gun for a time before slipping it out of its holster and checking the loads.

As Trace had taught him, he'd left the chamber under the hammer empty, so he wouldn't shoot himself in his thigh or foot while climbing off his horse or dropping his pants in the outhouse. Now, not knowing why but feeling compelled to do so, he plucked a .44 shell from his belt and thumbed it into the chamber.

Giving the cylinder a spin and liking the crisp, well-oiled clicks it made as it turned, he twirled the gun on his finger—again, as Trace had taught him to do while admonishing him to never show Ruth such a vulgar display of pistolero flamboyance—and dropped it into its holster.

He pulled on his red-and-black-plaid jacket that was missing a couple of buttons and, adjusting the angle of his hat, moved through the open door and then drew it slowly, quietly closed behind him, muting the hunchback's loud, inebriated snores. The barn was dark, though the side windows gave enough ambient light that he was able to make his way quickly to the front and on outside into the damp night.

He looked around. It was probably around one or two in the morning. One of the saloons up on the main drag was still open. He could see a couple of lit windows reflected in the damp street and hear the distant din of drunken voices. In the hills around the town, coyotes yammered. Nearer, an owl hooted. The rain was now only a drizzle, but heavy drops plopped from the barn roof onto the soggy ground below.

The sky was inky black, with no starshine at all. The darkness and the hushed quiet and chill, clinging dampness made Colter shiver.

Raising his collar, he pulled his hat brim low and, tucking his thumbs behind his cartridge belt, headed for the main street, his boots making sucking sounds in the narrow, muddy side street. His spurs chinged softly. He wished he had removed them back in the barn, but he didn't want to go back and start all over again.

He rounded the corner by the hulking church and, staying close to the church's massive blackness, looked around carefully.

Would Rondo or Bannon be out at this hour? Since the saloon up the street, not far from the sheriff's office, was obviously open, spilling its light and occasional whoops and hollers into the street, and a guitar was being strummed somberly in a small, dimly lit cantina farther off to the east, surely a lawman was out keeping an eye on things.

What would Colter do if he ran into either of the two lawmen? Gun them right then and there? Would he try to take them by surprise, disarm them, usher them off to a dark, secluded alley, and interrogate them at the point of his cocked Remy?

Continuing up along the side of the church toward the tree-lined square in the middle of the town, Colter felt his heart beating hard and regular. He drew up even with the Trail Driver Saloon, then stopped suddenly when he heard a man yell in Spanish as a chair scraped loudly across the floor.

A girl screamed.

Colter automatically touched his Remy's grips as he swung toward the saloon's big plate-glass window on the other side of the muddy street.

"Don't you dare slap leather on me, you greaser sonofabitch!" a man's voice boomed.

Colter knew who the voice belonged to before he saw, through the big window, Chico Bannon shoving a taller, dark-haired man up against a ceiling support post in the saloon. A scantily clad sporting girl backed away from the other side of the two men, nervously squeezing her hands together beneath her breasts.

Bannon gripped the Mexican's shirt in his fists and shoved his face up under the man's chin, shouting, "You hear me, Mex? I don't care if you was cheatin' or not! I wanna make sure right here and now you understand that if you ever—I mean *ever*—slap leather on me, I'll shove my own hogleg so far up your ass you'll taste gun oil in the back of your mouth!"

As much as he tried to suppress it, Colter felt another chill rake his spine.

As the Mexican muttered something in broken English while holding his hands high above his head and out away from his shoulders, a pained look on his face, the young cowboy continued up the street. The loud voice of Chico Bannon and the softer, strained, placating voice of the Mexican dwindled behind him.

Soon he found himself in the tree-lined square, the fountain across the church gurgling quietly.

He looked around the murky night, trying to pick out the small sheriff's office in the darkness. When he found it, he sat down on a loafers' bench under the arched branches of a couple of cottonwoods. The office was almost directly across the street from him. A light shone in the window to the right of the door—the light of a lantern with its wick turned low.

Colter adjusted the Remy on his hip and sat there on the splintery bench, comfortably hidden by the tree shadows behind him, and stared hard at the near-dark office. He was only vaguely aware of the night sounds around him—the dripping trees, the coyotes, a dog barking viciously for a short time before falling silent.

The town's sporting houses were on the far side of the creek, with a Chinese laundry and a Mexican café where Colter often ate his noontime lunches. While he couldn't see the brothels from here, he could occasionally hear a male or female laugh or a voice raised in brief anger.

He ground his teeth, thinking of Rondo and Bannon. He wanted nothing more than to shoot both men dead. But first he had to find out why they'd killed Trace. Avenging Trace would never be satisfying until he'd learned why he'd been killed so viciously, his still-living body nailed to the bed of the wagon and sent home as vulture bait.

Colter stared for a long time at the law office hunched between the bank and the harness shop with only a small gap on either side, as though he were trying to fathom the reason for Trace's murder from the structure itself. Finally, fatigued by fear and hate, he felt his eyes growing heavy. Before he knew it, his chin dropped to his chest and he slept.

Something slammed hard across his right jaw, whipping his head so painfully to the left that for a moment he felt as though his neck had been broken.

A gruff voice, thick with drink, said, "What the hell are you doin' out here, boy?"

For an instant, Colter couldn't remember where he was or what he was doing. Then, wincing against the burn in his cheek and the pinching ache in his neck, he looked up at the tall, broad, silhouetted specter of Bill Rondo.

# Chapter 13

"Easy, Bill," the girl leaning against Rondo said. "He's just a kid, for chrissakes." Her voice, like Rondo's, was thick from drink.

She was a tall, willowy blonde in pantaloons, high-heeled black shoes, and a red-and-green-striped blanket coat, which she held closed with both arms. She hunched forward against the cold.

Straw yellow hair curled over her shoulders and blew around in the wind. Her face was a pale oval beside and well below Rondo's, whose own face was a ruddy brown mask set dark and flat beneath his black Stetson.

Silver hair framed the man's face, glowing like dirty snow in the darkness; his silver mustache was a slash beneath his broad nose, trimmed in the starlight that was now starting to break through the clouds.

A long black duster was drawn back behind the silver-chased Colt sitting butt forward on Rondo's left hip. Another pistol rested in a shoulder holster mostly hidden behind the coat's left flap, just beside the sheriff's badge that also glowed in the darkness, a shade lighter than the lawman's hair.

"Don't care if he's still in knickers. Anyone caught loitering around the square after dark is damn suspicious," Rondo grumbled.

Colter glared up at the man standing before him and spit his retort out like unwieldy prune pits. "I was sitting here minding my own business, Sheriff. Any law against it?"

"There's a law against sass, you mangy pup!"

Before Colter could dodge it, the man's hand clubbed him again, this time along the side of his head. It was a hammering blow that sent Colter sprawling off the bench and into the leaf-littered dirt of the plaza. He felt the burning scrape of the man's heavy ring.

Automatically, the young drover's left hand clawed his .44 from its holster, but before he could bring the gun up, the whore screamed as Rondo shoved her away and laid a vicious kick against the underside of Colter's gun fist.

The Remy flew up and away.

Colter heard it hit the ground somewhere behind him with a metallic thud. His brain, still sluggish from sleep, shock, and fear, was slow to comprehend what happened next, though his eyes watched Rondo rake his big pistol from its holster.

"Bill, no!" the girl cried behind the sheriff.

The echo of her plea hadn't died before Rondo's Peacemaker roared, bucking in his hand and stabbing smoke and burnt-orange flames.

Colter's ears rang from the resonating *bang!* Then

he felt a wetness on his neck. A a couple of seconds after that, his left ear began burning as though someone had laid an iron against it.

Sitting on his butt, legs bent out before him, Colter raised a hand to that ear. The touch was like the pain of a savagely jabbed needle. He winced and looked at his hand. Blood made a slick smear across his fingers.

"Oh, *Bill!*" the girl protested, pressing both hands to her mouth and regarding Colter wide-eyed. "You didn't have to do that!"

Rondo held his gun down by his hip, smoke curling from the barrel. The gold ring on his middle finger glowed dully in the ambient light, beside the pistol's trigger guard. Colter half consciously noticed that a black S had been carved into the ring's green stone.

"I'll do the thinkin', if that's all right, Lucy? Thinkin' ain't your strong point. Never has been." His eyes blazed at Colter, who sat on his butt in shock, holding his hand to his bloody ear. "You go on back to the barn you came from—you understand me, boy?"

"Bill, come on," Lucy said, tugging on the sheriff's arm, trying to pull him away. "Let's go on over to my place for a nightcap."

Rondo jerked his arm from the girl's grip as he continued glaring at Colter. "I asked if you understood me, boy." Ever so slightly, the still smoking Colt edged left, so that the barrel was aimed at Colter's other ear. "Otherwise, you'll be leavin' town. And when I ask someone to leave Sapinero, they ain't likely to return. *Ever!*"

Colter hesitated. Bald fear was a fist wrapped taut

around his throbbing heart. Rondo was a nightmare specter looming before him—as diabolical and repellent as any he'd ever dreamed on the darkest, loneliest night—and Colter felt his courage hammered to a fine gray powder. "I—I understand," he heard himself stammer, inwardly sneering at his own cowardice.

Rondo smiled and nodded with satisfaction. "That's better." He gave a superior wink, meant only to humiliate his victim further, and holstered his six-shooter. "Stay off the street after dark from now on. Never know—I might think you're planning to rob the bank or somethin' and take off more than your ear."

With that, he gave Colter another evil nod, then let himself be swung around by the girl, who wrapped an arm around the sheriff's waist and led him off at an angle across the street. "Come on, Bill," she said, slurring her words and staggering slightly. "Let's go get a brandy."

The girl gave Colter a furtive, concerned look over her shoulder, then turned forward, and soon the darkness consumed both her and the lawman. A long time after the two had disappeared, Colter could hear the raucous, dwindling chings of Rondo's gaudy spurs.

Colter cursed as he pressed his hand to his torn ear, feeling the hot blood against his palm. The throbbing pain as well as fear and rage made him weak and sick to his stomach.

As he climbed to his feet, he glanced once more toward where Rondo and the whore had disappeared. With another curse at both Rondo and himself, for letting himself get caught off guard by the very man he'd come out here to consider killing, he turned and began stumbling across the square, toward the rushing fountain fronting the church.

He stopped suddenly, brushing his hand across his empty holster. When he'd retrieved the Remy from the horse dung and dirt into which Rondo had kicked it, he tramped heavily over to the fountain, knelt down close to the broad stone bowl, and dunked the burning, throbbing ear in the water.

He sucked air between his teeth as pain sliced through him. He lifted his head, probed the ear with his fingers. There seemed to be a notch torn from the rubbery flesh just above the lobe. The nerve endings there were dancing and sparking, and he continued to suck air painfully as he bathed the ear in the fountain before removing his neckerchief from around his neck, balling it up in his fist, and pressing it hard against the ear to stem the blood flow.

When he had the ear as clean as he himself could get it out there in the dark, hunkered over the fountain, he heaved himself to his feet with a weary groan. Then, pressing the wet neckerchief against his ear, he shuffled off in defeat and disgrace to the livery barn, where he burrowed down in the straw of an empty stall.

When the pain in his ear finally abated, he drifted slowly off into merciful sleep.

He woke later to the *rat-a-tat-tat* of a woodpecker seeking breakfast in the barn's outside wall. Lifting his head from the straw, he saw the bird in a near window—a large red-headed woodpecker—and ground his teeth at the ratcheting clatter that inflamed the raw burning in his torn ear.

The light silhouetting the woodpecker was soft gray edging toward pearl. Probably only dawn. Colter could hear the hunchback sighing and groaning and knocking around in the lean-to shed. Lowering his head back down to the straw, wondering vaguely if he could feign sickness and thus avoid facing the day—a day of pain and humiliation and the remembered specter of Bill Rondo drilling a .45 round through his ear—Colter pressed his cheek against the straw.

But he did not close his eyes.

A folded piece of lined tablet paper rested lightly in the straw only two feet from his head, in front of the stall's latched door. Frowning, he lifted his head again and plucked the folded sheet from the straw. He doubted that the paper had been in the stall when he'd returned to the barn late last night.

If it had, he likely would have stepped on it.

Blinking sleep from his eyes and gnashing his teeth at the burning in his ear, he sat up and, leaning a shoulder against the stall partition, opened the note. He wasn't a good reader—there'd been little time for school in the mountains—but he could read at about a third-grade level. He moved his lips as he ran his eyes slowly over the words printed in blue-green ink on the lined notepaper:

*Many tears have been shed at Barranca Verde.*

Frowning, staring hard at the befuddling sentence, he read it aloud to himself softly. The lone sentence was all that had been written on the paper.

Flipping it over, he found nothing more on the back, including anything to indicate the writer. A careful scrutiny of the penmanship likewise gave him no indication of the writer's sex. The letters were well formed, but they were neither sloppy nor overly neat or ornate. They were strangely, maybe purposely, sexless.

One thing was certain: Someone had stolen into the barn late last night, after Colter's encounter with Bill Rondo and Lucy, and had dropped the note over the stall door, letting it float down to the straw where he would easily find it in the morning.

"Well, I found it," he muttered, staring down at the note. "Now, what in hell does it mean?"

Shuffling footsteps grew from the direction of the lean-to. The hunchback yawned loudly, adding an exaggerated groan with his customary flare.

Quickly, Colter folded the note and shoved it into the back pocket of his wool trousers and, feeling as though the right side of his head was on fire, heaved himself to his feet. Kilgore's silhouette appeared before him, between tack-laden ceiling posts.

He shuffled along, grotesquely hunched to one side. As he approached Colter's stall, Kilgore stopped suddenly, light from the window behind Colter finding the hunchback's dull blue eyes.

The man frowned. "Figured you was with the hosses. What the hell you doin' out here?"

"Your snoring's likely to cause an early Rising."

The hunchback's face was drawn, and his hair hung over his pasty forehead. He merely smacked his lips at Colter's comment, and turned toward the front of the barn—likely to take his morning ablution. For some reason he preferred pissing in the street at the barn's front rather than somewhere out back where he was less likely to be seen, though few people were ever out and about on this remote end of town this time of the morning.

The half owner, Charley Manuel, never came in until around ten or so. Only when his wife kicked him out of the house did he sleep on the cot in his office.

Kilgore had taken just one more shuffling step before he turned back to Colter, canting his head sharply and frowning. "What the hell—a rat chew on your ear all night?"

"Nah," Colter said, face warming with embarrassment. "I reckon I was sleepwalkin' and ran into a rusty nail."

"Musta been one helluva big nail." Kilgore jerked his head to indicate the lean-to behind him. "Best wash it out with whiskey. Infection sets in, you won't be near so purty."

With that, he started toward the front of the barn.

Colter opened the stall door and stepped into the alley. He chewed his lip pensively. At the front of the barn, the hunchback slid the heavy doors open with a venomous grunt, then stepped a few feet into the street, opened his trousers, bending his knees and grunting, then loosed a strong flow with a relieved sigh, intoning, "Good mornin', Sapinero!"

He turned his hips this way and that with a defiant flare, sending his flow trickling into the street.

"Hey, Wayne," Colter said to the man's hunched back, "you ever hear of a place called Barranca Verde?"

The hunchback stopped swinging his hips. He glanced over his shoulder, sort of grimacing at Colter. "Where'd you hear about Barranca Verde?"

"Heard someone mention it in the café yesterday. I was just wondering about it."

As he continued to piss, the hunchback also continued to stare skeptically, almost suspiciously, over his shoulder at Colter. Turning forward, his stringy hair sliding over the side of his head, he said, "It's an old convent south of here, just over the New Mexico line. Between there and here is outlaw country. Badass bandits of every killin' stripe. Don't even think of ridin' out there."

"How far?"

Kilgore hiked a shoulder. "Half day's ride on a good hoss." He glanced at Colter again over his shoulder, narrowing one pain-racked eye. "Where'd you say you heard of this place?"

"Over to the café," Colter said, fingering his blood-crusted ear as he tramped toward the lean-to. "Don't worry—I ain't figurin' to head out that way. Can't a fella hear somethin' and be curious about it?"

# Chapter 14

Colter was more than merely curious about the convent called Barranca Verde. He couldn't get it off his mind.

Nor could he stop wondering who had dropped the note into the livery stall as he had slept. The note could be a trap, to lure him out of town and into an ambush.

But who would want to do that, and why?

The only two people who were aware of his reason for being in Sapinero were the Spurlock girl, Jenny, and Wayne Kilgore.

What reason could either of them have for killing him?

Of course, the Spurlock girl might have told someone else . . .

After their embarrassment at having lost the trail of the Standish bunch, one or both of the two local lawmen might want Colter to light a shuck out of their town. But he didn't pose enough of a threat for either of them to lure him into an ambush. That had become painfully clear to Colter last night, when Rondo, so drunk he could barely walk, had notched the young drover's ear. He could just as easily have killed him and claimed self-defense.

Despite the note's dubious origin, it might also have been intended to help Colter in his quest to find Trace Cassidy's killer. Trace had friends as well as enemies far and wide, and someone here unable to act himself might want the killer or killers brought to justice . . . or to see Trace's murder avenged.

But what possible connection could there be between Trace's killing and an old Spanish convent in New Mexico Territory, a half day's ride from Sapinero?

In spite of the throbbing burn in his torn ear, which he'd bandaged after cleaning it carefully with whiskey, Colter worked hard swamping out the barn and corrals. He wanted to ride out to Barranca Verde in the worst way, but if he left town today, Kilgore might get suspicious.

The rest of the day and half of the next, he pitched and shoveled manure, and hauled water, and, to earn some time off, he even reset a couple of cockeyed corral rails, greased the wheels on two rental buggies, and replaced a gate hinge.

In the early afternoon of the next day, when Charley Manuel had ridden off to inspect some draft horses for sale in Durango, Colter told Kilgore he was going to ride some of the corral moss off his coyote dun and pay a visit to an old prospector friend. He didn't mention he might be gone an entire day.

Before Kilgore, who'd been shoeing a big bay mare, had time to object, the young drover was in the saddle and trotting the dun out toward the main drag.

"Pardon me, amigo," Colter said, reining the dun up beside an old mestizo hoeing irrigated chili peppers at the south edge of town, near a stone shack and some goat pens fronting a dry wash. "Can you direct me to the trail to Barranca Verde?"

Ten minutes later Colter had crossed the wash, threaded several low, yucca-clad buttes, and was following a rocky old wagon road southeast of Sapinero, the midafternoon sun like a hot skillet on his neck and shoulders.

He brushed his left hand across the stock of his rifle jutting from the saddle boot, then touched the Remy sitting high on his hip, making sure both were near and ready. The mestizo had warned him in broken English that the trail to Barranca Verde was rife with killers and bandits, and when the old half-breed Mexican hadn't been able to convince Colter to reconsider his destination, he had crossed himself somberly as the young drover put the steel to the frisky dun's trail-eager flanks.

The trail led over low hills covered in scrub cedar, through a broad, rolling valley bordered on the east by the Sangre de Cristos and on the west by the San Luis range. The mountains were misty blue humps from Colter's position, with occasional snow-mantled crests above the blue-green timberline.

The blue and the green changed shades as the sun angled westward.

Shadows slid out from rocks, dusty green sage

clumps, cedars, and the occasional cottonwood copse sheathing an arroyo from which springs seeped. Rocky formations rose and fell along the twisting, rising, and falling trail. Besides the infrequent jackrabbit nibbling buckbrush in a rare patch of shade, or a coyote prowling a shaggy wash, there wasn't much out here.

There were no other riders that Colter could see. Remembering both Kilgore's and the old mestizo's warnings, however, he kept a close eye on his back trail and on the endless expanse of sage-covered hogbacks around him.

Nearly three hours after leaving Sapinero, he was watering the coyote dun at a spring bubbling up at the base of a slanting stone dike when a rider appeared seemingly out of nowhere—riding so quietly that Colter hadn't heard the squawk of his tack until the man was only thirty yards away. The rider, who was trailing five horses packing dead men facedown across their saddles, held a Winchester on Colter.

He lowered the rifle after a time, and Colter soon learned the man was a bounty hunter named Lou Prophet—a big, muscular, rangy hombre in faded, dusty denims, sweat-stained buckskin tunic, and a funnel-brimmed hat that looked as though it had been stomped and chewed by an entire remuda of wild mustangs.

He wore a Peacemaker .45 on his hip, and a savage-looking sawed-off double-barreled shotgun hung down his back by a leather lanyard. A bounty hunter he was—and an effective one, it appeared—but Colter found him a kindly, good-natured gent, with a friendly cast to the two blue eyes peering out from the shade of his hat brim. He had a soft Southern accent and an easy, conversational way about him.

While watering his horses, including the mean-eyed hammer-headed dun he was riding, Prophet told Colter that he'd taken down the dead men just west of Barranca Verde and was packing them off to Durango for the sizable reward on their heads. As he adjusted the hammer-headed dun's saddle cinch, he issued the same warning about this country as Kilgore and the old mestizo had.

"I appreciate the advice, Mr. Prophet," Colter said, tightening the latigo on his own horse and regarding Prophet over his saddle. "But I reckon I'll be ridin' on to Barranca Verde just the same."

"Purty place, but there ain't much there 'ceptin' a few pious women, far as I could tell," the big bounty hunter said, stepping into his saddle with a weary grunt. "But I learned after a hard struggle with a strong-headed girl I know—one about your age, I'd say—that you got to let everyone ride his own trail and dodge his own bullets. If you can't do that, you'll end up just one pure-dee miserable sonofabitch, and bad company for the cheapest of whores."

Prophet tipped his hat brim low against the western-ing sun, gave Colter a parting wink, and headed off, the hammer-headed dun nickering owlishly, the five packhorses carrying the bloody dead men lifting dust behind him.

An hour later, Colter was nearing the top of a saddle-back ridge. He hipped around in his saddle, placing his left hand on the cantle, to look behind once more for the telltale sign of a dust plume.

He'd just turned when something screamed through the air so close to his head that he could feel the air curl around his cheek. At the same time that the bullet slammed into a pine on the left side of the trail with a wicked *spang*, spraying bark, a rifle cracked somewhere up the pine-studded ridge to his right.

Colter looked around, disoriented, his inexperienced mind slow to comprehend that he'd just been shot at and missed by a hairbreadth. He gasped, then, as the coyote dun whinnied and jumped around at the flatting echo of the rifle report, shucked his own Henry, and threw himself out of the saddle.

He hit the ground off the dun's left hip, frightening the horse into a lunging, thumping gallop up trail. Racking a shell into the Henry's breech, Colter began scrambling on his hands and knees toward the brush off the trail's right side.

Two more bullets plowed into the ground nearby with a wicked thud, blowing up dust and gravel.

Diving into the brush, mindless of sharp rocks and rattlers, Colter hit the bottom of a shallow gully and landed flat on his back. Something sharp pricked his side, and he was vaguely aware of a wetness just above his belt. He held the old Tyler Henry straight up and down against him, grinding his gloves into the barrel and stock, his heart thudding wildly.

*Pish-teww!*

Another screaming bullet tore into the gully's lip, throwing rocks and sand over Colter and sending a small sage branch flying across to the cut's other side.

Colter gritted his teeth and blinked dust from his eyes. The gully was so shallow that he was afraid to lift his head even slightly for a look up the ridge. If the shooter was far enough above him, Colter would likely be rewarded with a bullet through his eyeball.

He waited, his face flushed with anxiety and with the vexing pain of the rock poking the exact center of his back, between his shoulder blades. He felt a chill sweat bead trickle down the side of his dusty face.

One minute passed. Then another.

No sounds except for an occasional bird up the ridge opposite the shooter.

Finally, tired of waiting and enraged by the ambush, he threw himself up out of the gully and ran as fast as he could across the trail and into the scrub cedars on the other side. He gained the base of the long, low, pine-studded ridge that the shooter was on and hunkered down behind a boulder.

Doffing his hat, he cast a glimpse up through the scattered trees and boulders. Nothing moved but an occasional breeze-jostled branch. Colter brought his head back behind the boulder, looked down at his rifle, then, steeling himself, thrust the rifle out from behind the rock and sent two quick rounds shrieking up the ridge.

He watched dust puff among the trees and rocks, heard the echoing thuds and spangs a second later.

He fired again to the right. His .44 round slammed into a low, flat rock with a witch's wail, blowing stone shards in all directions.

He lowered the rifle slightly and watched for movement. Seeing no sign of the dry-gulcher, he pulled the rifle back behind the boulder, donned his hat, and replaced the spent cartridges with fresh ones from his shell belt. He edged another look around the boulder, then, sucking a sharp breath, bolted out from behind his cover.

He scrambled up the hill on his feet and one hand, holding the rifle in the other hand before him. Zig-zagging around pines and boulders, he gained the crest of the rise and stared down the narrow valley on the other side. He was breathing hard, sweat trickling down his face and basting his shirt to his back. His lungs were raw.

Where the hell was the shooter?

Something moved in the corner of his left eye. He gave a slight, startled grunt and jerked his rifle around, but held fire.

A horse and rider had just galloped out from a jumble of strewn boulders on the valley's far eastern edge. Riding as though a twister were on their tails, the skewbald paint and its rider lunged up a rise, head-ing south toward another, slightly higher rise capped with scattered rock and cedars.

Colter slammed the Winchester against his left shoulder, took hasty aim, and fired. The slug blew up a little dust puff well behind the fleeing dry-gulcher.

The rider turned his head to glance back toward Colter—a lean hombre in a cream hat with a silver-studded band, red shirt, and black chaps that flapped like giant bat wings. Colter squeezed the Henry's trig-ger.

This shot blew up dust a little closer to the paint. The rider leaned low over the horse's neck, batting his heels wildly against the mount's flanks. Cursing, Colter ejected the smoking .44 shell, seated another in the chamber, but held fire.

He lifted his cheek from the rifle's stock and watched the rider, hunkered low over the skewbald's dancing cinnamon mane, bound over the crest of the rise and out of sight.

Colter rose onto his knees. He blinked as the ground pitched to his right and left.

"Whoa," he muttered, planting his hand on the ground to steady himself.

Again feeling a prick in his side, he looked down to see blood staining his shirt just above his shell belt and left hip.

"I'll be goddamned," he muttered. "Bastard pinked me."

# Chapter 15

The coyote dun came running to Colter's whistle. The young drover pulled himself heavily into the saddle, feeling more shaky than anything from the bullet that, after a hasty inspection, he'd decided had only nipped his side, just above his hip bone, carving a notch only a little larger than the one Rondo had shot from his ear.

"Well, I'm notched, that's all," Colter said, taking up the dun's reins and turning the mount toward Barranca Verde. "Sorta like the notch in a calf's ear—or a wild mustang's."

He chuffed wryly, trying to keep his spirits up.

All right, he'd been ambushed. By whom, he had no idea. It could have been one of the outlaws that haunted this remote country between mountain ranges, or it could have been whoever had left the note. But the bastard had missed. Or almost missed. And since Colter was more than halfway to Barranca Verde, he might as well ride all the way there and find out if there was anything genuine about the note before he went back to Sapinero.

When he'd ridden nearly a half hour, holding his hand over the raw wound in his side, he came upon a spring bubbling from a rocky hillside. He climbed down from the dun's back, knelt in the verdant grass beside the spring, lifted his bloody shirt, and began cleaning out the wound with his neckerchief, as he'd cleaned his ear last night.

The pain in his side had increased, sending ripples of misery through his body, and he thought he felt a weird chill coming on. He didn't think he'd lost much blood, though. The wound was fairly clean, as the bullet had gone clear through his hide after carving two ragged, nickel-sized holes.

Colter swabbed both holes, biting his cheek against the galling pain with each dab of icy water. When he had the bleeding stopped but was wishing he had some whiskey with which to clean the wound— he never carried the stuff, for Ruth didn't allow it anywhere on their ranch in the Lunatics—he stood, pulled his shirt down, and tucked it in behind his shell belt.

Moving heavily and wincing, he filled his canteen, then tightened the dun's latigo and stepped into the saddle once more. He looked around. The sun was a rosy ball in the west, silhouetting the low ridges around it. Swallows flashed in the green sky, and golden light burnished the endless sage expanses rolling out around him toward low bluffs and mesas.

The quiet gloom of evening had settled. He'd have to find a camp soon, build a fire, and cook up some coffee, beans, and fatback. He needed to stay strong. Tomorrow morning he'd ride on into Barranca Verde, maybe find someone with whiskey who could sew up his side.

He didn't admit it to himself, but his strength, as well as his spirits, was waning. Unconsciously, he yearned to be lying naked on the bank of Cow Creek with Marianna.

When his job was done here, when he could ride back into the Lunatics and proudly announce to Ruth that Trace's killing had been avenged, he would tie himself there among those piney ridges and faultless cobalt skies and creeks chuckling through wolf willows and yellow-blossoming potentilla shrubs. He'd marry Marianna. They'd build up their own herd and their cabin and raise a family, and he'd never leave home again.

*Marianna . . .*

Her name found its way into his consciousness, as did her face, and then her voice reached his hearing, calling his name as if from far away. Colter glanced over his shoulder. The Lunatics were a purple bulge low on the northern horizon, with only one or two pale splotches marking a snow-mantled peak.

A tear slipped down from his eye, and he blinked it away.

"Come on, Northwest," he coaxed the dun, turning forward and nudging the mount's flanks with his spurs. He worked some steel into his voice. "A few more miles, then we'll hole up for the night, hit the trail again first thing tomorrow."

The steel sounded tinny even to him.

A half hour later, as the first stars kindled in the cloudless sky, he set up camp at the bottom of an arroyo.

Despite his aching side, he carefully tended the dun, cooling the horse before watering it, then rubbing it down with a heavy swatch of burlap he carried for that purpose. He checked the mount's hooves for any stones or thorns it might have acquired that could cause it to go lame and leave him stranded out here. Then he looped a feed sack of oats over its ears.

His side was a raw, gnawing pain while he cooked supper, and it nettled him half the night as he tried to sleep under a slight overhang in the arroyo's south bank. Between the pain itself and the incessant yammering of coyotes that often sounded like the calls of wild banditos to his skittish imagination, he slept only a couple of hours.

Around dawn, he heard the distant thud of horses and rose to peer northward over the arroyo's lip.

Far out across the murky slope, he spied four or five figures on horseback. They were mere gray specks from a hundred or so yards away, but he could tell they were men—grimly silent riders with their horses spread out across the slope. In the quiet of the morning, their tack squawked and jingled softly, and there was the nearly inaudible chuff of one of the horses. A hoof clipped a stone with a dull thump.

And then they were gone, swinging wide around a pine copse at the base of the slope, heading northwest and, thank God, away from Colter.

That they were outlaws on the run, he had no doubt.

A half hour later, he had the coyote dun saddled and was on the trail, heading southwest once again. He'd been so nauseated from the pain in his side—a pain that seemed to settle deep inside him and make him sick all over—that he'd been able to eat only a few bites of cold beans and fatback for breakfast. Despite the rising sun's blanketing heat, he felt an eerie chill and his entire body frequently rippled with a shiver.

The wound had opened during the night, and he'd discovered a pool of congealed blood on the ground beneath his hip. He wondered how much blood he'd lost.

He needed to get the wound sewed shut, and to sleep soon. If not, he'd likely pass out, tumble out of his saddle, and become food for the coyotes and buzzards.

Remembering stories Trace's old roundup hands had told of sewing their own wounds closed—wounds from Indian fights or hooking cow or buffalo horns, or the sundry other injuries that were part and parcel of life on the old cattle or buffalo trails—a feeling of inadequacy added to the young drover's misery, making for a burning, all-consuming desolation.

According to such stories, the old salts practically threaded their wounds shut with catgut and rusty needles while still in the saddle, and afterwards were good for another thirty, forty miles!

Colter rode hunched on the dun's back, one hand pressed to his bleeding side, gritting his teeth against his misery. He was useless out here. A useless kid.

Trace deserved better. He deserved a man like the easygoing but obviously formidable bounty hunter Colter had run into just before he'd let himself be drygulched—Lou Prophet. There was a man to run the river with. There was a man to have Bill Rondo and Chico Bannon shaking in their boots.

Not some kid who let himself get his ear shot off and then be defeated by a little nick in his side.

Colter was mostly riding to Barranca Verde now because it was too far back to Sapinero. His vengeance quest all but forgotten, he was concentrating now on merely staying alive, not an easy feat for a wounded, inexperienced yunker alone in outlaw country.

As he continued riding, hang-headed, the hills covered in dry, spindly tufts of brush and sage gently troughed around him until the cool blue shade of two canyon walls swept over him. Here, the dry tang of sage, piñons, nut pines, and sun-scorched bunchgrass was replaced by that subtle musk of cool, damp rock.

Occasionally, as the canyon walls grew higher and began to lean away from him, and the shod hooves of the coyote dun rang like cracked bells, he could smell the nectar of flower blossoms. It was like the perfume that Angelique had been wearing when she'd visited the lean-to.

From somewhere nearby he heard a soft prattle of water. Probably in the gully running along the canyon's left wall. Sure enough—had to be a creek over there, with all that greenery. Here and there a shrub appeared, covered in pink or powder blue blossoms.

Colter's heart quickened. He held his heavy head up, looking around while squeezing his left hand against the biting wound, feeling the constant wetness of fresh blood. Dilapidated shacks of either stone or sun-bleached adobe, sometimes both, sprouted along both sides of the trail. Some sat alone on barren patches of cracked black lava rock, while others appeared to have been nearly devoured by rich green shrubs.

There were pens of sun-blistered cottonwood or cactus, and these, too, were covered in blossoming greenery.

There was so much green, indicating so much fresh water, that Colter found it strange that there were no people. No people of any age. No animals of any kind except chittering squirrels and songbirds that fluttered like little bits of winged sunlight among the leafy branches.

Giving the dun its head, he clomped along the stony main street of what had apparently been a small village at one time, between rows of overgrown adobe huts and shacks, with others climbing the low rises all around. One such hovel—a brush-roofed, doorless adobe-brick hut half hidden in the shade of the canyon walls—was nearly completely covered by the large pink blossoms and waxy green leaves of some tree or shrub that Colter, raised his entire life in the high mountains, had no name for.

Just beyond the hut with its pink blossoms, Colter reined up suddenly. The dun raised its snout and nickered apprehensively, fiddlefooting its back hooves, threatening to buck. Colter's eyes burned at the sickly sweet stench that had so suddenly replaced the aroma of the blossoms.

"Whew!" he grumbled tightly, releasing the wound

to hold the reins with both hands, looking around for the source of the stench. "Can't say as I blame you, Northwest."

His curiosity for the moment overcoming his need for a sawbones, he reined the dun right of the trail and soon sat the snorting, nickering horse, staring down at a dead man lying between two shrubs bearing fruit resembling small cherries, near a trash heap of ashes and rusted tin cans. The man, who was bearded and bald and wore a long cream duster, a navy blue bandanna, and green-checked pants tucked into high-topped boots, had been dead for several days.

Two bloodstains on his chest and a ragged blue hole in his sunburned cheek were obviously bullet wounds. He wore two holsters on his hips, both empty, as were the loops on his shell belt.

He was swollen up like a corn-foundered bull, so that his face resembled a ripe brown melon and his insides threatened to burst through his skin. His eyes had been pecked out, but otherwise the carrion-eaters had left him alone to rot among the shrubs.

Colter looked around warily, seeing nothing but the abandoned dwellings, the thousand-foot canyon walls, and the creek sheathed in a nearly solid line of trees and flowering bushes. Peering straight ahead along the village's main drag that out here, at the east end of the village, dwindled to a trail again, he saw another, much larger structure looming a hundred yards away, on a low rise backed by the dark red wall of a sheer, towering cliff.

Colter gave the dun its head, and the horse nearly

rose up off its front hooves as it sprang from deep down in its hindquarters, lunging away from the nauseating smell of the putrefying corpse. It headed toward the cliff wall, and Colter jerked it back down to a trot to keep his insides from slithering out the hole in his side.

As he did, he raked the structure ahead with his scrutinizing gaze—a sprawling stone building with two peaks in its red-tiled roof and what looked like a church abutting its right side. The main structure was surrounded by several humbler shacks and sheds, including a couple of pens, corrals, and a well house covered in corrugated tin. The tin roof shone brightly in the sun that was angling in against the cliff behind it, as did the silver ornaments decorating the large wooden cross atop the church.

All about the grassy slope upon which the structure sat—likely the convent that Colter had been looking for—cream and tan goats grazed, some with horns, some without. As the dun climbed the hill via the gently curving two-track trail, Colter saw a boy of about six or seven sitting on a rock near the trail, a shepherd's staff resting across his thighs.

The boy was barefoot, clad in only a baggy burlap blouse secured across his narrow chest with rawhide strings and ragged deerskin trousers. A silver cross hung around his tanned neck by a horsehair thong.

The cross looked terribly large and formidable against the boy's skinny chest. He had one foot resting on a knee, and he was picking at the bottom of his foot while holding his gaze on the approaching rider, the skin between his eyes creased with curiosity.

His thick cinnamon hair was sun-bleached almost yellow in places. His eyes were dark blue, betraying some Anglo blood. Something told Colter the boy did not speak English, however, because when he stopped and asked if this was the convent at Barranca Verde, the boy only stared at him, the lines between his eyes growing even deeper.

"Don't reckon there's a sawbones hereabouts?" Colter tried once more, wincing as he crouched a little lower in the saddle, pressing his hand against the bloody wound in his side.

The boy's eyes dropped to Colter's bloody shirt. "Bandito," he whispered as though to himself. He raised his befuddled eyes to Colter's.

"No," Colter said, shaking his head. "No bandito. Just an idiot gringo who got himself shot travelin' where he had no damn business."

He booted the coyote dun ahead once more, continuing up the hill. He glanced behind to see the blue-eyed boy standing now and staring after him, holding the staff in both hands across his waist.

At the top of the hill and in front of the sprawling structure, Colter half fell and half climbed down from the coyote dun's back. He fumbled with the saddle cinch, wanting to give Northwest some air, but he found himself too weak and his hands uncooperative. So he patted the horse's sweat-lathered neck and stumbled toward the base of a broad stone staircase rising toward two tall sun-bleached, iron-handled doors.

He stumbled up the steps, falling once when his toe caught a cracked riser.

At the top, he didn't bother knocking. He tripped

the iron latch, pushed the door open with a raucous squawking of dry hinges, and peered inside.

The musty air smelled faintly of candles, cool stone, and rodent droppings. There was also the smell of cooking and piñon smoke. From far off, the cries of a baby echoed.

Colter frowned.

A baby? But then, he hadn't expected to find a little blue-eyed boy on the grounds of a Mexican convent, either. Nor a bloating, bullet-riddled corpse nearby.

Leaving the door standing wide behind him, lighting the dark path before him, he moved forward, lurching down several dim, echoing hallways between heavy oak doors, following the baby's cries.

Cripes, he thought. Could the tears written about in the note be those of the wailing baby? Was some kind of bizarre joke being played on him?

For a moment, in his mind's eye, he saw Bill Rondo and Chico Bannon sitting around the sheriff's office in Sapinero, laughing their heads off.

The baby had stopped crying a few minutes before he paused in the broad-arched entrance to a long, narrow room. It was obviously a kitchen, because there was a big brick hearth on which several pots bubbled, and smoke wafted through the air.

A long, scarred plank table sat in the middle of the room. Several shadowy, black-clad figures milled about the hearth on the right end of the room, knocking pots and lids together.

But it was the figure almost directly across the table that made Colter's eyes widen and his breath catch in his throat.

The figure was a dark-haired girl, maybe in her mid-twenties, her ratty brown robe lowered to her waist, exposing her breasts so that the baby in her arms could suckle. She stood against the far wall fronting a small shrine and a stained-glass window. Her long brown hair brushed the baby in her arms as she cooed to it, rocked it, and clutched it tightly against her.

The baby made soft, wet sounds as it suckled.

The girl's breasts were large and sloping. She was pale-skinned and, though it was hard to tell because her rich hair hid her face, maybe Mexican or at least partly Mexican or even Indian.

Another figure sat hunched at the table with its back to him. Now, as the figure turned toward him suddenly, as though having abruptly sensed his presence, Colter's gut tightened with revulsion.

The face that had just turned to him was framed in the black-and-white hood of a nun's habit. It was a face as wizened as an ancient pine knot. It was shrunken, as dark as pitch, and appeared to have been devoid of life for years. The eyes that stared from that death mask—if you could call them eyes— were as large and white as duck eggs.

But when the lips moved in that horrific wreck of a blind visage, the voice that said in Spanish, "What have we here?" was as soft and high and innocent as that of a very small child.

Colter's knees weakened.

He felt them buckling.

He stumbled against the side of the arched entranceway, the room growing dark before him, and crumpled.

# Chapter 16

He didn't pass out completely.

He was dimly aware of women bustling about him, and then of being pulled to his feet by both arms. As female voices murmured in hushed Spanish around him, in tones more admonishing than concerned, he felt his boots moving heavily beneath him as, with arms draped around spindly shoulders on each side of him, he was led back down the echoing, musty hall.

His body felt as though it weighed a thousand pounds. His boots felt as though they were filled with cement. And he could not keep his eyes open.

But he caught occasional glimpses of the cracked flagstone floor sliding away beneath his plodding, stumbling boots while deeply lined, rope-sandaled feet the color of saddle leather shuffled along on either side, the black pleats of the nuns' habits swishing about stubby legs. He noticed, for some reason, that the sides of the nuns' feet were a shade lighter than the tops, and their toes were as cracked and yellow as the seashells he used to find in the creek beds around the Circle C.

The cooking smell receded behind him, replaced by the smell of ancient stone and candle wax and the floury, medicinal odor of old women. Vaguely, he was aware of someone's spidery fingers hooked behind the back of his shell belt, and the light tugs of someone scuffing along behind him.

The blind nun?

He must have blanked out for a time, because the next thing he knew he was lying on a squawky bed while the nuns, fluttering like vultures around him, were jerking his boots and clothes off. As his head bobbed with the brusque tugs while the nuns continued muttering reprovingly in Spanish, he glanced toward the small room's open door.

The blind nun sat in a chair beside the opening, leaning forward with her small, dark hands on her knees, white eyes fairly glowing in their mahogany sockets. A candle lantern fluttered and smoked on the wall above her, silhouetting her and accenting her specterlike countenance. She was saying something to the others, and her tone even in that eerily high-pitched voice was somehow commanding.

Colter had a strange acidic taste in his mouth and a strangely pleasant feeling in his head. The small, dark, white-eyed nun pitched and rolled from side to side in her chair, as though the entire room was moving around her.

No, it wasn't an earthquake, he realized as his eyes fell upon a small table beside the bed. He was drunk. He blinked groggily, trying to focus.

On the table was a washbasin filled with rose-colored water, several bloody cloths, and a needle threaded with what appeared to be catgut. There were also several open jars, two tin canisters, and a jug with its cork out. From here he could smell the strong alcohol emanating from the jug, and blinking once more and forcing his eyes to focus, he could just make out the faded letters that had been printed on the jug's smooth stone side—BACONORA.

Juventino had often sipped from a jug of *baconora*, and the Mexican cook had told Colter it was strong Mexican whiskey. "It will kill what ails you," the man had said with a wink, raising the jug to his lips. Then he added, "And then some!"

Colter realized, as the nuns finished removing every scrap of his clothing, that he no longer felt the bullet wound in his side. Glancing down his chest, he saw not the ragged, bloody wound but a large square bandage just above his hip. It was secured to his side by a broad cotton band wrapped tightly around his belly.

The nuns had gotten him drunk and sewed him up.

He felt a smile curl his lips, only half aware of one of the spidery old nuns running a wet sponge down his chest. Then his head fell back against a deep feather pillow, and darkness spilled like soft sand around him, and he slept the sleep of the dead.

His sleep was buoyant with pleasant dreams at first, then racked with nightmares. Spooks and demonic beasts chased him through an isolated darkness that seemed to have no end.

As the alcohol wore off, he dreamed that a lion was

ripping into his side, the jaws hungrily lunging and tearing. He tried to reach for his gun to shoot the beast or to scare it off, but he couldn't quite reach far enough for the weapon, which kept sliding away from him as though tugged by an invisible rope.

At one point he heard what sounded like a girl crying. He opened his eyes slightly and saw rain streaking the window to his right.

Lightning flashed and thunder rumbled. There was more darkness and silence, and then he opened his eyes again, jarred into half wakefulness by a loud thunderclap that shook the entire room, and the wavering image of a balding, tough-eyed, middle-aged man in a green bib-front, brass-buttoned shirt and leather jacket hovered over him. The man moved his lips as he turned a glance over his shoulder, and the candlelight touched the gray in the thin, sandy hair behind his pronounced widow's peak.

The man's name seemed to wing up out of nowhere to catch in Colter's brain: Paul Spurlock. The rancher Colter had met in Sapinero.

"Two and a half days," he heard the little girl's voice say somewhere in the shadows behind him, and he glimpsed the white eyes staring like a wolf's out of the darkness.

Then he could see the wolves themselves, staring straight into his own eyes, tongues slick with saliva drooping over their jaws.

Another figure appeared, dancing and laughing, and it took Colter a moment to remember the name of Spurlock's daughter, Jennifer.

Why was she dancing? Colter wondered vaguely.

Couldn't she see the wolves waiting to devour them both?

"Want I should take care of him, boss?"

This was a strange, slightly high-pitched voice—louder than the others, as though a product of the storm raging outside the walls of wherever Colter was; he couldn't remember that he was in the convent nor what had brought him there. A darkly handsome, mustached face appeared in the shadows at the foot of his bed. It belonged to a tall, rangy man in a yellow rain slicker over a pinto vest, wearing a battered Stetson with a snakeskin band. His large, rope-burned hands were tucked down behind his wide brown leather cartridge belt, near his walnut-gripped Schofield .44. Another .44 was wedged behind his belt buckle, as were a pair of deerskin gloves.

The man's eyes were filled with liquid shadows, and as Colter tried to study them to learn their intent, the young cowboy's own eyes rolled back into unconsciousness once more.

But the menace in the man was like a heavy, cloying odor in the room.

Total, welcome darkness enshrouded Colter for what seemed a long time.

Silence.

Then a strange sound lured him back toward consciousness. He could not tell if the sound was part of another dream, but as he lay there listening, it composed itself into the uncontrolled weeping of a heartbroken young woman. It came from far away, and Colter lay listening to it for a long time, the grief so poignant that it became Colter's own.

He felt—or thought he felt—tears rolling out from under his closed eyelids to dribble down his cheeks and make an uncomfortable wetness against his neck.

"Trace . . . ," he heard himself croak.

He woke later. It was the middle of the night, and the fogs and mists of his dream- and nightmare-riddled slumber cleared like the sky after a rain.

He lifted the covers and inspected his side by moonlight. Someone had apparently changed the bandage, for it looked as fresh as the first time he'd seen it, though he knew he'd been here a couple of nights.

He felt better, stronger, and he tested his strength by getting up and using the chamber pot he discovered under the washstand in the room's corner. He swooned like a bride at first, but then he got his feet under him and steadied his knees. He'd no sooner padded naked back to the bed than he stopped suddenly.

He'd heard something. For a moment he had the eerie feeling his dreams were calling to him, for what he heard sounded like a much fainter version of the crying he'd heard in his sleep.

But no. The sound was coming from outside.

He reached forward, unlatched the shutter over his bed, and swung it outward, gritting his teeth at the audible rake of the hinges. Cool night air pushed over him, rife with the fresh, aromatic smell of a recent rain. There was the rush of a night breeze . . . or was it water?

The cries rose and fell beneath the whispering, rushing sound. They were almost like the faint tinkle of wooden wind chimes in the far distance, carried on fickle air currents—fading, clarifying, then fading again when the breeze waned.

Colter stood with one hand on the shutter, the cool air lifting gooseflesh on his arms, down his chest and belly. He stared out at a small courtyard surrounded by low, vine-shrouded adobe walls. Beyond it rose a velvet mountain ridge so steep that he had to crouch and tip his head back to see the stars sparkling beyond the jagged peak.

The breeze freshened, blowing his long hair back from his neck and filling his nostrils with the perfume of nectary blossoms. At the same time, the cries became so clear that the girl shedding the tears could have been kneeling just below him in the courtyard. In fact, for a moment he lowered his head to peer around the low green shrubs lining the courtyard walls, at the stone benches and the statue of one of the saints limned in silvery moonlight.

The breeze waned, and so did the cries, though they continued faintly. They seemed to be coming from somewhere in the velvet mountain wall—so anguished that with every softly uttered note, Colter felt as though his heart were clenched in a tight fist, and a knot swelled in his throat. They were cries not of physical pain but of emotional pain.

A pain that Colter understood. A pain more penetrating and lingering than most physical maladies.

He was still weak, too weak to do what he was about to do, but curiosity gripped him even tighter than that anguished fist, and he turned from the window to begin looking around for his clothes.

His trousers, shirt, and longhandles—all freshly

laundered—were on a chair in the corner opposite the washstand. His boots had been polished and set neatly beneath the chair. Everything was there except for his Remington and his shell belt.

He dressed quickly, pleased with the strength he felt in spite of the hitch in his side. If he had to, he could ride out of the convent right now, tonight, if he could find his horse. But first he had to find out who was shedding so many tears at Barranca Verde, and why.

When he'd removed the spurs from his boots and stepped into them, he went to the door, half expecting it to be locked from the outside. But it opened as creakily as all the doors and shutters he'd encountered in these hulking quarters, and he stole quietly into the dark hall, not wanting to wake anyone.

For fifteen minutes he wandered the cavernous corridors on the balls of his boots, untucked shirttail flapping with his suspenders around his hips. Once he heard deep snores, and he thought they were those of a man, though he'd never seen a male besides the goat-tending boy on the premises. But each snore was punctuated by a high, female sigh, and something told Colter he'd just passed the room of the nun with the hideously blind white eyes.

Finally he came to a door on what he figured to be the convent's first floor, as he'd descended several stone staircases, perilous with chipped rocks and flaking mortar. The door's locking bolt was open, and the door itself was unlatched, showing a long vertical line of pearl moonlight.

Colter went out, finding himself in the small courtyard beneath his room. Wincing against the heat in his side, the wound having been aggravated by his milling about the convent, he drew the door closed behind him and left it unlatched, as had the person who'd gone out before him.

The courtyard was all moon-silvered planes and angles and deep, dark shadows. He saw benches and shrubbery, and as he stole forward from the convent wall, heading toward a gate that he'd spied from his room, he paused to regard a large stone shrine flanked by a wrought-iron fence.

Within the fence lay a mounded, grass-covered grave fronted by an elaborately scrolled wooden cross adorned with a juniper wreath. On the shrine had been scored a long Spanish name—likely the name of some important nun who'd lived here long ago. Maybe the very first one.

Colter didn't linger at the shrine. Continuing to hear the intermittent cries that he'd heard from his window, and incredulous at the despair that could keep one crying with such vigor for so long, he continued through the courtyard gate and out onto a rocky, night-cloaked flat flanking the convent.

Following the cries, which grew louder with every step of his worn boots, he headed into a narrow defile in the wall of the black velvet ridge. As he moved along the canyon, the walls so close he could reach out and touch both pitted and fissured slabs at the same time, the hairs rose along his neck. It was not from horror of anything he could see or even hear, for the cries were heart-wrenching rather than terrifying.

But there was something else here—an inner dreadfulness, a terrible awareness.

He didn't want to go on, because he felt that he wasn't going to like what he discovered here at Barranca Verde. But go on he did, brushing at his empty hip and wishing like hell he had his Remy.

# Chapter 17

Colter had smelled the faintly pungent humidity before he'd even entered the defile.

Now he saw the fog rising from the rocks down a steep gully along the base of the canyon's left wall. The little stream was being fed by a waterfall just beyond.

It wasn't much of a waterfall, but the water—apparently heated underground before bubbling up somewhere atop the ridge—fell from a lip high above the creek. It tumbled over black slabs of volcanic boulders at the head of the stream, where it formed a pool among the rocks. The creek was formed by runoff from the fog-enshrouded pool.

The cries sounded now like a strange kind of singing in accompaniment to the water's tinny splatter onto the rocks and into the pool below. The singer, if you could call her that, sat on a flat boulder at the bottom of the falls, just above the pool.

Colter hunkered behind a gnarled cedar and a small boulder at the lip of the warm creek steaming down the gully on his left. The falls were just ahead. He doubted that he'd have been able to see the girl on the boulder if it hadn't been for the moonlight angling like the wash of liquid pearls into the defile. The mist would have concealed her.

As it was, the moonlight revealed her and the mist and the water tumbling over her—a single, surreal image like those from his fever dreams of the past several hours. He couldn't see much of her inside that watery, oddly ambient sarcophagus—but that she was a girl was plain not only by the pitch of her sobs but by the roundness of her body just barely concealed by a wet, clinging nightgown that seemed to shimmer and dance in the mist-woven moonlight.

Soaked hair was pasted to her head and shoulders, one of which was laid bare by the fallen strap of her nightgown. She sat atop the boulder with one knee up. One arm was hooked around that knee, and she was leaning her head forward. She kicked her other leg out with each upbeat in the keening wails that seemed to originate from a source as infinite as that from which the warm water flowed.

Suddenly she lifted her head and loosed a wail that made Colter jerk with a start. The shriek echoed hollowly in that tight cavern, for a moment drowning out the murmur of the steaming water. Then the girl rested her head against her knee once again and continued sobbing steadily, occasionally shaking her head as if in utter exasperation and rage.

Colter felt his face grow taut, and his heart swelled. The girl's misery recalled his own, and he suddenly wanted to leap out from behind the boulder, run t her, pull her head to his chest, and wrap his arms around her shoulders.

But he held his ground. Befuddlement, even more than empathy, raked through him.

As well as fear and apprehension.

He wanted to know what had caused the girl to spill so many tears here at Barranca Verde—but what possible connection could this girl and her sorrow have with Trace's killing?

Again the haunting dread chilled him.

But then, steeling himself—he'd come too far to leave without completing his mission—he started to rise from behind the boulder, to begin walking toward the falls.

The faint slap of a sandal sounded back the way he had come. He jerked down behind the rock and pressed his back to it, hunkering low. Looking back along the trail, he saw a pinprick of yellow light shining, swinging slightly, eerily haloed by the fog.

Soon a bulky silhouette appeared beneath the lantern, and Colter scrunched himself even lower, hoping the boulder's shadow and a small, gnarled piñon would conceal him from the newcomer.

The nun holding the lantern passed within six feet of his position. He could see little of her but the heavy brown hooded robe she wore and the tan rope-and-hide sandals slapping her heels.

As the nun passed him, she yelled, "Jacinta! Jacinta!" A string of Spanish followed, and from what Colter remembered of Juventino's lessons, the woman was ordering the girl, Jacinta, to come down from the boulder and to return to the convent at once.

"You will catch a chill and die of sickness . . . and what of the little ones?" the nun barked, her shrill voice echoing above the clattering of the ragged falls. "Besides, your ridiculous caterwauling is keeping all the sisters awake!"

Colter waited, his head turned sideways to the boulder, listening, wondering what the girl's voice would sound like speaking instead of crying. But there was only the noise of the water over the rocks.

His heart thudded. If the girl and the nun returned to the convent before he did, they'd likely lock him out.

He pushed up onto his knees and edged a cautious look over the small boulder. Beyond, the girl was climbing slowly down from the boulder she'd been sitting on, facing the rock, her nightgown clinging to her round bottom and long legs, her hair pasted against her back.

The nun waited in stonily patient silence at the edge of the pool, holding the lantern aloft.

Knowing he had to make it back to the convent before the women did, and not wanting to be discovered out here like a peeper in the night, he quickly turned away from the boulder and moved as quietly as possible back along the trail toward the mouth of the defile.

Once out of the canyon, he hurried back to the large stone building hulking in the darkness, every tile in its multipeaked roof delineated by the moon. He was careful not to trip in the ghostly darkness, lest he rip open his side again.

On the other side of the courtyard, he found the

same door he'd left the convent by standing slightly more ajar than how he'd left it. He slipped through it, closed it carefully, then stole back to his room, where he shucked out of his clothes and climbed into bed.

He lay there for a short time, pondering the girl, Jacinta, and her uncontrollable tears. Sooner than he expected, sleep swept over him like a giant crow's wing.

A metallic click sounded. Hinges squawked.

Colter opened his eyes, blinked against the gray morning light that angled through the window he'd left open last night. The door to the hall was pushing wide. A young woman with long brown hair stepped sideways into the room. She carried a wooden tray in front of her. There was a heaping breakfast plate and a steaming stone coffee mug.

The blood raced audibly in Colter's ears as the girl turned toward him, kicking the door closed behind her—a pretty young woman with large brown eyes, hair pulled back in a ponytail, bangs hanging over her brows. She had a sullen, almost angry look, full lips stretched in a straight, hard line. A very faint mole was visible just to the left of her mouth.

Colter hadn't seen her face before now. But there was no doubt who she was—the girl who'd been nursing the baby, the girl who'd been crying in the canyon of Barranca Verde.

Suddenly feeling careless and bold, he said, "Hello, Jacinta."

She stopped some distance from the bed, but her expression did not change. She stared at him for a time, her eyes holding his obliquely, and then she said in a tight, bitter, Spanish-accented voice, "You better get your ass out of here, sonny. Unless you want to be hauled out feetfirst!"

Colter shook his tangled hair back from his face, frowning. "Why would that happen?"

Jacinta moved forward and set the tray on the bed beside him. "Sister Graciella says she heard someone in men's boots stealing around last night."

"She the blind one?"

"Eat. Then you must leave." Jacinta stared at him, as though pondering a problem. "I put your pistol in the barn. It's with your horse and your rifle and your tack. Go back to where you came from."

"I'm not a bandit," Colter hurried to say, sensing she was about to swing around and leave before he could find out what he needed to know.

She looked at him again, and the skin between her eyes wrinkled faintly. Then she did as he had feared she'd do—she swung around and began moving toward the door, the folds of her brown robe buffeting about her legs.

"I came here because somone left me a note."

The girl continued moving toward the door, reaching for the knob.

"You know what it said?"

She stopped, her hand on the knob, facing the door.

" 'Many tears have been shed at Barranca Verde.' "

She didn't turn around. She stood frozen, facing the door.

"The note wasn't signed," Colter said. "But whoever wrote it wanted me to come here."

Jacinta turned from the door to face him squarely. "Who are you?"

"Colter Farrow. Trace Cassidy was my foster father."

Her face changed suddenly. Her eyes widened, her chin came up, and her throat moved as she swallowed. Her clean-boned oval face, already pale, turned one shade paler.

Colter didn't want to ask the next question. Steeling himself, rubbing his thumb nervously over the second knuckle of his index finger and clearing his throat, he said, "Are your tears for him? For... Trace?"

She swallowed again and moved silently forward. She dragged a chair out from the table by the wall, not looking at it, moving stiffly. She pulled the chair over to the bed and straddled it.

Her eyes were wide, dark, and grave.

She stared at Colter, and he could see the thoughts racing behind those dark eyes. Her lips were slightly parted, and he thought she was on the verge of saying something, but when she said nothing, only stared at him as though deeply, keenly vexed, he prodded her with, "How well...?" His voice caught. He cleared it again and continued. "How well did you know Trace?"

"Those little ones out there," she said so suddenly that her soft voice startled him, turning her head slightly toward the door, her eyes remaining on him, defiant, challenging. "They're his."

Colter felt his entire body tighten. Heat rose in his

neck, instantly drying his throat. A voice inside his head screamed very shrilly as if from far, far away, *"Noooo!"*

At the same time, he remembered the several supply runs Trace had traditionally made to town each spring, summer, and fall, buying only a little each time. He said he bought so little because he couldn't bring himself to spend more than a few dollars each time, money being so scarce in the Lunatics.

In the spring and again in the fall, he trailed a few beef at a time to the railhead in Walsenberg . . . alone. Said he liked the quiet ride. Besides, Colter was needed at home, to watch over Ruth, David, and little May.

Colter lifted his hand from the bed. He moved it toward his steaming coffee cup. The hand trembled.

The next question came automatically, and he heard only sadness and defeat in his voice, minus the rage from before: "Who killed him?"

"What does it matter?" she said, lifting her gaze to the window in which the morning sun now blossomed like a giant yellow rose. "If you came to settle things for Trace, you're wasting your time. Things can't be settled. There are powerful men involved, my father being one."

Colter felt his insides coil and tighten.

"Who's your father?"

"Spurlock."

Colter looked at her in surprise. "Paul Spurlock? The rancher?" He remembered seeing the man and his *segundo*—what was his name? Surtees?—in his fever dream. Or had it really been a dream?

She nodded slightly.

"You're . . . Jennifer's sister?"

"Half sister."

Colter mentally digested that, then asked, "Who're the others?"

"Rondo. Surtees. Bannon. What does it matter?" She was staring at the sunlight in the window. She chuckled dreamily, caustically, her lips trembling and showing her teeth, and a tear rolled out of her eye to dribble down her cheek. "And half the town of Sapinero!"

Her voice broke. She pulled her head down, slapped a hand to her mouth, and convulsed, shoulders jerking as she sobbed.

# Chapter 18

Colter swallowed. His heart ached, and his limbs felt rubbery, but he had to know the whole story.

"What do you mean—half the town of Sapinero? They all had a hand in Trace's murder?"

Jacinta Spurlock sat in the chair, one arm draped across the back, staring at the window brightly adorned with soft lemon sunlight, as if she were seeing it all right there, in the gradually intensifying light.

"Oh, they didn't all take a hand in it. But they didn't help him. I saw after I'd ridden to town after Trace. They stood along the street, watching, doing nothing to stop Rondo and his deputy and Surtees. They were all quite happy, in fact.

"The men were jealous of Trace, because all the women in town were in love with him. The women were jealous of me, because they all loved Trace and wanted to be swept off their feet by the charming gunslinger who rode out of the Lunatics every few months to spread his charm."

Her face hardened slightly. "Only, I was the one

who became the most susceptible to that smile of his, the joking, the gifts, the tender lovemaking. . . ."

Colter shook his head and gritted his teeth. She couldn't be talking about Trace Cassidy. Trace was in love with Ruth. He was devoted to his family.

"No," Colter said, shaking his head slowly. "You're lying. You gotta be lying."

"You think so?" Jacinta continued staring at the window, laughing and crying at the same time, her smooth, pale cheeks awash in tears. "I don't think so, amigo. You came here to learn the truth. Well, I'm telling you the truth. Not pretty, huh? Well, then, you better go on back to where you came from before you get all mixed up in the ugliness."

She turned to him then, dropped her suddenly hard eyes to the breakfast tray. "Eat. Then, go!"

Colter stared at her dumbly, his mind racing, unable to believe what she had told him and, at the same time, unable not to believe it. He knew from stories others had told him that Trace had had many women in the past. He'd been a handsome, rakish young gunslinger, very good with the ladies.

But when he'd met Ruth, his childhood love from the Tennessee mountains, and brought her out here with him to the Lunatics, he'd hung up his promiscuous past with his guns and settled down to ranching and raising a family.

Colter shoved the breakfast tray away and pressed the heels of his hands to his eyes, trying to steady his thoughts, to quell his thudding heart. He felt warm and dizzy, and he wanted to get out of there.

But first . . .

"Tell me about the last time," he said. "You said you followed Trace to town. I don't understand. . . ."

"He came to my father's ranch," the girl said, looking directly at Colter now, as though challenging him to believe what she was saying, as though she were assaulting him with the facts. "My father caught us together in the old bunkhouse, where we often met and where I would give Trace some time with the baby. Miguel, you see—the boy—has been here with the sisters since he turned one year old. My father saw to that, since Miguel had no father—at least, none that my father knew about."

She laughed caustically. Her lips trembled, and she pressed her hand to her mouth, stifling them. Slowly lowering her hand, composing herself, she stared grimly at the carving of Our Lady of Guadalupe on the wall behind Colter.

"My father caught us together. He yelled for Surtees, and there was shooting. It was crazy. Trace was wounded. He ran to his horse and rode to town. My father and Surtees and several other men followed him there. That's when Rondo and Bannon became involved."

She sighed deeply, wetly, sniffing but holding her wide brown gaze on the wall.

"They scoured the town, found Trace in the doctor's buggy shed. The doctor, McCallister, had been a friend of Trace's, and he tried to help, but there was no help for Trace. He was too weak to run anymore, or to put up much of a fight."

She stopped and just stared at the wall.

"Go on," Colter heard himself prod her thinly. "Tell me."

She sniffed again, and brushed a tear from her cheek with the back of her wrist.

"They caught him and dragged him out into the street in front of Rondo's office," she continued in an almost singsong voice, as though to compensate for the horror of what she was relating. "Bannon and Surtees went to work with quirts and bullwhips. I ran to Trace, and they whipped me, too, and then all I remembered as I lay in the street, sobbing and only half conscious, was the horrific sounds of the whips and quirts and Trace's screams for help. But no help came. . . ."

Her voice trailed off.

Slowly she turned her stricken gaze to Colter. "When I woke in the street, they were nailing Trace to the bed of his wagon as he screamed and sobbed. The street was lined now—this was four o'clock in the morning—with a hundred men and women, at least. All watching, doing nothing to help. Many of the men were laughing and congratulating my father and Rondo for their handiwork. Finally ridding the town of the old Confederate gunslinger who owned the hearts of all the women."

The corners of Jacinta's wide mouth rose in a hard, mirthless smile. Her brown eyes flashed fatefully. "And then they slapped the mules up the trail with the wagon. They wanted to torture Trace, of course, as well as send a warning to his people in the mountains about what would happen if they tried to avenge his murder. Normally, they would have branded him, like they do the men they don't want to see in town again. With a big S for Sapinero. I guess killing Trace was enough."

She paused. A sunlit tear dropped from her chin to a fold of her robe. "The next day, my father brought me and the baby here to be with Miguel . . . for the rest of our lives, as far as that old killer is concerned."

Colter tried to speak, but no words would come. He was hearing the hammers nailing Trace's arms and legs to the wagon. Hearing the screams . . .

He squeezed his eyes shut and tried again, thickly. "And . . . and that was him—Spurlock—here the other night. . . ."

Jacinta nodded. "He stops by occasionally. His range is just a little ways from here. For taking me in, he pays the sisters in beef and keeps the outlaws from harassing the convent. He has many gunmen on his roll . . . and commands much respect in this part of the territory. There are still bandits around Barranca Verde, but not nearly as many as before I came here."

She smiled with phony affability. "There you have it. Are you happy now, Colter Farrow? You've learned the truth, and there is nothing you can do about it."

Colter had been staring at the door. Now he turned to her, anger sparking in his eyes. "Don't be so sure."

Jacinta Spurlock shook her head. "My father knows you're here. He's suspicious of your intentions, and, while he *is* above killing a wounded boy in his sleep, he's ordered the nuns to make sure you're gone by the end of the week. You can bet he has ordered Rondo to make sure you don't show yourself in town again, either."

"He owns Rondo, I take it?"

"My father owns half the town. More than half the county, for that matter. Rondo once rode for him. Same with Bannon. And believe me, gringo *rojo*, if my father wants you out of the country, Rondo and Bannon will make sure that you're out of the country. If you defy them even a little, they will kill you. Or worse—they'll brand you so that you'll wear the mark of Sapinero till the end of your days!"

Colter grimaced at the grisly notion. He'd heard the name Spurlock before, from the men he'd worked around in the Lunatics. But he'd paid little attention; the name hadn't meant anything to him. Now he felt a stubborn defiance of the rancher. But fear chilled him as well. Obviously, if Spurlock had been able to kill Trace Cassidy, Colter Farrow would be easy prey.

He had no idea what he was going to do now. But, clearly, remaining here at the convent would be suicide. If Spurlock returned, he'd kill him. Besides, he'd regained enough of his strength to ride—and he'd learned what he'd wanted to know.

Or, at least, his questions had been answered. What he was going to do about those answers, he had no idea. He needed time to think.

He nodded slowly, staring at the breakfast tray. He hadn't eaten in many hours, and while he knew he needed sustenance, he felt as though he'd drunk a quart of sour milk. "I'll go."

"*Sí.*"

Jacinta stood slowly, regarding him grimly, and walked to the door.

"You always fall in love with married men?" Colter

asked her suddenly, his voice pitched low with brooding anger. After all, it took two to tango.

She stopped at the door and turned back toward him. "I don't expect you to understand my feelings for your foster father. I . . . and he . . . have hurt you too badly. Just know that it was not my intention. I simply"—tears glistened in her eyes once more, and she shook her head as if to clear them—"found myself too much in love to turn him away. And then Miguel came, and . . ."

She let her voice trail off, leaving the words to fade like echoes around a canyon before adding, "If it makes you feel any better, I will be a prisoner here for a long, long time. Until my children are grown, at least. All because I loved a man—and continue to love him and miss him—more than I could help. More than I knew was right."

She opened the door and went out silently, latching the door softly behind her.

When her retreating footsteps had faded, Colter stared for a long time at the breakfast tray on the bed beside him. He thought of Ruth and David and little May.

What would he tell them?

"Goddamn you, Trace."

Bunching his lips and gritting his teeth, he sent the tray and all the food and utensils flying across the room.

Colter found the blind nun standing at a side entrance as he left the convent with only what he'd entered the place with—the clothes on his back. She stood just outside the door, taking in the morning sun with her back to the crumbling stone wall of the staircase.

Facing east, she held a jeweled crucifix in her dark, deeply lined hands up close to her neck. The sun had found those eyes set in the deep, coffee-colored sockets, and they glowed like backlit eggshells. She was smiling celestially, and her expression did not change as Colter moved through the open door, though she'd likely heard the ching of his spurs and the thud of his boots several minutes ago, as he'd worked his way down from his room.

He hesitated in front of the blind nun. "Thanks for your hospitality," he said finally. *"Muchas gracias."*

Celestial smile in place, she hiked a shoulder. In a thick Spanish accent she said, "Travel safely, young one." Her high voice dropped a note. "And you best travel south."

Colter had started down the steps. He hesitated again, glancing at her, frowning. Sapinero lay north. Though she smiled like an angel fresh from heaven, there had been a definite note of warning in her tone.

"Obliged for the advice," he grumbled, and started down the steps.

"If you see Miguel in the barn," the nun called behind him, "please to inform him it is time for his morning prayers, *por favor.*"

Colter threw up a hand in acknowledgment and continued down the steps and across the gravelly yard, heading for the large, thatch-roofed, white adobe building he assumed was the barn. A corral flanked the structure, around which several cottonwoods tossed their shade as the warming sun climbed higher, and in the barn were several horses.

The coyote dun stood off to one side, staring toward Colter and twitching its ears and working its nose. Northwest threw up a welcoming whinny that was nearly lost on Colter's own ears, for he was so deep in brooding contemplation of the horrible things he'd learned about Trace, and racked with such bitter anguish, that he almost ran into the barn's one closed door before swerving left and entering through the open right one.

The sudden switching of his course had, for the moment, jarred him from his reverie. He stopped suddenly and looked inside the dim barn, which was rich with the smell of hay and straw. The blue-eyed, brown-haired boy Miguel knelt on the floor before an empty stall, his back to Colter.

The boy had Colter's shell belt and holster on his lap, and he was fiddling with Colter's Remington .44, lowering his head to inspect the cylinder and barrel, his little thumb caressing the hammer. Colter heard the boy grunting and breathing raspily, lost in his fascinated inspection of the six-shooter.

Colter stepped forward. "Hey, kid, what the hell're you doin' with my pistol?"

The boy gasped as he turned with a fearful start to regard Colter. Colter reached down and grabbed the Remy from the boy's hand. Then he snagged his shell belt from the boy's lap.

"Urchins like you aren't supposed to play with guns," he admonished, sliding the pistol into its holster. "Didn't anyone ever teach you that? You could shoot your damn—"

No point in taking his anger out on the boy. Miguel was as blameless as David and little May.

"It's dangerous," Colter said, softening his tone as he wrapped the shell belt around his waist and buckled it. *"Peligroso."*

The boy stared up at him, the fear leaching from his blue eyes—the same blue, Colter realized now, as Trace's. Deep down, he'd noticed the resemblance when he'd first seen the boy, and that realization had fueled his dread.

He felt the boy's eyes on him as he loaded the Remy, then grabbed a lariat off a heavy ceiling joist. As he started for the corral to rope the coyote dun, he heard the crunch of dirt and straw as the boy gained his feet behind him.

The boy's eyes haunted him. It was as though Trace were staring at him through Miguel, his bastard son. Colter was glad when he remembered the nun's order.

Stopping at the other end of the barn, he glanced back. The boy had been following him slowly, tentatively, blue eyes wide with interest.

"Sister Graciella wants you," he said in his halting Spanish, canting his head to indicate the barn's front door.

The boy continued staring at Colter, lines forming between those haunting eyes. Then he turned suddenly and sprinted to the other end of the barn, out the door, and into the yard. His rope-soled sandals slapped wildly, the sound dwindling quickly.

Then there were only the snorts of the horses in the corral behind Colter, and the barn's musty, tomblike silence.

# Chapter 19

Not by any conscious design, Colter headed back north.

He didn't know where he was going, or what he was going to do when he got there. The mission that Ruth had sent him on now seemed poignantly pointless. In fact, nothing at all seemed to make sense anymore.

He rode blindly, his thoughts murky and his side and his torn ear aching. The brush and rocks rolling down from the ridges around him, the low, puffy clouds in the cobalt sky, all seemed part of the same hokum, a meaningless gathering of random objects, a dream dreamed by a long-dead God.

He was so lost in despair, and wondering what story he was going to make up to tell Ruth, that he didn't see the five horseback riders angling down a sloping, cedar-stippled ridge toward him until they were a hundred yards away. No, not five riders. Six riders on five horses. Two of the rough-garbed, unshaven, heavily armed men were riding double on a beefy sorrel.

They were trotting directly toward Colter, one ominously sliding his rifle from his saddle boot. It wasn't hard to decipher their intentions. They'd obviously ridden a long way hard, probably up from Taos with a posse dusting their trail, and they needed another horse.

Colter's pulse beat a war rhythm in his ears, and the hammering of his heart made his wounds bark.

He reined the dun off the trail and spurred it hard. At nearly the same time, a couple of the oncoming riders whooped like coyotes on the blood trail. Colter put the dun up a long, gradually shelving bluff on the west side of the trail, hearing beneath the frenetic thumps of his own mount's hooves those of his savage pursuers.

More of the men howled and called, their voices pitched high with lobo-like menace. They'd kill Colter and take his horse as easily as shooting a coyote off a fresh calf carcass. The young drover cursed his stupidity. Licking his wounds when he should have been scouting his own trail was a good way to get himself beefed and tossed in a gully.

As he closed on the bluff's crest, he glanced behind.

Two of the riders were peeling away from the other two—or three, counting the doubled-up sorrel—and it wasn't hard to figure their intent here, either. The two would swing around Colter, hoping to cut him off on the other side of the bluff, while the other three continued fogging him up to the bluff's crest.

He cursed loudly, his voice quivering with the jarring of the hard, fierce ride. Fear jelled low in his belly, and as he crested the bluff, he saw the two cutthroats racing around the base of the bluff in the northeast.

They'd already cut him off.

Well, at least he had the high ground. Trace had always told him that high ground in a fight was as good as draw speed or having the best weapon.

Colter shucked his old Henry from the saddle boot and leapt off the dun's back, hitting the ground on one foot, then the other, and falling from the force of the dun's momentum. Northwest whinnied and half turned toward him; then the horse swung around its head, reins whipping, and lunged off across the broad, flat-topped bluff, buck-kicking its fear.

As Colter rolled, desperately clutching the Henry in his left hand, gunfire cracked and bullets kicked up dust and sage branches around him. A rock shard bit into his eye, instantly making it water.

Brushing his gloved hand across his cheek, he rolled up against a low rock, racked a shell into the Henry's breech, and aimed at the three riders bounding toward him, forty yards away and closing. The single rider was on the right and slightly ahead of the two riding double on the sorrel.

The two on the sorrel whooped and hollered. The one riding in front jerked a big pistol out in front of him, lowering his head slightly and slitting one eye beneath his broad, slightly troughed hat brim.

The big Dragoon puffed smoke and spat flames.

A wink later, the gun's roar reached Colter's ears. The bullet screamed past his right cheek. Flinching slightly, Colter planted the Henry's sights on the shooter's chest, between his bending, buckled suspenders, and squeezed the trigger.

The Henry's ripping shriek echoed over the valley. Colter saw dust puff from the middle of the shooter's chest as the .44 slug slammed through his breastbone and punched him back against the man riding behind him.

"Vernon, damn it!" the man behind the heart-shot shooter screamed.

Then they both rolled off the lunging sorrel's right hip. The man behind the first hit the ground and rolled in a cloud of dust, snapping sage and rabbitbrush. The heart-shot shooter got his boot caught in a stirrup and, as his upper back and head slammed against the ground, was whipped forward, his lifeless body bouncing and flopping as the sorrel continued toward Colter, screaming, the dust rising.

Before the horse reached Colter, it swerved sharply left, and the dead rider swung far out from the horse's side, throwing up sand and gravel over Colter's head and shoulders. Then, boot and spur firmly wedged in the stirrup, the dead rider and the sorrel careened off across the bluff as though following Colter's own coyote dun.

The single rider had drawn his buckskin mare to a skidding halt when his two cohorts had been blown out of their saddle by Colter's Henry. Holding his buckskin's reins taut in one hand, he raised his Sharps carbine, propping the barrel on a forearm.

The carbine exploded. The bullet cut the air with a savage *whush!* to hammer the ground where Colter would have been if the young drover hadn't flung himself to the right and rolled.

Pushing up on an elbow, Colter quickly pressed the Henry's brass butt plate against his shoulder and fired three rounds—levering and firing, levering and firing—until through his own wafting powder smoke he watched his attacker throw his carbine straight up over his head with a loud grunt and tumble back over his mare's stiff tail.

The mare lunged forward and swerved sharply right, galloping eastward while screaming and shaking her head.

Behind her, her rider pushed up on his knees, grunting and groaning and folding his arms across his chest. He'd lost his hat, and he was bald as an egg, with a thick, tangled salt-and-pepper beard nearly covering all of his sun-blistered face.

Blood glistened in the brassy light. He walked a ways back down the hill on his knees, steadying himself with a gloved hand, before collapsing to lie belly down against the ground, shivering as though with a monumental chill.

About ten seconds had passed between Colter's first shot and his last.

Hearing hooves pounding behind him, he turned to see the other two riders lunging up the back side of the bluff. Smoke puffed around the pistol of the second man, while the man in the lead—a tall, gaunt-faced outlaw with stringy black hair hanging below his shoulders—extended a sawed-off double-barrel shotgun in his right hand like a pistol and closed one eye to aim down the broad twin bores at Colter.

Colter froze as he opened the Henry's breech to eject the smoking cartridge. The black-haired gent had him dead to rights.

Time slowed.

Colter watched the man bearing down on him from atop the lunging pinto, hearing, seeing everything as though in an especially vivid dream. The man had him and he knew he had him. He stretched his long lips back from his large brown teeth, and his dung-colored eyes fairly sparkled in the midmorning sunlight.

The twin bores of the savage-looking barn blaster yawned darkly as the man closed, the pinto blowing and snorting, the drumming hooves making the ground quiver beneath Colter's rump. The man's head lowered as he peered down the barrels, his hair flopping wildly all around his shoulders.

Colter's clenched jaw ached as he watched the outlaw's grimy index finger begin to squeeze both of the shotgun's curved triggers.

The shotgun exploded with a deafening roar . . . but only after the bores had jerked up suddenly. Buckshot screamed two feet above Colter's head to pepper the ground behind him.

He blinked as the barrels blossomed. When he looked up again, the shotgun dangled from the man's right hand. The man himself sat staring with a befuddled expression at Colter.

Just then his pinto reared, screaming and sunfishing, and as the man was thrown sideways from the horse's back, the sunlight flashed on the brain-flecked blood spilling down from above his right ear.

His head wobbled like that of a puppet with a broken string. As the horse wheeled, the man's long body came flying toward Colter as though it had been dropped from a passing cloud, the man's broad-brimmed black hat flying away on the wind and his black hair stringing out around him.

Colter grunted as he began to push off his heels, but before he could dig them into the loose red gravel between sage shrubs, the shotgunner slammed into him, punching him back against the ground hard, his ears ringing and a throbbing starting at the back of his head. The bulk of the man's weight lay stretched out across Colter's chest and shoulders.

Colter lay staring up at the sky, stunned, the shotgun's blast and the horse's screams still echoing inside his head. The dead man was a lead weight pressing his back into the rocks and gravel and a splintery sage branch.

The man's long, coarse hair, speckled with white, was spread like a thin curtain across Colter's face. It smelled like horses and rancid sweat and, improbably, mink spray.

Colter's insides recoiled at the smell and what could only have been lice peppering the man's hair. He gave a disgusted grunt and, pushing off his elbows and shoulders, bolted straight up off his back, flinging the man's body off his own. As the man rolled into the sage and gravel, his head swung around, lifeless eyes staring blindly up at Colter.

Blood dribbled from a corner of his mouth. More of it—much more—gushed from the right side of his head to stain the ground beneath him.

Just as Colter realized that the hole in the left side of the man's head had been made by a bullet, he also realized he'd been hearing distant rifle cracks. He looked down the back side of the bluff to see the man who'd been riding with the shotgunner galloping off across the bluff's sloping shoulder, heading north, crouching low in his saddle and casting wary glances behind him.

Dust puffed once to his left, then to his right. There was another puff behind him, followed by the whip crack of the rifle, and then the man disappeared into a depression.

Colter looked to his right.

A hundred yards away, dust wafted atop a low, rocky knoll. Behind the smoke, the shooter hunkered on the knoll, just his head and shoulders showing, ejecting a spent cartridge from his rifle's breech.

Colter couldn't see much of the man—just his cream hat, long yellow hair, and red shirt.

The man pressed his rifle stock against his shoulder once more, sighting down the barrel, and squeezed off one last shot. It kicked up dust on the far hill that the rider he was shooting at was just cresting. To the left of the rider, Colter saw another man walking in the same direction but a good distance south.

It was the man who'd been riding double with the outlaw Colter had drilled through the chest. As he walked, casting wary glances behind him, he shouted at the fleeing rider. He was too far away for Colter to clearly hear his words, but he was apparently wanting another ride.

If the rider heard him, he gave no sign. He crested

the rise and, in a full thudding gallop, disappeared down the other side. He reappeared a moment later, lunging up another rise toward a pine forest higher up the slope.

The walker shouted again, so angrily that it sounded like a shriek. He turned full around, limping slightly, then turned forward and broke into a jog, emphasizing his limp.

Thuds rose to Colter's right. He turned that way to see the rifleman who'd saved his life trotting toward him. Colter frowned as he studied the horse. A skewbald paint.

The rider who'd given him the hitch in his side to go along with the hole in his ear had ridden a paint. And he'd been a long-haired blond, too . . . wearing a red shirt and black chaps.

Caution rippling through him, Colter pushed to his feet and took his Henry in both hands, ready to raise it if the need arose. But the horsebacker held his own rifle across his saddle bows, and as he chewed up enough ground between them for Colter to get a better look, he saw that the rifle's hammer was uncocked.

The rider thudded up the rise, tack squawking, bridle chains jangling, hair bouncing on his—no, *her* shoulders. The red shirt was unbuttoned almost halfway down the girl's chest, and the two full globes of her breasts pushed it out while the blond curls danced across the green embroidery that formed two saguaro cacti just beneath her broad but feminine shoulders.

# Chapter 20

Jennifer Spurlock wore a small-caliber revolver in a soft black holster on her left hip, positioned for the cross draw. The hammered silver disks on her hatband flashed in the sun. Her blue eyes beneath the hat's slightly curled brim flashed as well, but it was only a trick of the light.

The girl's expression was grim, brooding, as she drew rein in front of Colter.

The heated paint blew and shook his head, jostling his cinnamon mane. Colter felt the slight spray of horse sweat across his cheek and neck, but he barely noticed. He was too busy scrutinizing the girl. His incredulity must have shown in his eyes, because she said, "Surprise, surprise, huh?" with no emotion whatever.

As the paint dropped its head to graze, she leaned forward, resting her rifle's breech across her saddle horn, clutching the rifle in both fawnskin-gloved hands.

"What made you change your mind?"

"What's that?"

"Seems like a lot of work you just went to—savin' my hide when just the other day you tried to ventilate it." Colter pressed his hand to the lumpy bandage on his left side. "And did a fair-to-middlin' job of it, too."

Genuine chagrin sounded in her voice. "I hit you?"

"Don't tell me you were just tryin' to make me dance."

"Shit," she said glumly. "I wasn't tryin', Colter. I swear."

"Oh. You were just takin' potshots to brighten up your day."

Jennifer slid her rifle into its sheath, then swung down from her saddle. "Where's your mount?"

"Last I saw, he hightailed it into them pines yonder, around where them owlhoots are headin' now."

She started walking in that direction, jerking the paint along behind by its reins. "Come on. Let's walk."

Colter twisted around slightly and frowned at her slender back, down which her blond curls danced. She didn't turn to look at him but kept walking, apparently confident that he would follow her like a calf on its mother's tit. Her tight jeans clung to her round rump, and he absently appreciated the sway of each firm buttock as she strode resolutely away from him.

He gave an annoyed chuff and walked after her, quickening his pace until, holding his rifle on his shoulder, he was striding beside her, the paint on her far side.

"What the hell's your game, Miss Spurlock?"

As he glanced at her, his eyes brushed her breasts, clearly delineated by the slightly sweat-damp red blouse. The open buttons revealed the orbs' first tan rise, and he looked away quickly, not wanting to get caught up in any automatic male attraction to a girl who'd tried to kill him.

"There's no game," she said, her voice shaking slightly as she walked across the bluff's flat top. "I was trying to save your hide the other day, too, though I'll allow as how it was probably less obvious than today."

"You got that right."

She stopped suddenly and swung toward him. "I didn't mean to hit you. It must have been a ricochet. If I'd wanted to hit you, I'd have hit you exactly where I'd aimed." She dropped her chin and looked at him squarely, her blue eyes crossing slightly, unexpectedly, causing a tender little hitch in the back of his brain. "I'm *that* good with a Winchester."

Colter chuckled caustically, as taken aback by the girl's saucy confidence as he was by her sexual allure, which he wouldn't have expected after seeing her in her gray work dress the first day he'd ridden into town. But then he realized she was dead serious, and he frowned, canting his head slightly to one side.

"All right—let me put it another way. Why the hell are you so intent on saving me? There must be plenty of other boys you could save in Sapinero."

She stared at him, a slight flush rising in her fine-boned cheeks. Then her haughty certainty flickered, and she turned her head sideways and dropped her chin. She doffed her hat, beat it against her chaps a few times, puffing dust, and plopped her butt down on a rock, splaying her legs in a very unladylike fashion and resting her elbows on her knees.

"I was trying to save you from the truth. I was trying to scare you back to your people in the Lunatics, so you wouldn't find out why Trace Cassidy died."

"Was murdered," he corrected.

"All right—*murdered*." Jennifer entwined her hands and stared down at the ground in front of her pointed-toe black boots. "But since you're riding from Barranca Verde, you likely found out."

Colter turned away. His emotions were so mixed up that he couldn't have said exactly how he was feeling. But anger was there. Almost as much rage at Trace as at those who had killed him and at the entire convoluted situation.

"I found out a lot of things at Barranca Verde."

"Including that my half sister is there."

"And her two kids." Colter sucked a sharp breath. "Hers and Trace's."

"Well, there you have it."

Colter chuckled dryly as he stared up the piney ridge rising in the north. "You two really are sisters. Jacinta said the same thing. And she was right—here I have it. More than I ever wanted to know. Sure as dried shit on a cow's tail!"

"The best thing you can do now," Jennifer said, "is go home and forget everything."

Colter turned to her. She sat as before, looking up at him now. The mockery had left her eyes, replaced by caution and sympathy.

"Was it me you were trying to protect, or your family?"

She laughed. "Believe me, my family can take care of themselves!"

"Who, then? The town? I'd imagine Rondo and Bannon are pretty good at taking care of themselves, too."

"I told you who I was trying to protect—an ignorant, innocent-eyed mountain boy sent down here on an errand he couldn't possibly follow through with. A boy about my own age but with no knowledge of anything that goes on in Sapinero. I was trying to keep you from ending up like Cassidy."

Colter stared at her. Her eyes held his. They were clear and direct, and he believed her. What other possible reason could she have had for not wanting him out at Barranca Verde? He certainly hadn't been much of a threat to anyone but himself.

"You're lucky my father didn't have you killed. Since finding you at the convent, he's become damn suspicious of your intentions. If he scrutinized that coyote dun of yours, saw the mountain brand on it . . ." She shook her head and slid a strand of breeze-brushed hair back from her cheek. "As it is, he's told Rondo and Bannon to make sure you don't spend any more time around town."

"You mean he's afraid of me?"

"He's afraid of what you might find out. In case it hasn't worked its way into the aptly named Lunatics yet, killing is a hanging offense."

"Sounds like your pa's got the law stuffed pretty good in his pocket."

"The law around *here*."

"You don't like your pa very much, do you, Miss Spurlock?"

She took a moment to answer. "I like him just fine. It's what he's done since he's grown so big I don't like. He sees himself as a god around here."

Colter turned and stared back toward Barranca Verde. His thoughts chased each other around like echoes in a deep canyon. Finally he sighed and started tramping north. "I'm not getting nothin' accomplished here."

"Where are you going?" Jennifer asked, leading the horse up behind him.

"I don't have the foggiest notion, Miss Spurlock."

Colter was only vaguely aware of the girl leading her paint behind him as he climbed the slope through the pines.

Neither of them said anything. There was only the singing of chickadees and mountain jays and the crunch of pine needles and branches beneath Colter's boots and faintly trilling spurs. Occasionally the horse snorted as it thudded along beside the girl, who stayed about thirty yards behind. The sounds offered a solemn accompaniment to the drover's wretched mood.

He kept an eye out for the two fled outlaws but neither saw nor heard anything threatening. He'd begun to worry that the horseless rider might have gone Northwest, when the horse gave a bugling whinny, and Colter found it standing on a relatively flat shelf above a dry, boulder-strewn creek bed, charred trees from a recent fire concealing the mount in their dingy shadows.

The horse's latigo had come loose, and the saddle had slipped down to one side.

Colter reset the saddle, tightened the strap, and adjusted the bridle. He stuffed his Henry down in the saddle boot, turned out a stirrup, and toed it. He remembered the girl, and turned to her. She sat the paint some distance away in the fire-blackened trees.

She regarded him silently, with a curiously doting, worried look. Her presence puzzled him. She'd done her good deed for the day. Why hadn't she ridden off?

He pulled himself up into the saddle, took the dun's reins in his right hand, and pinched his hat brim at the girl. "Well, thanks for the help, Miss Spurlock," he said, hearing a wry note in his voice. "I reckon our trail forks here."

"Not so fast." She looked at his side. "That bandage needs changing, and you need a rest. I know a place."

She reined the paint down the slope toward the creek bed. Colter sat the dun, frowning warily after her. She glanced over her shoulder as the dun dropped in short, choppy lunges down the slope. "Come on. I didn't save your Lunatic hide just to lead you into a trap."

Colter glanced down at his side. Sure enough, blood spotted his shirt that the nuns had patched and laundered. During the dustup with the outlaws, he'd loosened some stitches. He'd lost enough blood a few days ago that he couldn't afford to lose any more.

As the girl bottomed out in the brushy creek bed, Colter touched spurs to the dun's flanks and started down the slope behind her. No longer caring what happened to him or where he ended up, he found himself surrendering to her totally.

He followed her blindly across the rocky creek bed, up the bank on the other side, and across rugged country northwest of the main trail.

They'd passed a couple of old prospectors' shacks and a small abandoned ranch headquarters of crude scrub picket fences and a stone cabin, when the girl gasped suddenly. Colter, who'd been riding numbly in his saddle, head down, looked up.

She'd reined in the paint at the top of a low rise about twenty yards ahead. He couldn't see her face, but she'd drawn her shoulders taut, her head lowered as she peered down the other side of the rise. Suddenly she neck-reined the horse around, her face pale, eyes grim, and rode back down the rise, dust stirring from the paint's chopping hooves.

"Damn," she hissed. "Of all the lousy luck!"

"What is it?"

Just behind Colter, she leapt smoothly out of her saddle, dropped her reins, and strode stiffly back up the rise through her own sifting dust.

Colter's blood warmed. More outlaws?

He slipped his Henry from the saddle boot, stepped down from the dun's back, and hurried up the rise behind the girl. She'd dropped to her hands and knees and was lifting her head to peer cautiously over the crest of the rise.

Colter dropped down beside her and followed her gaze into the broad, shallow valley.

His knees tightened, and he grimaced. Quickly

doffing his hat, he ducked his head behind the rise before lifting it again slightly so that he could just barely see over the bending weed tips into the valley below.

The girl did the same, and together they hunkered tensely atop the butte, staring down at two men and two horses clustered around a small, sparkling spring bubbling up from sun-bleached rocks.

The horses were a buckskin and a white-socked black. Sheriff Bill Rondo sat the black, smoking a long black cigar, while his deputy, Chico Bannon, lay in the dust beside the spring, lapping water like a dog.

The men were about fifty yards out from the base of the rise, their horses idly switching their tails in the dry breeze. Rondo sat partly facing away from Colter and Jennifer, staring off toward the northeast. The short, stubby Bannon lay so that his head was facing the slope, his close-cropped sandy hair lying thinly against his pink scalp. He had his hat in one hand, a rifle in the other.

Now, as Bannon lifted his head, water glinting in the sun as it dribbled down from his knife-slash mouth, Colter jerked his head down. Beside him, Jennifer flinched and pulled her own head back from the top of the rise. She looked at Colter, eyes bright with fear.

"They must be on the scout for outlaws," she whispered tensely, stretching her rich lips back from her fine white teeth. "Rondo prides himself on keeping the country clean of rustlers and the like. The sonofabitch is an old border rustler himself!"

Colter edged a slow, careful look over the rise

again. Bannon was swinging one stout, muscular leg over the buckskin's rump as he stepped into the leather. Rondo turned toward him, cigar smoke puffing around his head, his long gray hair blowing in the breeze. He had one tan-gloved hand on his holstered revolver's grips.

Turning his head forward, he pulled his hat brim down over his eyes and savagely ground his large-roweled spurs into the black's flanks. The horse gave a startled whinny and lunged into an instant, ground-eating gallop, hooves thudding.

Bannon threw his bulldog head back on his broad shoulders, laughing loudly enough for Colter to hear, and put his buckskin into a gallop after his boss. Soon the lawmen were little more than two specks—one black, the other tan—galloping up a low jog of hills in the northeast. They dropped into a cut in the cedar-stippled slopes and disappeared.

Their tan dust glinted in their wake.

"Whew!" Jennifer said. "That was close."

Colter sat up, scrutinizing the girl curiously. "Don't reckon your pa would appreciate your bein' found with me. Why risk it?"

She studied him in return, seemingly as befuddled by her actions as Colter was. She pursed her lips and, climbing to her feet, said, "Best not give me any second thoughts, Colter Farrow."

# Chapter 21

The place where Jennifer Spurlock led Colter was a small, boulder-strewn box canyon about a mile northwest of where she and the young cowboy had almost run into Bill Rondo and Chico Bannon. A spring murmured out of the black rocks at the base of the canyon wall, well concealed by boulders that had long ago tumbled from the ridge above, and by scrub cedars, willows, and rabbitbrush.

There was a fire ring near the runoff freshet, and it was heaped with gray ashes and a half-burned log. Jennifer must have seen Colter regarding the ring skeptically.

"Those are my old ashes," she said. "See that bison tooth in the middle?"

Colter's eyes picked out the white object about the size of his small fingertip.

"I put it in the ring whenever I leave, so I'll know if anyone's been here since I left."

Colter dismounted and began loosening the coyote

dun's latigo cinch. "Don't seem like a place a pretty girl should be runnin' loose."

"Most of the badmen around here know who runs this county." Jennifer swung down from the paint's back and narrowed an eye at Colter. "And that they'd harm me at their peril."

"Who're they more afraid of—your old man or you?" For the first time in what seemed a long time, he felt like making a joke. It sort of caught him off guard, but it made him feel a little better.

Jennifer kept her narrowed eye on him as she stripped the tack from her paint. "Apple don't fall far from the tree."

She tossed her saddle and saddle blanket onto the ground near the fire ring, and Colter followed suit. When they'd hobbled both horses only a few yards up canyon, among the willows and thick grama grass lining the little stream formed by the spring, Colter sat down against his saddle with a weary sigh.

Jennifer was rummaging around in one of her saddle pouches. "Take your shirt off."

Colter looked at her.

"Don't get all excited," she drawled. "Gotta change that wrap."

Colter doffed his hat, then sat up straight to remove his shirt and to slip his longhandle top down his arms, leaving his torso bare.

He looked down at his powder white chest and flat, ribbed belly. He needed to put a little meat on his bones. His arms were long-muscled and corded. His thick, rope-burned hands looked oddly large at the ends of his narrow wrists. Feeling self-conscious in front of the girl, he wished he had a little more bulk all over.

Inwardly, he snorted. What the hell was he talking about? His shredded ear was enough to repel anyone but the cheapest pleasure girl. What would Marianna say . . . if he ever saw her again?

Guilt pinched him as he watched Jennifer walk toward him, carrying a pin-striped blouse in one hand, a small tin and a small folding knife in the other. Her breasts jostled under her red blouse as she walked.

He remembered his conversation with Angelique, about the contrition of disloyal men, and he looked away as Jennifer knelt beside him. She set down the tin and the shirt and pulled the loose bandage away from his side, leaning toward his chest to peer at the wound.

She made a face. "My handiwork, huh?"

He only groaned as she pulled the wrap away from his belly and began cutting through it with the knife. When she'd removed the bloody bandage, she complimented the nuns on their needlework, then smeared some of the salve over the sutured wound with her fingers. It smelled gamy and green—not an unpleasant odor but one he wasn't familiar with.

"What's that?"

"Bear grease and crushed cottonwood leaves. Old family remedy."

"Your father's side of the family?"

She shook her head as she thoughtfully smeared the salve across the stitches and the bits of dried blood. "My mother's."

She glanced at him, probably saw the question in his eyes.

"Pa's first wife was a Mexican woman he met when he first came out here from Texas with a herd of maverick steers he'd branded in the Brasada country. She died the year after Jacinta was born. He married a woman from Arizona a few months later and brought her out to the ranch. I didn't come along for several years, and the very same year I did, my mother left— went back to Arizona."

"She left you?"

"Never really have known why, though I got a hunch. Pa's not an easy man, and he probably wouldn't let her take me. Haven't heard from her in all these years, so my guess is she's either dead or didn't really want me in the first place."

Wiping her hands on the pin-striped blouse, she glanced at Colter. "How'd you come to be taken in by Trace Cassidy?"

He watched her tear a sleeve from the blouse. "My folks died in a plague when I was six. I didn't have anybody else. Trace was our nearest neighbor and . . . and I reckon he and Ruth just naturally took me in." He wasn't sure why, but his throat felt thick, remembering Trace's easy nature, the way his blue eyes crinkled at the corners when he smiled, the sound of his laughter. "He was good to me—I'll give him that."

Watching him as though weighing his words, Jennifer folded the shirtsleeve, pressed it against the freshly greased stitches, then leaned even closer to Colter's chest as she pulled up the long wrap from beneath him. She drew its ends closed over his belly, securing the pad over the wound.

"You love him like a father?"

"I suppose I did, yes."

"I'm sorry."

"It ain't your fault. It's his."

"And my sister's?"

Colter watched her hands deftly tying the ends of the nuns' wrap. "I reckon she wouldn't have gotten involved with a married man if she'd known. I can't figure Trace for doin' that, and I reckon I never will."

Jennifer leaned back and rested her hands on her thighs. "And now you don't know how to think of him?"

"No, I don't." Colter looked off toward the horses grazing up canyon, near a cottonwood sapling whose leaves fluttered like small silver disks in the softening light. "It grieves me."

"What're you going to tell Ruth?"

Colter shrugged and drew a breath. "I don't know I'd tell her anything if I ever saw her again. How could I? What would I say?"

"Colter?"

He turned to her.

The corners of her mouth rose slightly, and she shook her head. "Don't think about it anymore. Some things are best set aside to cool. When and if the time comes, you'll know what to say."

Colter stared at her. As she gazed back at him, he felt a warmth rise in his loins and on the back of his neck. She glanced away, flushing slightly, and then she turned back to him. Her eyes were grave, her lips slightly parted.

He could sense the heat rising off her.

He didn't know why—maybe it was the escape

from the horror of his situation—but he suddenly
found himself overwhelmed with a physical desire
for this girl. It was more than just how she looked,
kneeling beside him, shoulders thrown back, breasts
thrust out.

He could have avoided his reaction if that was all
that had caused it.

But now he saw his left hand close around her
right arm, and he leaned toward her. Her eyes widened slightly in surprise. He pressed his lips to hers,
and she did nothing at first but accept the kiss. Then
she pushed away from him, setting her hands on his
chest and pushing him back.

Leaning back on her heels, she stared up at him,
confusion in her eyes. He still had his hand on her
arm. Now he put the other hand on her other arm and
drew her to him once more. She did not resist, but slid
her hands around him and placed them on his back as
he closed his mouth over hers once more, pressing his
lips against hers, savoring their warm, moist, silky
feel, which caused his blood to rush and his heart to
thud.

He held her tightly, kissing her, and all the tension
left her limbs and her back and her neck, and she
turned herself over to him. He could feel her finger-
tips pressing into his back as their tongues entwined,
could feel her breasts against his chest.

When she finally pulled away from him, there was
a wild, hungry spark in her eyes. She rose slowly and
began unbuttoning her blouse, her breasts rising and
falling heavily, several strands of hair hanging in her

eyes. Those and the moist flush in her cheeks and the wanton gleam in her eyes added to her wild allure.

Colter's ears rang with need.

Desire consuming him, he rose to his feet, kicked out of his boots, unbuckled his shell belt, and let the belt and holstered pistol drop to the ground near the cold fire ring. As he shucked out of his pants, he tripped and almost fell.

She laughed and kicked out of her boots, then squirmed out of her jeans with a quirky little smile, and then her shirt was off, her camisole was off, and she stood facing him naked, her full, pale breasts standing up proudly.

A blond swirl of hair clung to the curving side of one tender, perfect orb.

Colter's breath caught. His erection throbbed. He moved toward her, stopped only inches away.

Her eyes crossed again slightly as she reached down, caressed his belly with her fingers, then wrapped her hand around his shaft, fondling him for one long, excruciating minute before she leaned into him and hooked her right leg around his left.

Colter wrapped his arms around her and kissed her, and then, limbs entangled, they dropped slowly down to the ground together. He mounted her quickly, if a little awkwardly, with her help, and she groaned and wrapped her long, slender legs around his waist.

Colter enjoyed the bliss of the afternoon and evening the way a man sentenced to hang enjoys a last meal and a cigarette.

He and Jennifer made love several times playfully, experimenting with different positions. Then they built a fire together and cooked supper—all the while laughing and joking and hopping around barefoot like two young lovers playing hooky from school or work in the fields.

A couple of times Colter caught the girl regarding him with a wistful smile. Obviously, she was consciously helping him escape from his problems, and knowing that did nothing to dampen his enjoyment of another slow, purposeful coupling by the fire after they'd indulged in a leisurely meal of corn cakes, bacon, and pinto beans.

They talked as the fire died, wrapped together in their blankets, and at no time did either one mention Trace, Rondo, Bannon, Jennifer's father, or anything at all that might have jolted them back to grim reality. They might have been the sole survivors of a shipwreck, happily stranded together on a desert island.

They watched the stars in silence.

Jennifer fell asleep with her head on Colter's chest. A few minutes later, his own heavy lids closed over his eyes, and his breathing grew slow and even through slightly parted lips.

Something woke him. He opened his eyes.

A light shone in the darkness—the flickering light of a fire. He could feel the warmth pushing against him through the cold night air.

Jennifer slept with her face snugged against his side, one arm thrown across his belly. She must have stoked the fire.

She lifted her head suddenly from Colter's chest

with a clipped gasp. Colter had heard the sound, too—the trill of a jinglebob chain. At almost the same time a silhouetted figure stepped around the fire to Colter's left. He saw another crouching on the fire's other side. The flames flickered redly across the broad, pugnacious face of Chico Bannon, the deputy's elbows resting on his knees, his thick, stubby hands entwined before him.

He smiled.

Colter jerked his head up and reached toward his holstered Remy.

"Uh-uh," a low voice grunted. "It ain't there."

A hand came down on Colter's left hand, grinding it into the ground. Wincing, Colter looked up to see the tall silhouetted figure of Bill Rondo towering over him, silver hair and badge glowing in the firelight.

Jennifer said, "What the he—?"

She screamed as Rondo grabbed her arm and pulled her off of Colter as though she weighed no more than a feather pillow. She streaked off into the darkness behind Rondo—a pale figure disappearing into the rocks and shrubs, groaning. Colter pushed himself to a sitting position, but he hadn't completed the move before Rondo's shoulders swayed, and something dark and shiny—Colter's own cartridge belt—slammed against his head, smashing him sideways and setting up a deafening shriek in both ears.

He clawed at the ground, breathing like a landed fish, trying to push himself up. His muscles wouldn't work. A dense fog filled his vision.

Then, with a grunt, he cleared the cobwebs and pushed up onto his outstretched arms and his knees.

"Bastard!" Jennifer screamed from the darkness.

"Girl," Rondo said calmly, "your pa ain't gonna be at all happy you was found out here with this brindle calf from the Loonies. No, sir. He ain't gonna be happy at all!"

The sheriff dropped to one knee beside Colter, who, on his hands and knees, stared at the ground and felt blood dribbling down the right side of his face, bells tolling in his head. Rondo grabbed his long hair and jerked his head up savagely.

Rondo's face pushed up close to Colter's. The drover could smell whiskey and tobacco on the lawman's breath. Rondo's gray-blue eyes sparked like bits of glowing steel, and his lips stretched back from his gritted teeth.

"What'd you think you was gonna do, boy?" The man chuckled angrily. "You think you was gonna get even for ol' Trace, didja? *You?*"

Colter gritted his teeth as Rondo pulled his hair so hard that his eyes watered. He thought his scalp was going to rip loose from his skull. Despite his pain and misery, he told the sheriff to do something physically impossible to himself.

Still crouching on the other side of the fire, Chico Bannon chuckled.

Rondo's breath quivered in and out of his flaring nostrils as he glared down at Colter. He held his hands together, frenziedly turning the large gold ring with the carved S, which he wore over his glove on his right middle finger. "That ain't no way to talk to me, boy. In fact, you're gonna be right sorry for that there little bit o' blue nastiness." He glanced over his shoulder. "The iron hot?"

Bannon glanced at something in the fire. "I'd say it's hot enough. That shaver's skin's probably purty tender."

"Rondo!" Jennifer screamed, lunging out of the darkness.

Rondo released Colter's hair suddenly. He stood and wheeled in time to meet the girl bolting toward him. Jennifer screamed as she threw a fist toward Rondo's face. The lawman laughed as he dodged the blow, and the girl's fist thudded against his shoulder.

He grabbed Jennifer's flailing fists in both his own and held her up in front of him like a slab of meat. "Look at this, Chico. What do you think of old Spurlock's youngest daughter, huh? Look at them titties jiggle." Bannon jerked the girl's arms up and down and roared with laughter as her breasts quivered. "Look at 'em jiggle!"

"Let go of me, you sonofabitch!" Jennifer screamed so loudly that her voice cracked.

"Let her go," Colter groaned as he got his knees under him and pushed himself up, staggering and swinging around toward Rondo, clenching his fists.

The sheriff shoved Jennifer back into the darkness beyond the fire, laughing. As Colter grabbed the man's arm, Rondo swung toward him, his face a mask of indignant, bunch-lipped rage, and hammered a vicious right cross into Colter's left jaw.

As Colter grunted and stumbled back into his and Jennifer's blankets and saddles, Jennifer lunged toward Rondo from behind, snaking both arms around the man's neck.

"Goddamn it, bitch!" the lawman roared. He whirled around, raising his right arm and slamming the back of his hand against Jennifer's face. The girl gave a grunt and dropped instantly out of sight with a sharp, slapping thump and a snapping of shrub branches.

"*Jennifer!*" Colter screamed, getting his feet under him and lunging toward Bannon.

Bannon showed his teeth again in a savage grimace as he buried his right fist in Colter's belly. Colter lunged forward with a great *hahhh!* of expelled air and dropped to his knees. Futilely sucking breath and making only a froglike croak, he once again fell to his hands as barking misery flooded over and through him.

Above his own raking gasps, he heard Rondo say, "Bring it."

Colter had no idea what the "it" was. He couldn't even guess. Still, his insides coiled tightly at the numerous savage possibilities.

Even after Rondo had kicked him onto his side and he lay staring up at the tall, gray-haired, black-clad lawman, and saw the glowing branding iron that Chico Bannon brought over from the fire, he couldn't quite work his mind around what the brutal lawman's intentions were.

"Piggin' string?" Rondo asked.

Bannon chuckled and pulled the string out of a back pocket, dangling it in the air over Colter.

Colter's eyes narrowed with incredulity. Fear was a giant, chill hand engulfing him.

"Tie him," Rondo ordered, holding up the branding iron so that the glowing S at the end of it lit up his entire face and made his eyes flash wickedly.

"Christ," Colter gasped, sucking a short draught of air into his pinched lungs. "Get that goddamn thing—"

Bannon kicked him again, but Colter's hands somewhat eased the blow of the pointed boot toe. Still, the young cowboy was too weak to fight the man off him, and in less than a minute he lay belly down in the dirt, hog-tied with piggin' string that cut painfully into his wrists and ankles.

Colter cursed and grunted and squirmed, but the more he fought the bindings, the tighter they became. He turned his cheek to the dirt and looked up.

Rondo stood over him, holding the branding iron up close to his face. The tall lawman placed his left boot on Colter's shoulder as if to steady him.

"A little trick me and Chico came up with last year," Rondo growled. "Owlhoots we don't want returning to Sapinero we mark with this S brand here. The S, of course, standin' for Sapinero. That way we remember—and so do they."

He grinned as he lowered the glowing branding iron toward Colter's face.

An icy wave of bald terror swept through the young cowboy. Christ, the man was going to brand him like a damn cow!

Colter jerked his head so that the opposite cheek was against the ground.

"Turn him."

Bannon dropped down so that his knee ground painfully against the young drover's side. He clapped his thick hands on Colter's head and turned it so that Colter's left cheek was angled up toward Rondo. The deputy held it there, and there was no moving it.

Colter could only jerk his shoulders and grunt, eyes wide as he watched the glowing branding iron drop toward him.

"Let me go, you crazy sonsabitches!" he raked out, dirt and gravel pasting against his lips.

One of Bannon's hands dug into the top of Colter's head while the other was wrapped around the front of his neck, up beneath his chin, holding him taut.

"Only take a second," Rondo said as the glowing S grew to the size of a wagon wheel before Colter's horrified gaze. "Of course, it'll feel like a whole lot longer!"

Colter shuddered.

Bannon's fingers dug painfully into his flesh, the hand around his neck nearly cutting off his wind.

The deputy laughed.

Rondo grimaced savagely, showing his teeth, as he suddenly jerked the branding iron down to Colter's face and pressed the S hard against his left cheek.

At first, it felt cold. Like ice.

Colter squeezed his eyes closed and gritted his teeth. The blazing-frigid iron burned into his skin with a deafening hiss.

As the fetid odor of his own burning flesh filled his nostrils, and pain like he'd never felt or even imagined filled every nook and cranny of his being, he tensed every bone and muscle, and wailed.

Beneath the wail, Rondo and Bannon were laughing.

# Chapter 22

Colter dreamed that he was drowning in the burning tar pits of hell and that the devil's warlocks were prodding his face with glowing pitchforks.

A voice called from somewhere far out in the leaping flames and billowing smoke: "Wake up, boy. *Kid!*"

Someone nudged his shoulder. He opened his eyes. Beneath him, sand, dirt, and gravel. An ant was crawling over a bit of cedar branch with a few clinging needles.

The hand nudged his shoulder again, and his lips bunched as the burning in his left cheek bit all the way to his toes.

"You awake?" The voice grew a little softer, as though the speaker turned to speak to someone else. "You get a look at his cheek?"

"I saw it," said a grim, Spanish-accented voice. Both voices were vaguely familiar, but Colter was having trouble thinking about anything but the burn that fairly devoured his face. "And I figured as much when I saw Rondo and Bannon. The mark of Sapinero, uh? *Christos!*"

"We got trouble, boy."

Colter turned slightly and raised his eyes. The hunchback, Wayne Kilgore, was on one knee beside him, a hand wrapped around Colter's arm. The hunchback's breath was spiced with whiskey. Beyond him, Juventino Escobar was crouched at the base of the canyon wall, near the spring. He crossed himself and knelt on both knees, staring down.

An invisible hammer smashed against the back of Colter's head. He pushed himself up to a sitting position, his naked butt against the ground.

"Jesus, that looks bad!" Kilgore said.

Colter tried to look around the hunchback toward Juventino, but the man's head moved as Colter's did. He was inspecting the burn on Colter's cheek, and, judging from the expression twisting the hunchback's mouth, the blaze looked as bad as it felt—burning, icy, wet, and itchy.

Kilgore's eyes met Colter's. He shook his head. "They killed her, kid. That's why we gotta get you outta here, before her pa comes lookin' for her."

Colter shoved the burning pain that encompassed his entire face to the back of his head and, naked and covered in dirt and grit, crawled forward toward the hairy, bearded Mexican. Juventino looked over his shoulder at him, a large silver medallion dangling down his buckskin shirt and flashing in the midmorning sun.

He shook his head gravely as Colter approached.

"She's gone, amigo. Hit her head on a rock. They

probably didn't know they killed her. They returned to town last night, cocky as hell and complimenting the blacksmith on the branding iron he forged for them."

"No," Colter groaned as he approached Jennifer Spurlock's lifeless form, covered in a saddle blanket and lying at the base of the canyon wall. She lay on her back, and a surreally contrite expression lazed on her face, her blond hair pillowed out beneath her head. There was a mark on her bruised, swollen cheek. The indentation left by a large square ring with a carved S on it.

Rondo's ring.

"Those bastards!" Colter's voice broke, and he ran his eyes up and down her slender, unmoving form beneath the striped wool blanket. A sob racked him. "They . . . they *killed* her?"

Kilgore sighed. "Musta been dark when they jumped you."

Colter glanced over his shoulder at Kilgore standing over him, hunched slightly forward, eyes a little bleary from drink.

Colter frowned. "How . . . ?"

"We backtracked 'em," the hunchback said. "Started early this mornin'. Figured we'd find you somewhere along their trail."

Juventino explained, "Wayne and me used to prospect together till he got uppity and retired to town. Wayne knows everything happening in Sapinero. It's those big ears that came with the hump on his back."

"Yeah, that and watchin' them two lawmen like a hawk, cause I never know when they're gonna come gunnin' for me. Something about my hump gets their dander up."

"It's not your hump, fool," said Juventino. "It's all the bad things you say about them to the whores when you're drunk. It makes its way back to them—I've warned you!"

Kilgore lifted his upper lip. "It's on account of how much better I please the girls—" He stopped abruptly and crouched to take Colter's arm. "Oh, hell, let's save the palaver for later. If Spurlock finds us out here with his girl, he'll hang all three of us."

The hunchback wrapped an arm around Colter's shoulders and began pulling the boy to his feet. "Come on, kid. We got us an old shack out here, and we best get you there, tend that ugly burn on your face. Christ, I can't believe them sonsabitches did that to you!"

"Why can't you?" Juventino said as Colter got his feet beneath him and Kilgore draped his shirt over his shoulders. "They've done it before, haven't they? Even threatened me a time or two when I looked at 'em wrong!"

"Shit, he'll wear that forever."

Kilgore brought Colter's pants to him, and as Colter took the trousers in one hand, he stared down at Jennifer, his eyes wide with disbelief. "We gotta . . . bury her. Can't . . . leave her to the . . . coyotes."

"We'll take care of her," Juventino said. "You get dressed. We gotta pull out soon, amigo."

Colter dressed slowly, tiredly, as though moving through deep water. The burn was an incessant ache, and he could feel it weeping over his jaw and onto his neck. But even worse than the burn were the flames of his rage, and he set his jaw hard against it.

He glanced at the grave Juventino and Kilgore were digging for Jennifer, and squinted one eye as he brushed at the pus dribbling over his jaw. He knew now what he was going to do. What he had to do. The resolution in him was as solid and unmoving as the wall of a mountain that had tumbled down to block a canyon for centuries.

He buttoned his shirt. He buttoned his pants and drew the suspenders slowly up his arms.

He swallowed the burning, leaping, shrieking rage. For now.

He had to bide his time, tend his courage, and get damn handy with his six-shooter.

Then he'd pay a little visit to Sapinero, the town that would be forever burned into his face.

When he'd dressed himself, he sat in a stupor beside the grave, which Juventino and Kilgore had hastily dug in a relatively soft patch of dirt. The Mexican used the folding shovel he carried with him everywhere in case he found a gold vein, while Kilgore used a tin cup and a fork.

When the grave was a few feet deep, they laid the body into it, then covered the girl with dirt and rocks. They erected a small cross—two willow branches secured with rawhide—and then Colter mounded more, heavier rocks over the loose earth, to keep scavengers away.

Juventino and Kilgore, looking around warily as though expecting Spurlock's men to appear at any time, wandered solemnly away from the grave, leaving Colter alone. The boy stood over the mounded earth, and he wished he could have felt something more than anger.

But all he could do was glare at the cross while feeling the icy sting of the large S burned into his face, hear Jennifer's scream of the night before as she'd tried to help him, then watch the glowing S move slowly toward him, Rondo grinning behind it.

Slow hoof thuds sounded.

He glanced around to see Juventino and Kilgore riding toward him, leading both his own coyote dun and Jennifer's paint. The paint wasn't saddled, as the men had used its saddle blanket to wrap Jennifer's body in, but they'd bridled the mount so they could lead it by the reins.

"We'll take her horse," Kilgore said. "Release it a ways up the trail. It'll head on home, but not before we're long outta here."

"Think you can ride by yourself, amigo?" Juventino asked Colter, his eyes pinched with concern.

Colter nodded, moved heavily over to the dun, turned out a stirrup, and poked his boot through it. He swung into the leather, sucking air through his teeth as the movement increased the flow of blood to his cheek, making his entire head feel as though it had been doused with burning kerosene.

Then he urged the dun after his two companions, and they ambled back out of the box canyon to which Jennifer had led Colter only a few hours earlier. Such a short time. And now, after an evening of playful lovemaking, he was leaving her here, covered with sand and rocks and cedar needles, hoping the coyotes wouldn't dig her up and strew her about the canyon.

He half wished her father would find her. But then Spurlock would have an easier time of tracking Colter, and he doubted he'd be able to convince the rancher that the two renegade lawmen had killed his daughter. The young drover didn't care so much about himself. He didn't care at all anymore what happened to him, in fact, as long as he took Rondo and Bannon down before he ended up like Jennifer. But he didn't want to endanger Juventino and Kilgore.

And what did it matter, anyway, where and how Jennifer was buried?

She was as dead as the rocks that covered her, and no fancy headstone or softly spoken words read from the Good Book would change that.

So swaddled in pain was Colter that he was only vaguely aware of Juventino turning the girl's horse loose. And then, after what must have been nearly three hours of slow riding in deference to Colter's condition, they climbed a chalky, seemingly endless trail to a lone, forlorn-looking shack sitting atop a broad tabletop mesa.

The shack, a lean-to shed, a brush corral, and a leaning privy were the only structures on the mesa, and the place seemed virtually swallowed by the massive sky arching above and sweeping out around it. The hovel's flat roof of cottonwood poles whistled softly in the hot, dry wind.

The men led Colter into the shack, and when he'd sagged down on one of the two-room hovel's two cots, they fed him whiskey until he was drunk enough to sleep in spite of the pain. When he woke a few hours later, he automatically touched his cheek. It still burned, but there was a soothing coolness amid the heat, and his fingers touched moist, sticky salve that smelled of aloe and mint.

Juventino's homegrown medicine, no doubt. Likely handed down from his ancestors.

Colter looked around the dark cabin. The room smelled of roasted meat, pepper, tobacco smoke, and liquor. He could see stars twinkling between the roof poles, and he heard the snores of only one other person. The snoring wasn't loud enough to be that of the hunchback. Kilgore must have gone back to town, to the livery barn. But Juventino was here.

Colter was glad he wasn't alone.

He dropped his hand to the cot and spiraled instantly back into sleep.

He woke in the morning when Juventino got up from his own cot on the other side of the room, yawning, farting, scratching himself, and hacking up phlegm. Colter just lay there, cloaked in pain and fury as Juventino shuffled around the cluttered little room, cooking breakfast on the small cookstove.

If Rondo and Bannon had left him alone, he probably would have been out of the country by now. He'd either have gone back to the Lunatics with a lie about his dealings down here, or he'd have drifted on toward another territory, another life, in which he wouldn't have to meet Ruth's gaze, or David's or little May's, and he wouldn't have to harbor his secrets, his own lies, about their husband and father's double life in Sapinero.

About Trace's woman and his two bastard children being raised by a weeping mother and a covey of malicious nuns in the convent at Barranca Verde . . .

He was saddened that Trace had been taken from him and Ruth. But, then, Trace himself had done that a long time ago. So it wasn't so much his murder that Colter grieved, but Trace's own deception. Because of that deception, Trace's murder wasn't worth avenging.

But Jennifer's murder was.

As was the murder of Colter's own face and identity at the hands of two rogue lawmen in the employ of one rogue land baron who fancied himself a god.

Those men would pay. Likely Colter himself would die extracting payment. But they would die just the same.

Colter sucked a breath as pain fired through his left cheekbone. He touched his face, touched the gelatinous wound. Repelled by the feel, he pulled his hand away, threw the blankets off himself, and swung his stockinged feet to the floor.

Juventino turned away from the eggs and sausage he was frying in a pan atop the range. The Mexican wore only his threadbare longhandles, moccasin boots, and beaded deerskin vest. Surprise lit his brown eyes as he turned toward Colter rising from the cot.

"*Cual es este?*" What is this?

Colter had spied a mirror hanging above the washstand on the left side of the cabin's only door. He shuffled toward it now, kicking a chair out of his way and ramming the square eating table with his hip. He continued to the washstand, grabbed the chipped mirror off the nail above the tin washbasin, and raised the warped, tarnished looking glass to his face.

The mirror shook in his hand. He held his wrist still with his other hand.

The S that had been burned into him was angled across his left cheek, the top of the S curving just beneath and to the left of his eye. The bottom of the S hooked just off the corner of his mouth.

The serpentine blaze was about the size of the palm of his hand, and it glistened pinkly in the morning light that pushed through the open door.

He'd known it was there. He felt the burn every waking moment. But he hadn't been prepared for its ugliness. It would mark him, be the first thing people saw when they looked at him till the end of his days.

Colter dropped the mirror. It hit the floor with a scream of breaking glass. He staggered backward, fell into a chair, turned toward the table, and lowered his forehead to the scarred, food-stained planks.

He convulsed with a sob and dug his hands into the table in a rage.

# Chapter 23

Colter Farrow spent the next two months at the cabin atop the mesa with Juventino when the Mexican wasn't off prospecting in the hills, mountains, and nearby barrancas. Kilgore paid occasional visits, but mostly he remained in town, working at the livery barn and keeping an eye on the two renegade lawmen and their boss, Paul Spurlock.

Apparently the rancher, not finding Jennifer's body in the box canyon, had given up on ever finding his daughter. According to Kilgore, the rancher sent out no more search parties. Spurlock remained in town—an angry, brooding man who, when he wasn't over-seeing his business interests, including the hotel, the mercantile, and the livery barn, could be found drink-ing heavily in one of the Mexican cantinas on the poor side of Sapinero's central plaza. Occasionally he'd shoot up the place, and once, he slit the throat of a young Mexican whore who'd made the dire mistake of serv-ing him out of the wrong *baconora* jug.

Meanwhile, at the little cabin hunkered atop the

sprawling mesa, Colter's wounds healed. At least, the outside ones healed, leaving a knotted scar on his left earlobe and a far grislier one in the shape of the slanted S on his left cheek.

Every day with his Remington he practiced shooting at tin cans and at Juventino's empty tequila and pulque bottles. On one such afternoon, he tossed a dark glass bottle high in the air, slapped the Remy from his greased, tied-down holster, and, crouching and taking hasty aim from down around his left hip, fired three times quickly.

His first shot clipped the bottle in half.

His second shot blew it into thirds.

His third shot quartered it.

Juventino, who'd returned to the cabin late the previous night to check in on his scarred young charge, laughed from the wicker chair against the cabin's front wall. He was leaning back in the chair. The October wind owned a knifelike edge, and the burly Mexican was wrapped in a shaggy, knee-length bear coat, his sombrero pulled down low over his ears.

"*Bueno! Maravilloso!*" He tucked the jug he was currently drinking from under his chin and clapped his gloved hands. "You are just good enough to get yourself thoroughly ventilated. Deader *matado que infierno!*"

"*Vaya al infierno, viejo hombre!*" Colter said, telling the old man to go to hell in the Spanish he'd been picking up from Juventino himself.

"I will meet you there, huh?" the old prospector yelled, throwing up his arms and sloshing whiskey from the mouth of his jug.

Colter flicked open the loading gate of his .44 and began punching the spent shells from the cylinder. Juventino continued berating him in Spanish mixed with English. Beneath the Mexican's drunken harangue, a crack sounded.

Colter jerked his head up, frowning. "Be quiet."

Juventino let the tirade die on his lips, frowning at Colter from under the cabin's brush arbor. *"Cual es el?"*

"Shut up!"

Just then, another crack sounded from the direction of the trail leading up the mesa behind the cabin. Juventino gasped and heaved himself drunkenly from his chair. As he scrambled into the cabin, Colter, hearing a couple more cracks, the last slightly louder than the first, quickly reloaded the Remy from his shell belt.

His heart beat insistently, and his breath grew short. He was both eager and scared. He'd been wanting a fight for two months, but he'd wanted to make sure he was ready.

He spun his Remy's cylinder and stepped around the cabin, holding the pistol straight down by his side, his thumb gently caressing the cocked hammer, his index finger curved through the trigger guard but resting lightly on the trigger.

As Juventino's boots sounded behind him, the old man's breath rasping loudly and rife with the smell of pulque, Colter picked the rider out of the afternoon shadows.

He was coming along the trail that was two floury ribbons leading toward the back side of the mesa,

with a strip of wiry grass and sage between them. The
rider sat hunched in his saddle, extending a revolver
off both sides of the trail and seemingly firing at ran
dom. The pistol barked about a second after each
flash and smoke puff. As the rider continued toward
the cabin, the time between the flash and the sound
dwindled, and the man's figure took shape—an oddly
built gent in a wolf coat, with a grubby hat on his
head, and what appeared to be a hump pushing his
right shoulder forward.

"Ah, *Christos*!" Juventino said when it had become
obvious to him as well as Colter that their potshooting
visitor was Wayne Kilgore. "I should have known—
it's Friday night, and he probably got paid. I hope he
brought his own hooch for a change!"

The pistol cracked again. The bullet whined off a
rock. And then Kilgore's crazy laugh sounded above
the horse's thudding hooves. "Good evening, gents
It's Friday night and I'm *flush*!"

"Flush, amigo?" Juventino called, his voice not
quite as hooch-garbled as his friend's. "I hope you're
flush with forty-rod, then, too, because I'm almost out
of pulque, and you're not getting any!"

As he came within forty yards and closing, leaving
the trail to head toward Colter and Juventino, Kilgore
holstered his old cap-and-ball revolver and lifted a
croaker sack above his saddle horn. "I not only come
bearing drink, but five pounds of beefsteak, *mi amigos*
And not only that, but I come bearing news, *mi amigo*
Colter."

Kilgore drew rein in front of the young drover and
Juventino. He leaned heavily forward and appeared

to have some trouble keeping his drink-bleary eyes from rolling back in his head. The fur of his wolf coat blew in the cooling breeze, and the salmon color of the west-angling sun burnished it.

"Well, what's the news, Wayne?" Colter said. "They get a new whore to replace the one Spurlock cut?"

Since his branding, his sense of humor had grown as sour as the rest of his character. As Juventino had told him, he would have gotten along well with the orneriest of Irish gandy dancers.

"Uh-uh." The hunchback grinned down from his saddle. "Your friend and mine, Chico Bannon—he's drinkin' and playin' stud over to Pilgrim's Hole not two miles north of here."

Pilgrim's Hole was an old Spanish mission church, part of which had been converted into a cantina that served some of the roughest drifters south of Sapinero. Many a lawman had met his bloody end in the place, but Bill Rondo and Chico Bannon played poker there often . . . and enjoyed the whores, who were said to be the finest outside of Arizona's border country.

Juventino groaned. "Ahhh . . . Now, why you go and tell him that, *pendejo*? Don't you know what he is foolish enough to try?"

"Hell, he's gonna try it anyways, *pendejo* your ownself! And I say if he's gonna make a play on them two yellow-toothed demons, he might as well do it when they ain't watchin' each other's backs!"

Colter turned to Juventino. "What's the fastest way to Pilgrim's Hole?"

"*Dios mio!*" The Mexican threw up his hands in defeat. "Wait until I am sober, and I will *show* you."

"You won't be sober till tomorrow, and that killer'll likely be gone by then." Colter stared hard at his old friend, who stared back at him darkly, the breeze brushing his long hair and his beard. "If you don't tell me, I'll just backtrack Wayne's horse. Just take me a little longer's all."

"Hell, he don't need to tell you," Kilgore announced, swaying in his saddle, his eyes lit fiercely. "I'll show you! Hell, together we'll take down the sonofabitch in a hail of hot, burning lead. Won't even know what hit him!"

"You're going to lead him into that death trap?" Juventino railed at the hunchback. "Javelina shit! You can barely even sit that old cob of yours, *pendejo* dog!"

Colter didn't have time to wait for the two drunken fools to stop arguing. He turned and, hitching his shell belt higher on his lean hips, stalked across the yard to the corral. He lifted the latch chain from its nail, drew the gate open, and headed into the lean-to shed, where he retrieved his saddle, saddle blanket, bridle, and throw rope. He dropped his gear in the dust in the middle of the corral as his coyote dun and Juventino's two mules and his saddle horse edged away from him skeptically.

When Colter had collared and saddled the dun, draping his saddlebags over Northwest's back in front of his bedroll, he led the animal outside.

Juventino was sitting in the wicker chair in front of the shack. The sun was low, illuminating all the deep lines in the Mexican's round, brown, bearded face, the dark eyes regarding Colter stubbornly, grimly. Colter had been so immersed in his murderous thoughts of Chico Bannon that he hadn't noticed that Kilgore had apparently passed out and tumbled out of his saddle.

The hunchback lay snoring on his side in the sage almost exactly where his grulla had been standing a few minutes ago. Now the grulla was standing in front of the corral, eyeing the other horses affably and no doubt wanting feed and water.

With a muttered curse, Colter let the horse into the corral and, because he knew that neither Juventino nor Kilgore was in any condition to tend it properly, quickly stripped the tack from the mount's back so it could roll and eat from the hay crib.

Leaving the corral, Colter stepped into the dun's saddle and trotted over to the shack, where Juventino continued to sit, bottle propped on his thigh, regarding Colter pensively. Colter leapt out of the saddle, stomped into the shack, retrieved his rifle from under his cot and two boxes of .44 shells from a cupboard pounded together from tomato crates, and headed back outside.

When he'd stepped into the leather and slid the Henry into its boot, he drew the dun's reins up close to his chest and looked at the Mexican.

Before he could open his mouth to speak, Juventino said, "Follow the two-track to the potbelly butte, hang a left in the draw. You'll see a razorback ridge. Ride toward it. Pilgrim's Hole is at the base of it. You'll see the red roof. Probably hear the girls' screams and the gunfire and the yells of the savage banditos sticking each other with rusty knives."

"Good."

Colter reined Northwest away from the cabin and booted the dun into a lope.

Two hours later, sitting beneath a hackberry tree trimmed with starlight, Colter slipped his Remington from its holster. He filled the empty chamber beneath the hammer, flicked the loading gate closed, and quietly spun the cylinder.

A belligerent yell rose from the hulking dark mission house a hundred yards away, beyond a corral and a softly clattering windmill. Another man yelled, and then there was the sharp crack of an open palm striking flesh.

A man laughed loudly, thoroughly pleased with himself. It was the laugh of Chico Bannon. Colter would have known the laugh anywhere. He would remember the laugh on his deathbed—as it had sounded beneath the hiss of the glowing iron sinking into his cheek.

Things quieted down inside the saloon after the slap, as the men, evidently, settled back down to their card game inside the great, hulking mass of the mission house. Only a small part of the house, the part directly across the yard from Colter, was being used as a saloon. It was marked by soft umber lamplight showing between arched porticoes and from several windows in the second story, beneath the red-tiled roof.

Colter spun the Remy's cylinder once more and slipped the iron back in its sheath. He closed his gloved hands around the Henry, lifting the rifle slightly, hefting it, liking the heavy, ominous weight of the gun in his hands.

A peculiar calm had settled over him after the short, anxiety-racked ride from Juventino's cabin. Sitting here under the hackberry, with the corral containing several milling horses ahead to the left, the soft, tinny clatter of the windmill in the night breeze, and the occasional jovial or angry outburst from the saloon, an almost ethereal peace had settled over him.

A grim resolve.

Grave determination.

Fate had brought him here, and fate would see him through to the end of what was about to begin.

He sat clutching the rifle and dozed.

A steadily loudening din of conversation rose from the saloon. He pulled his head up. The conversation grew into an argument among at least four men.

"Bannon!" The exclamation rose clear and crisp on the silent night, for the breeze had died and the windmill had stopped turning. "That's the last time you'll cheat me, you—"

*Blam!*

A shouted curse.

*Blam-blam-blam!*

A scream. Someone wailed, and there was the thud of a chair hitting the flagstone floor.

Bannon laughed.

Two more quick shots pierced the night—*Blam-blam!*

And then one more, as if fired inadvertently. It was followed by the sharp clank of a gun hitting the floor and the heavier thump of a body doing likewise.

Beneath the hackberry, Colter watched grimly, expectantly, his heartbeat increasing only slightly. His finger caressed the Henry's eyelash trigger.

Only silence from the saloon. In the wake of the bloody violence, the lamplight seemed to glow a little more brightly.

Suddenly a girl shouted something in Spanish—a savage harangue, only a few words of which Colter was able to decipher in spite of his recent renewed tutoring by Juventino. The sharp crack of a hand meeting flesh cut the tirade off.abruptly, and that report was followed briefly by sobbing and the clatter of high-heeled shoes fleeing up a flight of stairs.

The clatter dwindled to silence.

Colter watched a shadow move under a gaping arch at the front of the saloon. There was the soft ring of a spur. His interest growing, Colter climbed to his feet slowly and stood holding the Henry low across his thighs, his finger lovingly caressing the trigger.

The man-shaped shadow sidled up against one of the stout, pale pillars, and there were the raucous smacks of louvered doors slapping shut behind him. The man groaned. His spurs trilled as he staggered a few feet into the yard, then dropped to his knees.

The silhouetted figure threw his head back, and the shout he sent careening to the stars was harrowing: *"Mierda!"*

When the echo died, the louvered doors squawked and smacked again, and another shadow moved out from the front of the saloon, boots clomping with a leisurely, self-satisfied flare, crunching grit on the flagstones. The short, stocky figure stood between the two pillars, looking out into the yard. It was hard to tell in the dim light and inky darkness, but Bannon seemed to have his thumbs tucked back behind his cartridge belt.

The man who'd shouted remained on his knees, grunting loudly, a gurgling rising from his throat.

As Colter turned and walked back to where his coyote dun cropped grama grass, he heard a shot. He leaped lithely into his saddle and, facing the saloon, saw the flash of Bannon's gun a half second before he heard the report.

The kneeling man grunted shrilly. He flopped forward and hit the ground with a soft smack. He groaned again, and Bannon, laughing, fired two more shots into him.

By this time Colter had heeled the coyote dun into a lunging, ground-eating gallop toward the saloon. Bannon didn't hear Northwest's hoof thuds above the echoes of his own blasts until Colter was within fifty yards and closing like a cyclone.

# Chapter 24

Standing over the prone form of the man he'd killed, powder smoke from his own gun wafting around him, Chico Bannon jerked his head suddenly toward Colter as he hammered toward him on the charging dun.

Bannon's eyes snapped wide. He lifted his smoking, ivory-gripped .45.

Colter had shoved his Henry into his saddle sheath, deciding his Remington was more the tool he needed here.

It was.

It roared.

"*Ach!*" Bannon cried as his own revolver was punched from his hand.

Clutching the hand that had held the gun and staggering back and sideways, tripping over the dead man's boots, Bannon looked from his hand to Colter, his jaw dropping in shock.

Colter checked Northwest down quickly. As the plug pony skidded to a stop on all four hooves, lurching back on its hindquarters, Colter holstered his six-shooter and grabbed the lariat off his saddle horn. He was as fast and clean with a throw rope as he was now with a hogleg.

The coyote dun was still skidding toward the shocked, enraged Bannon, when Colter began shaking out a loop above his head. He twirled it twice, letting it grow easily in the dark air, and released it.

The loop settled over Bannon's head and shoulders before the drunk deputy knew what was happening.

"Hey!" Bannon shouted, lifting his arms to shed the loop.

But he hadn't moved it more than six inches before Colter neck-reined the coyote dun around sharply and ground his spurs into the horse's flanks. The dun lurched off its rear hooves with an anxious whinny, and the lariat's loop slapped Bannon's arms down close to his sides, jerking his head and shoulders up and evoking a scream of indignant pain.

"*H-yahhhh!*" Colter shouted, slapping his right hand against the dun's hip.

As Northwest lunged back in the direction from which Colter had come, the young drover glanced over his shoulder to see Chico Bannon, eyes wide as fresh cow plop, jerked up and forward with such force that his hat was still turning end over end in the air after the deputy had been smashed facedown in the dirt and then jerked forward like a human missile.

Bannon's screams quavered as he was pulled savagely along the ground behind Northwest's chopping rear hooves.

"*Stawwwwwp*, damn you!" the deputy shrieked as he fishtailed along behind the horse, holding the rope with both hands to keep his head out of the dirt and above the rocks and brush he plowed through or over at a wild, hoof-drumming clip. "Gawddamn you, stop right now, you sonofabitch! You know who I *ammmmmmmm*?"

"Yeah, I know who *you* are!" Colter shouted, turning forward in the saddle and tipping his hat against the wind. "You know who *I* am?"

When he'd traced a broad circle around the saloon/mission house twice, noting a definite diminishment in the deputy's threats and, more recently, pleas for mercy, he reined Northwest to a halt between the saloon's wan lights and the corral. Bannon was an unmoving lump in the dirt behind him, the taut rope angling down from the horse's rear.

The cowboy swung out of the saddle and stood beside the dun, staring back toward Bannon. His jaw was hard, and his chest rose and fell slowly.

A footfall came from his right, and he turned toward the saloon. He saw several shadowy figures silhouetted by the light from the windows and the louvered doors, standing on the gallery between the pillars. He couldn't tell for sure in the murky light, but several seemed to have long hair and were skimpily dressed.

A little man with black hair and a mustache, and wearing a white apron, stood in front of the doors, arms folded across his chest. Cigarettes glowed brightly as they were raised to painted lips, and smoke wafted like gauzy gray curtains.

Colter could smell the harsh Mexican tobacco, and

he could smell the girls' perfume mingling with the odors of sage, horses, and dust.

His senses were alive. His heart beat regularly, purposefully. Absently, he raised a hand to trace the knotted S scar on his left cheek.

Ahead of him, Bannon groaned and turned slowly onto his back, a spur grinding into the ground beneath him.

Colter's pulse quickened slightly.

He reached into his saddlebags and dragged out a braided rawhide quirt, about two feet long from leather-wrapped handle to the two dangling whip ends capped with small metal poppers. Holding the quirt down low in his left hand, he walked over to Bannon, turned so that he faced the man's head, and dropped to his haunches.

Bannon grimaced and arched his back.

He was so covered with blood, dirt, and bits of sage and ragged rabbitbrush blossoms that he blended well with the ground. Only a few patches of light skin shone in the starlight and in the dim light from the saloon. The deputy groaned, grunted, and shook his head slightly, muttering curses under his breath.

When his pain-racked eyes found Colter's, they hardened.

Colter's voice was just above a whisper. "Can you see me, Bannon?"

The man only grunted.

"You see the S on my face?"

The man only stared at him, flinching now and then when pain spasmed in his body. By the harsh way he breathed, Colter could tell several ribs were probably broken. He swallowed and continued staring darkly at Colter with rage.

He didn't say anything.

Colter rose from his haunches. The quirt hung down by his side. Bannon's eyes dropped to it, rose to Colter's face. The skin between his eyes wrinkled. Then both eyes snapped wide in horror as Colter brought the quirt up behind his left shoulder.

Bannon screamed and turned his head to one side.

The quirt whistled through the air before striking Bannon's cheek with a sharp crack. Colter brought the quirt back behind his other shoulder, and Bannon sobbed as the quirt raked across his other cheek with another savage whip crack.

Bannon's head fell back in the dirt, and his chest rose and fell sharply as he panted and wheezed, spittle frothing over his lips and down his chin.

"Those scars ain't as deep or as purty as mine," Colter growled, "but you won't have to wear 'em long."

He tossed the quirt down on the man's chest. Stepping over Bannon's torn, filthy frame, he strode to the corral, where Bannon's buckskin stood hanging its head over the gate in sullen interest at the activity in the middle of the yard.

Colter went in, saddled and bridled the horse, and led it to where Bannon lay, the rope still holding his arms taut against his sides. The outlaw deputy was groaning, half unconscious, and slowly carving furrows in the dirt with his spurs, his cheeks shiny with bloody mud.

Colter tied his buckskin's reins to its saddle horn

Then he untied his own throw rope from his own horn and dallied it around the buckskin's. Moving purposefully, not hurrying, his face a mask of grim intent, he went back to where Bannon was now pushing up on his elbows.

He kicked the deputy down onto his back. Bannon was too broken up and addled to do much except fling his arms up weakly toward Colter and curse.

"What the hell you think you're doin', boy?" the man grunted as Colter lifted the throw loop from the man's chest to his neck. A look of bald horror swept the deputy's face when he realized where the loop— or noose—now lay. He shoved up on his elbows.

Colter backhanded him, then stepped down on his chest with all his weight.

"Please," Bannon begged, his chest thumping against the sole of Colter's boot. His eyes were large and frantically beseeching. "Please don't do this, boy. I don't have this comin'."

"Oh, I wouldn't say that."

Colter waited until the man had fought all he could. When he felt the tension ease beneath his boot, he crouched over the man and tightened the noose about his neck, adjusting the slipknot.

Bannon stared up at him, his forehead deeply creased in horror. "Don't," he raked out, shaking his head from side to side. "Please . . . I'm . . . I'm beggin' ya now. I apologize for . . . for what we did."

His boot pressing the man's chest down once again, Colter stared at him coldly. "Kinda late for that, don't ya think?"

Bannon's eyes brightened with tears. They dribbled down his bloody, filthy cheeks and scraped lips. "I reckon you're right. I don't reckon you have any reason to show me any mercy. Just the same . . ."

"You're really sorry?"

"Of course I'm sorry!" Bannon sobbed. "That was an awful damn thing we did, scarrin' one so young!"

Colter stared down at him, one eye narrowed pensively. "If I take that noose off your neck, will you ride into Sapinero and tell Mr. Spurlock it was you and Rondo who killed his daughter?"

Bannon's eyes snapped wide as he lifted his head hopefully, the cords standing out in his neck around the noose. "Sure I will!"

The corners of Colter's mouth rose slowly. Stepping back away from Bannon, he laughed.

He walked over to the buckskin, and pointed the horse toward Sapinero. Then he stood up near the horse's left hip, the rope stretching from the buckskin's saddle to Bannon's neck now a taut, slanting line.

Colter slipped his Remington from its holster.

He cocked the Remy and held its barrel toward the sky.

"Please, goddamn you!" Bannon screeched. "You get me outta this noose, boy, or I'll carve you up in little bits and send you in burlap back to your ma!"

"Say hi to Rondo for me. Tell him he's next."

"No! Please, *nooooooo*!"

Colter licked his lips and squeezed the Remy's trigger. The pistol roared.

The buckskin whinnied and lunged forward, lay

ing its ears back against its head. Bannon's eyes nearly popped out of his skull as he clawed feebly at the noose. He tried to scream, but the rope squeezed off his wind and the scream was a stillborn gurgle in his throat.

The buckskin galloped out of the yard and traced a bend in the trail between buttes, Bannon's body bouncing, eerily silent, along behind it.

Slowly, the buckskin's thudding hooves and squawking tack dwindled into silence.

The breeze had picked up again, and it blew a little dust devil in a short curvet around the yard.

"Amigo," one of the girls called from the saloon's gallery—a husky, Mexican-accented female voice that the breeze shunted eerily. "Come on in and have a drink on us."

Colter glanced toward the saloon. A slender, long-haired figure in a pale wrap leaned against a gallery pillar. She held one arm beneath her breasts. The other hung down by her side, a cigarette glowing faintly in her hand.

Colter looked back down the trail along which Bannon had disappeared. Then he hiked a shoulder and began strolling toward the saloon, his thumbs hooked behind his shell belt.

"Don't mind if I do."

An hour after sunup, Colter drew the coyote dun to a halt on the outskirts of Sapinero. He'd donned his black-and-red-plaid jacket against the crisp fall chill, and he raised the collar as an icy breeze funneled down the town's main street and stung the S scar on his cheek, which had all but healed but still pained him occasionally, especially in a cold wind.

Dawn was well past, but little moved among the shacks and pens around him. Smoke wafted from the brick chimney of a blacksmith shop on his right. Through its open doors he heard the smithy hammering on his anvil inside the stout building, but he couldn't see the man in the dreary inner shadows.

Straight ahead along the trail that became the town's main drag, he saw no one except one shop owner in a long green apron, wolf coat, and black wool cap, sweeping the low porch in front of his store. Dust blew up around his broom and drifted into the street.

As the shopkeeper tried to dislodge a pesky tumbleweed from his broom at the edge of the porch, Colter glanced cautiously at the rooftops around and ahead of him. Spying nothing unusual, he touched spurs to the dun's flanks and started forward again at a walk.

He wondered if Bannon had made it back to town. And, if he had, he wondered what Rondo's reaction had been. Colter had half expected to see riders galloping out from town, but on his way from Pilgrim's Hole he'd run into only a few deer grazing along the trail.

As he continued forward, dust and leaves blowing around the dun's hooves, the town's old central plaza coming up on the street's left side, he noted a faint flutter of excitement at the edge of his consciousness.

There was a strange silence here today. A grim air of waiting. A tension like that in a cocked gun hammer.

Colter felt a faint, grim smile touch his mouth.

The rasps of the shopkeeper's broom ceased. Colter glanced to his left. The man had stopped sweeping to stand atop his porch, leaning forward on his broom and eyeing Colter darkly, strands of gray-brown hair blowing around his cap.

Colter pinched his hat brim to the man as he passed. He saw now, as he neared the plaza, that the shopkeeper was indeed the only man on the street. The rest of the main drag was abandoned, only a couple of horses tethered here and there in front of saloons and cantinas.

One horse stopped drinking from a stock trough and craned its neck to regard Colter with a look, Colter fancied, very much like that of the shopkeeper. Water dripped from its lips.

"It's all right, fella," Colter mumbled, wincing slightly as the cold breeze bit his scar. "This shouldn't take too long. Not too damn long at all."

Halfway along the street, he drew up sharply and touched his hand to his Remy's grips. A cottonwood stood among the sycamores and pecans at the edge of the central plaza. It was the largest tree of all. Only a few frost-burned leaves remained on its thick, gnarled limbs.

From one of the low branches that jutted out into the street, the bloody, battered, half-mangled body of Chico Bannon hung, twisting in the chill breeze.

Looking up at the gently turning, blindly staring carcass, Colter smiled.

# Chapter 25

Colter raked his gaze from Bannon's wrecked face to the dusty plaza behind the dead man, the cantinas and brothels behind that, and the shops on his right. The sweeping shopkeeper had abandoned his porch so that the only movement on the street now was a couple of tumbleweeds and a tabby cat prowling the weed- and trash-choked gap between a leatherwork store and a photographer's.

Smoke continued to billow from the chimney of the blacksmith shop farther west, but the hammering had died.

The shop windows all around Colter were dark squares through which he could feel the heat of secret, calculating gazes. Keeping his hand on the Remy's grips, a wistful expression on his scarred young face, he urged the dun across the street, to the Trail Driver Saloon. He put the horse up beside the lone cow pony tied there, dismounted, and tied Northwest to the hitchrack.

Leaving his Henry in the saddle boot—he'd become good enough with the Remy that the long gun

would only get in his way—he mounted the Trail
Driver's porch steps. In front of the batwings, he
turned to look at the street once more. His eyes caught
on a figure moving toward him from across the square,
partially obscured by the trees and the slowly turning
boots of Chico Bannon.

The girl wore a long green hooded cape. Chestnut
hair blew out from the hood to dance about her round
face and shoulders.

As the slender, gently curved figure approached
the edge of the square, turning her head stiffly toward
the hanging dead man, one hand brushing her dancing hair back from an eye, Colter turned and sauntered through the batwings. Just inside the dim room
that smelled of last night's beer, liquor, tobacco smoke,
and even the perfume of the sporting girls, he stopped
and looked around.

The mahogany brass-railed bar ran along the back
wall. A beefy gent with carefully combed red-blond
hair and matching mustache stood in the direct center
of it, leaning on his fists and regarding Colter without
expression. Several longhorns loomed over him from
above the backbar. A clock ticked on the wall to Colter's left.

To his right sat the only man in the room and likely
the owner of the cow pony outside. The man was
facing the saloon's back wall, lifting a shot glass to his
lips. If he'd heard the shudder of the batwings, he
gave no indication, but continued to stare woodenly
toward the back of the room.

He was a lanky gent with a handlebar mustache
and close-cropped brown hair, the skin powder white

where his hat protected him from the sun. The rest of his face and his neck had been burned to a choke-cherry red color. He wore an old cap-and-ball pistol in the cross-draw position on his right hip, but he didn't look like trouble. He had the look of a slightly down-at-heel drifter who'd merely stopped for a drink to ease the chill of the cold ground from his bones.

Colter kept the man in the corner of his right eye, however. From this day forward, he'd likely have to keep everyone he saw in the corner of one eye or another.

He sauntered forward along the center alley between the tables that still had the chairs upended on them for sweeping. The bartender held his ground, watching Colter with cowlike, heavy-lidded eyes.

"You come to the wrong place, boy," the bartender grunted as Colter approached the bar. "Don't you know what happens to folks dumb enough to come around here wearin' that S brand on their cheek?"

Colter tossed a coin on the bar top and turned slightly to his right, setting his arm on the bar and leaning on it. "Give me a whiskey."

"Shee-it," the barman scoffed, running his gaze from Colter's gaunt, scarred face to his thin neck and bony shoulders with sneering disapproval. "Why, one sip of my forty-rod, you're liable to—"

"Just pour the shot."

The man sighed and reached under the bar. "All right."

The man had just filled a shot glass when footsteps sounded on the porch, and Colter turned to see Angelique push slowly, tentatively through the batwings.

The drifter didn't look at her as she entered, arms crossed beneath her breasts, but just kept his eyes on the back wall near the stairs.

Angelique moved slowly across the room. She lowered her head and said in her heavy French accent, "So, you came back."

Colter's right cheek faced her. She hadn't seen the scar yet. He threw back half the shot and enjoyed the burn. He'd been enjoying the burn since he'd started drinking in earnest two months ago, to ease the pain in his face and sundry other places, including that between his ears.

"Well, you had it right," he said, staring toward the stairs as the girl approached him. "Many tears have been shed at Barranca Verde."

"You're a fool," she said, lowering her chin and narrowing her eyes. "I left that note so your questions would be answered and you'd go back to where you came from."

Colter turned to her now, holding up the bottle. "Drink?"

Her eyes found the S scar on his left cheek. Her lower jaw dropped as she took a step around him to see the scar better. She stopped, and gasped, bringing a hand to her mouth. Instantly, tears glazed her eyes.

"What's the matter?" Colter said. "You don't like the tattoo?"

"Colter!"

He extended a hand toward the bartender, who stood staring grimly, fatefully, at both him and the girl. "Another glass."

When the bartender had handed over a glass,

Colter took both glasses and the bottle to a near table. He put two chairs onto the floor and sagged heavily into one, his back to the east wall. From this position he was able to keep the barkeep, the drifter, and the front door in clear view.

Angelique stood staring at the S brand on his cheek, tears dribbling down her own, arms still crossed beneath her breasts, as though she were deeply chilled.

"You gonna join me?" Colter said, kicking out her chair. "Or you gonna make me drink alone?"

Stiffly, brushing a tear from her cheek with her right hand, she sank down in the chair. As Colter filled her glass from the bottle, she said, "Colter, you're crazy to come here."

"How's that?"

"They'll kill you."

Colter snorted and sipped his drink. "They'll try."

"Did you kill Bannon?"

"Sure." Colter took another sip, smacked his lips. "But I didn't hang him."

He changed the subject easily, glancing outside, where he watched four men moving toward the saloon from the hotel west of the plaza—one bull-chested, well-dressed gent and three others in rough trail garb, with guns thonged on their thighs. "Did you know Trace?"

"Sure," she said sadly, staring down at the table now. She hadn't touched her drink.

"Were you in love with him, too?"

A faint, wry smile pulled at her mouth. "Every woman in town was in love with him."

"But Jacinta got him."

Angelique nodded slightly. "They met in the general store. Trace was very fast. Very charming."

"You could have told me yourself."

"You would have gone off half-cocked and gotten yourself killed."

Colter threw back the rest of his shot. "I'm about to do that, anyway, aren't I?"

The men—Spurlock and three of his gunslicks, including Blaine Surtees—were moving across the street now, following the path that Angelique had taken. Spurlock's corduroy coat blew out behind him in the wind, and he had the brim of his Stetson pulled low over his forehead. Surtees wasn't hard to pick out—as tall as Spurlock but leaner, darkly handsome, with longish brown hair, matching mustache, and wearing a pinto vest under a denim jacket.

"I didn't realize what a fool you were," Angelique said, lifting her gaze to Colter's now. "I thought you would be reasonable, when you'd heard the story from Jacinta . . . and seen the children."

"All they had to do was let me go. I wasn't plannin' on comin' back here."

She frowned. "Why, then . . . ?"

"They found me with Jennifer. Didn't like that, I reckon, any more than they liked Trace bein' with Jacinta." Colter splashed more liquor into his glass and chuckled dryly. "Damn jealous town. Men got their claws in all the pretty girls. Women got theirs in all the handsome men. Of course, that ain't my problem. 'Specially not now."

He laughed again and began to close his lips over his glass. Hearing boots and spurs on the porch, he stopped, pulled the drink back down. Paul Spurlock burst through the batwings and stopped a few feet inside the saloon, fists on his hips. Surtees stood beside him. The rancher's *segundo* had two Colts thonged low on his black denim–clad thighs. The other two gunslicks moved in to flank Spurlock and the dark, faintly sneering Surtees, all standing there with hard looks on their faces and poking their hat brims back off their foreheads with gloved fingers.

"What in Sam Hill?" Spurlock intoned, his big voice filling the room.

His clothes hung on him, the skin of his face loose. He'd lost a good twenty pounds since Colter had last seen him.

The man jerked his thumb over his shoulder and glowered through the morning shadows at the young cowboy. "Don't tell me *you* did that to Bannon?"

"Yessir—I did at that," Colter said dully.

He looked at Angelique and jerked his head toward the doors.

The girl stared at him, pleading with him silently. He didn't look at her but kept his gaze on Spurlock and his cold-steel artists, anxiety whispering at him softly and setting up a slight throbbing in his temples. He took a deep breath through his nose, repressing his fear, scouring his mind of all thought, letting the cold rage take control once more.

The scar on his cheek burned as though it had been blazed there yesterday.

Angelique climbed out of her chair. She shoved the chair under the table, staring hard at Colter, her eyes angry and sad. Wheeling suddenly in frustration, she started back toward the front of the room.

She stopped in front of Spurlock, looking up at him. The two men flanking him and Surtees grinned. Silently, she moved around the four men and pushed out through the doors, descended the porch steps, and was gone.

Surtees said in his faintly raspy, feminine voice, "He's the one, boss. Ain't no one dumb enough to ride into town wearing that brand less'n they're dumb enough to do what they did to Bannon."

"Dumb, huh?" said a familiar voice at the top of the stairs.

Despite his attempts at self-control, the small hairs rose on the back of Colter's neck. He looked up at the top of the stairs, across the room and above him. Rondo stood there, buckling his cartridge belt around his lean waist. A girl with long red hair and clad in only a pale wrapper stood behind him, holding his black hat.

"I'd say the one who did that to Chico was one smart hombre, since he went ahead and did it, an' all. Chico— he's the dumb one. But he done paid for his sins."

Rondo turned and grabbed his hat from the girl's hands. He donned it, chucked the girl under the chin, and turned to look over the banister at Colter. A grim smile lifted his pewter gray mustache, and his eyes flashed wickedly.

"What the hell are you gonna do about this, Rondo?" Spurlock barked. "You were supposed to run him outta the country. You know I don't like getting involved in gunplay in town."

"Thought I did run him outta the country."

Rondo casually descended the stairs, running his right hand along the rail as he did. His large spurs jingled like bells. The heel thumps and spur jingling nearly filled the room until the renegade lawman gained the bottom of the stairs and stopped, facing Colter, his black duster pulled back behind the silver-plated Peacemaker .45 thonged low on his right thigh. His striped trousers were shoved down into the tops of his mule-eared boots.

"Go on," Rondo said, cutting his eyes toward the rancher. "Take your gunnies and vamoose, Spurlock. I'll take care of this."

"Ah, hell," Colter said. "I was hopin' the three of us could talk."

All five men looked at him now. Rondo was too far away for Colter to be sure, but he thought a faint flush had risen in the man's weathered cheeks.

"What about?" Spurlock said, his voice resonating off the walls.

The drifter on the other side of the room continued sipping his single shot of whiskey. He might have been in the room alone, for all the attention he paid to the men around him.

Colter squeezed his shot glass in his right hand. He kept his left hand on his thigh, near the butt of his Remington .44. He would no doubt need the gun in about three jerks of a pig's tail.

He kept his eyes on Rondo as he said to the rancher, "About your daughter, Mr. Spurlock. About Jennifer. Thought you might want to know where she is . . . and who killed her."

# Chapter 26

"Chew that up for me, boy," Spurlock ordered. "Where's my daughter?"

Colter shuttled his gaze between the rancher still standing in front of the batwing doors beside Surtees, and Rondo, who stood at the bottom of the stairs, his duster thrown back behind his Peacemaker.

The lawman's face had not only paled but tightened dreadfully.

Before Colter could answer, the drifter sitting about midway between Rondo and Spurlock sighed suddenly and threw back the last of his whiskey. He raked his chair back, stood, and donned his hat, letting the chin thong swing down against his shirt. Adjusting the hat, he sauntered casually toward Spurlock, to whom he nodded cordially, and left.

The batwings shuddered behind him.

Glaring at Colter, Rondo set his jaw and said, "I suggest you don't indulge the boy. You can't believe a word this damn little mountain scoundrel says!"

At nearly the same time, their voices mingling, Colter said, "You'll find her in Cottonwood Canyon, buried in some shrubs against the south ridge. You'll find the Sapinero S on her left cheek, about the size of Rondo's ring."

Silence.

Rondo's jaw clenched as he switched his gaze from Spurlock to Colter and back again.

As though his own head were sitting on an unoiled swivel, Spurlock turned toward Rondo. The sheriff's right black-gloved hand hung low by his side. The light from the window behind him shone on the large gold ring on his middle finger, outside the glove—the ring set with the large square emerald studded with the single letter S.

Rondo opened and closed his fist as though half consciously trying to shake the ring from his finger.

Spurlock stared at him. Rondo turned his head toward Colter. Half a second later, his head dropped as he crouched and swept the Peacemaker from his black leather holster.

The Colt thundered. Smoke and flames blossomed.

At the same time, Colter threw himself straight back in his chair. His back hit the floor as Rondo's bullet screeched through the air where his chest had been and slammed into the bar behind him.

Spurlock's voice boomed in the wake of the Colt's roar. "Rondo, you sonofabitch!"

Rondo's Colt roared again. The bullet slammed into the floor as Colter rolled to one side, clawing his Remy from its holster.

He pushed up on an elbow, thumbing the hammer

back. As he did, Spurlock extended a silver-plated, horn-handled Smith & Wesson and fired on Rondo.

The bullet slammed into the ball atop the newel post just behind the sheriff. Rondo crouched and returned two quick shots at Spurlock and the rancher's gunnies. Spurlock jerked back and, as Surtees and the other two gunmen triggered lead toward Rondo, their bullets chewing splinters from the back wall, the newel post, and the stairs, Rondo wheeled with a grace unusual for a man of his size and sprinted toward the bar.

Colter snapped off a shot from his position on the floor, aiming over his raised left knee. His bullet lifted the hair at the back of the man's head and carved a thin red line across his neck just before Rondo launched himself airborne and disappeared behind the mahogany.

He hit the floor behind the bar with a loud bang as Spurlock's gunmen, lined up at the front of the saloon, with Spurlock down and groaning miserably, peppered the bar and the backbar mirror with screeching lead. The shattering of mirror glass and bottles sounded like a hundred screaming children.

Beneath it, Spurlock groaned loudly, pounding the floor with his boots while the three gunmen yelled like banshees.

Colter knocked a chair over for cover.

Rondo lifted his hatless head up from behind the bar, showing his teeth under his mustache, and snapped off two shots toward Spurlock's men with his Peacemaker. He hit only one of the batwings and a window before angling the weapon toward Colter.

Colter had the man's head in his sights, but as he squeezed the Remy's trigger, a bullet plowed into a table leg to his right. Another blew his hat off his head. His own shot was nudged wide of the sheriff, who drilled a round into the chair in front of Colter's face, peppering his cheeks with wood slivers.

Colter cursed. He was in a crossfire between Spurlock's men and Rondo. As Blaine Surtees sent another lead bumblebee buzzing toward him, he scuttled back on his hands and knees, putting a small woodstove between himself and the gunmen.

He edged a look over the stove.

The room was filled with smoke. Beyond the haze of wafting powder, two of Spurlock's men had dropped down behind tables while Surtees knelt where he'd been standing, in front of the doors. He was shouting for the others to cover him while he reloaded one of his Colts. The other pistol lay on the floor in front of his right boot.

As Surtees flicked the Colt's loading gate closed, Colter, wincing as a bullet burned across his left cheek, extended his Remy over the stove and fired two rounds into the kneeling man's forehead—one beside the other and spaced exactly one inch apart.

Surtees fell back against the legs of Spurlock, who'd managed to push himself halfway outside the saloon on his back. The rancher was flopping around like a landed fish, wailing, while Surtees spasmed on top of his legs.

Colter dropped to the floor as several bullets careened around him from the direction of the bar as well as from the two tables where the other two gun slicks were crouching. The lead spanged loudly off the stove and slammed into table legs and the floor.

When Rondo's firing stopped abruptly, Colter lurched to his feet, fired at each of the two surviving gunslicks, who were well concealed by overturned tables, then leapt up onto the stove. From the stove he leapt to a table and dove onto another one.

As both gunslicks rose, shouting like lobos and triggering six-shooters in all four hands, Colter hit the floor, rolled once as lead shrieked around him, plunking loudly into wood, and rose to his haunches. Both shooters were still tracking him, squinting through the wafting powder smoke.

The Remy bucked in Colter's hand twice, three times—and both men were sent stumbling back across the room, screaming and triggering their own pistols into the ceiling, eyes rolling back into their skulls as though to get better views of the .44-caliber holes bored into their foreheads. One had a hole in the dead center of his forehead and one through his right eye as well.

He wailed the loudest but also for the shortest time, as he was dead before he hit the floor near the other one, quivering in his own quickly pooling blood.

Colter dropped down behind a table, glancing toward the bar, noting an eerie silence in the room. He thumbed the spent shells from his Remy's cylinder, the brass clinking like coins on the floor around his boots and sounding as loud as cymbals in the sudden silence. Not even Spurlock was wheezing and wailing anymore.

Behind the bar, grunts and whispers rose. It was

Rondo and the barman, who'd dropped out of sight before the shooting began.

Colter flicked the loading gate closed and rose to his feet. "Rondo!" He started walking toward the bar, holding the cocked Remy out before him. "Rondo, you're gonna wish to hell you'd never crossed my path, you ring-tailed sonofabitch!"

He took two more steps.

"Just like you done to Trace, you're gonna be buzzard bait, you bastard!"

Suddenly Rondo lifted his head above the far left end of the bar. He whipped a double-barreled sawed-off shotgun atop the bar and angled the savage twin bores toward Colter.

The young drover had been waiting for such a move. He slid the Remy toward Rondo and fired. The slug screeched and barked wickedly as it slammed into the side of the shotgun. Both barrels exploded half a wink later, the twin wads of buckshot peppering the ceiling above Colter's head.

Throwing the shotgun down and bellowing like a poleaxed bull, Rondo whipped around and bolted down the dim hall behind the bar, taking long, loud, spur-chinging strides. Colter dropped to a crouch and fired two quick rounds, but both bullets only clipped the corner of the backbar as Rondo disappeared.

Colter shoved between the tables, vaguely noting all the bullet holes in the wood around him and the ruined backbar mirror. When he reached the end of the bar, he swung around it, holding his gun out.

The barman sat on his butt against the broken glass

and spilled liquor. He tucked his chin against his neck and held both hands above his head. "Don't! Leave me be, goddamn it, kid! I got no dog in this fight!"

Beyond him lay Rondo's Peacemaker, likely empty. The lawman had had so much confidence in the effectiveness of the double-barreled gut-shredder that the barman apparently kept behind the mahogany that he'd left his pistol.

For the moment he was unarmed.

But that wouldn't save him. Colter would put him down like any rabid dog, even if he had to backshoot an unarmed man.

He didn't pause to consider the strange calm he felt. No shaking in his limbs whatever. In fact, there was an odd peace in him, beneath the burning intent he could feel guttering just behind his eyes, making his scar tingle faintly.

Nor did it amaze him that he enjoyed the sensation.

He continued to the back of the saloon, taking long, stiff strides, and went out the door that Rondo had left open when he'd fled the building. He stopped at the door, listening.

Spurs chimed to his left, dwindling with running boot thuds. He walked over to the building's west side and saw Rondo running through the narrow, weed-choked gap toward the main street.

Colter could have shot him then, put an end to it. But why show mercy to someone as unmerciful as Bill Rondo?

Colter strode after the man. Soon he was on the

main street, heading west, Rondo stumbling ahead of him, jerking on the locked doors of the shops on the left side of the road.

"Someone give me a gun!" he shouted. "Anyone— a gun, goddamn it!"

Colter strode down the middle of the street, holding his cocked Remy down low at his side. Besides the gently twisting body of Chico Bannon, there was no one else on the street.

A block farther west, a man stepped out of his shop, stared toward Colter and Bannon, then jerked back inside his store, closing the door behind him. The street was so quiet aside from the rustling morning breeze that Colter could hear the man pull the shade down over the door and ram the locking bolt home.

Colter felt a smile touch his lips.

"You're finished, Rondo!"

He continued striding down the middle of the street while the sheriff shouted for a gun as he ran along the boardwalks to Colter's left, thirty or forty yards ahead. "The citizens of Sapinero need a bell cow to follow, and your bell doesn't ring anymore, Rondo!"

Rondo stepped out to the edge of a boardwalk and looked frantically up the street. Half a block ahead, smoke puffed from the brick chimney of the black-smith shop.

"McCallum!" Rondo shouted, breaking into a half run, half trot toward the shop. "McCallum, lend me a pistol! This little viper is tryin' to kill me! He already killed Spurlock!"

Rondo ran through the shop's open doors. Colter

could hear voices inside the shop, the slight trill of Rondo's spurs.

The young cowboy was twenty yards from the shop and still striding purposefully, his gun down by his side, when Rondo ran out of the shop's open front doors. The bulky, bearded blacksmith in his long black apron was behind him in the shadows, slowly backing away from the door, from which emanated the smell of smoke and hot iron.

The forge glowed hellishly in the shop's dense shadows, the low orange flames dancing.

Rondo gritted his teeth as he held a big Dragoon Colt in both hands, cocking the heavy trigger. He marched out toward Colter, eyes flashing with menace, extending the Dragoon in his right hand and lowering his head and squinting his right eye to sight down the barrel.

Colter kept walking as he brought up his Remington and extended it straight out from his left shoulder.

*Pow!*

Rondo grimaced as the .44 round plunked into his left thigh. His own gun roared, blowing up dust in the street to Colter's left, as he reached for the ragged hole in his pin-striped trousers.

He'd no sooner gotten a hand over the wound that Colter's Remy barked again, drilling a hole through the sheriff's right thigh.

"*Sonofabitch!*" Rondo screamed, dropping the big Dragoon as he stumbled straight back and plopped onto his ass in the dust. "You've crippled me, you little redheaded bastard!"

"And I'm not finished yet!"

*Pow!*

Rondo wailed as another round plowed through his left shoulder, jerking him backward.

*Pow!*

Rondo wailed as the next round tore through his right shoulder, again jerking him straight back. He looked at both ruined shoulders, then glanced up at Colter, tears streaking down his dusty red cheeks, and sobbed. He sank back against the ground, snarling and shaking his head like a wolf in a leg trap.

His legs and arms flopped, bloody and useless.

Colter twirled the smoking Remy. He stared down at the sobbing, grunting, cursing lawman, who stared up at him with animal eyes. Dropping his pistol into its holster, Colter moved into the smoky darkness of the blacksmith shop.

The bearded smithy stood behind the glowing forge, staring at Colter warily.

There were several irons in the fire. Colter found the one he was looking for, and lifted the glowing S from the flames. Rondo probably had the smithy keep the iron hot, as he never knew when he'd need it.

Colter held the glowing S up to his face. Gritting his teeth, he turned and strode slowly back to where Rondo lay flat on his back in a growing pool of blood. The man arched his back and lifted his head, yelling. His arms and legs stayed flat against the ground.

"Don't you dare, you bastard," he growled when he saw the brightly glowing iron.

Colter stood over him.

*"Don't you dare!"* Rondo raged, stretching his lips far back from his teeth. His eyes flashed like steel in

the sunlight. Several knotted blue veins stood so far out from his forehead that they appeared about to burst through his flesh.

As Colter lowered the glowing iron to Rondo's face, stark horror darkened the man's eyes. His chest rose and fell like a wildly pumped bellows. He tried to push away from Colter, but his arms were as weak as straws.

He could only lie there, panting and grunting, white-ringed eyes nearly popping out of his head as he glared at the wickedly glowing S.

Tears rolled down his cheeks. "Pl-please . . ."

When Colter pushed the iron to within an inch of the lawman's face, Rondo turned his head to one side, gritting his teeth so hard that Colter could hear them crack.

With both hands, and propping one boot against Rondo's chest, Colter pressed the glowing S into the man's left cheek.

Rondo arched his back, lifted his chin, and wailed.

Colter pressed the iron down hard against the man's face. He held it there until the sizzling of the flesh began to dwindle and the stench of burning flesh nearly made him retch.

He pulled the iron away.

Rondo's mouth yawned wide, but his scream was now so shrill as to be nearly inaudible. His eyes were squeezed shut. His head fell back in the dirt and he lay writhing in unbearable agony, able to move neither his legs nor his arms.

Colter tossed the iron away.

He looked at the smithy, who now stood in the

open doorway, grinding his palms as he stared sicken-
ingly down at the spasming lawman. "Best get a sawbones in a hurry," Colter told him. "Wouldn't want
him to die, now, would we?"

The smithy looked up at Colter. Understanding lit
his brown eyes, and his lips quirked in a faint, devil-
ish grin. Stepping wide around Rondo, he strode off
toward the central plaza in search of a doctor.

Colter looked once more at Rondo. The lawman lay
writhing and shaking his head as he sobbed and
ground his teeth against the infernal burning in his
face. The mark of Sapinero continued to sizzle softly
as it smoked.

"Maybe see ya again sometime," Colter said as he
started back in the direction from which he'd come.

A figure stepped out of the trees on his left, not far
from Chico Bannon's hanging, twisting body. Angelique pushed her hood back from her head and regarded Colter grimly.

Colter stopped in front of her. She didn't say anything. Colter stared up the street toward his horse still
tethered to the hitchrack fronting the saloon.

"Do me a favor," Colter said. "Write another one of
your notes. Send this one to Barranca Verde. Tell Jacinta she can take her kids back to her ranch. No one
else livin' there now."

He glanced at Angelique. Staring at him sadly, she
asked softly, "Are you going back to the Lunatics?"

He lifted his gaze to the white-mantled mountains
rising in the blue northern distance and shook his
head. "And tell 'em what?"

For an instant, the face of Marianna Claymore

floated across his mind. He pushed it away with all the others.

Brushing his fist at the S brand on his face, he continued up the street. As he did, the shop, saloon, and cantina doors began to open, and men stepped out onto the boardwalks, regarding Colter with wary interest. He turned his head, looking around at all those faces regarding him silently. He thought of the night Trace was killed here, before those very same cow-faced men who did nothing but stand there and watch.

He gave a caustic snort, mounted his horse, swung around, and rode back past the silently writhing Rondo. He rode past Juventino and Wayne Kilgore, who were just now riding into town, both looking miserable with hangovers.

He said nothing to either man as he trotted between them. They stopped their horses and hipped around in their saddles to regard him gravely.

Colter spurred the coyote dun into a westward lope.

It was as good a direction as any.

## About the Author

**Frank Leslie** is the pseudonym of an acclaimed Western novelist who has written more than fifty novels and a comic book series. He divides his time between Colorado and Arizona, exploring the West in his pickup and travel trailer.